Richard Hooker, W. Henry Winslow

Cruising and blockading

Richard Hooker, W. Henry Winslow

Cruising and blockading

ISBN/EAN: 9783337373795

Printed in Europe, USA, Canada, Australia, Japan

Cover: Foto ©Andreas Hilbeck / pixelio.de

More available books at **www.hansebooks.com**

A Naval Story of the Late War.

CRUISING

AND

BLOCKADING.

BY

W. H. WINSLOW, M.D., Ph.D.

" Libera terra liberque animus."

PITTSBURGH, PA.:

PUBLISHED BY J. R. WELDIN & CO.

1885.

SHERMAN & CO., PRINTERS,
PHILADA.

PREFACE.

———o———

THIS book contains an exact description of life in the United States Navy during the rebellion, and traces the career of an officer from midshipman to lieutenant.

The author believes that in other modern naval stories personal thoughts and actions and the minor matters of life in the navy have not been adequately described, and he has endeavored from his experience and his diary of the war to make an instructive, interesting and amusing story.

To his critics, the boys, both young and old, he offers the labors of a winter's evenings, serenely confident that, if the book is not a success, it will at least save him many repetitions of the adventures therein to his own boys at home.

W. II. W.

950 PENN AVE., PITTSBURGH, PA.

CONTENTS.

———o———

CRUISING AND BLOCKADING.

CHAPTER I.

HARRY CARESWELL was born on the New England sea-coast. His paternal ancestors could be traced back in historic pages to those hardy pilgrims, who established a home upon the bleak hills of Plymouth, in the piercing winds of December, 1620.

Harry's father had lived and worked upon a farm and attended school during the winters, in a little yellow school-house upon the hill a mile away, until his desire to know more of books and men and the great world, induced him to go to a neighboring town, where he found employment as a clerk in a general store. Here he worked by day and studied by night, saving his wages carefully, until he was able to enter one of the New England colleges, from which he graduated so well, that he was offered the chair of English Language and Literature. He preferred to teach a country school during the winter, and to pursue the study of architecture, for which he had a great liking, during the rest of the year in the city of Boston. After some years, he settled in the same town where he had been a clerk, and carried on the business of an archi-tect, though he still kept up his nomadic habit of teaching a country school in winter when the heavy snows of that climate prevented all building operations.

The leading merchant of this town was of pure Dutch de-scent, an honest, able, courageous man, who had crossed and recrossed the ocean many times upon his commercial ventures. He was proud of his enterprise, his warehouses and ships, but prouder still of his English wife and his seven beautiful chil-dren. He felt that, " whosoever commands the sea, commands the trade of the world ; whosoever commands the trade of the

2

world, commands the riches of the world, and consequently, the world itself;" but the sea, the riches of the world, and the world itself, were only the means whereby he could educate his family and give them a luxurious home, and he lavished his money for these objects. His children were given the best education attainable, and his home was adorned by curiosities and treasures of art, brought to him by his ships from distant parts of the world.

The young teacher-architect had been in this great merchant's employment and confidence; he had entered his charming family circle, and fallen deeply in love with one of the daughters. He was looked kindly upon by her, but he felt there was too great a difference between their positions in life, that he must win fame and competence, before he could ask her to be his wife. He worked, watched and waited.

A great commercial crisis came; business cares multiplied, became oppressive, crushing; the great merchant's health gave way; he involved his affairs in confusion, and sank into a fever which terminated his life. The former trusted clerk was employed to take charge of the disordered business. He put to flight the rascals, who had taken advantage of their principal's feebleness to rob him; fought step by step the cormorants, who had seized upon the assets by false and fraudulent claims, and succeeded in clearing and saving a slender estate for the family.

The eldest daughter had materially assisted the young architect in settling up affairs, as she had been her father's favorite and confidante. The daily intercourse had increased his love and admiration for her, and revealed to her that she could not be happy without him. It was a true love match, and, one year later, they were married.

Harry Careswell was the first-born of this union. He grew to be a well developed, shapely lad, with brown hair and eyes, and a graceful and energetic movement, and took great pleasure in all kinds of athletic sports.

Harry was not particularly brilliant at school. The objects and incidents of the busy world attracted his attention, now here, now there, and led his mind from the pursuit of knowledge in books to studies in nature; but he managed to graduate at the High School at the age of sixteen years.

His curriculum of studies embraced much more than those ordained by the very efficient school-boards of New England. He knew every hill and valley, field and forest, brook and lake, within ten miles of his native city. He knew where the best berries and beech-nuts grew, the squirrels were most numerous, the rabbits had their hiding places, and the flocks of partridges hid in the dark, damp copses. He could tell a chub from a perch, a trout from a pickerel, and a flounder from a sculpin, the moment one seized his hook. He had rowed, sailed, fished and skated over all the neighboring ponds and the beautiful bay near his home, and had followed every stream around, from its source, through woods and fields, until it broadened in the sunny meadows, and furnished poor fishing, but excellent wading-places for the lazy cows. He delighted to roam along shore, to gather queer stones and shells, to have clam-bakes by driftwood fires, and to spend hours and days in swimming, and boating, and climbing over the schooners, brigs and ships, that were always lying at the wharves in the harbor. He had inherited one grandfather's love of rural scenes, and the other's love of adventure and fearlessness of the sea, and wished to become a sailor. It is not surprising that the greatest business of his native city, that of ship-building and maritime commerce, attracted Harry's attention. His parents had other hopes for him, however, and set him to work to prepare for college. He said all he could against it, droned over his classics, and slipped away to the woods or the vessels whenever he had an opportunity, but his parents kept the one object in view, and made him very unhappy. They were awakened to their folly one afternoon rather painfully. A great ship was to sail for New Orleans, and one of Harry's playmates brought them the intelligence that Harry was going in her. His father went to the vessel and learned that Harry had shipped as a boy before the mast, and already had some of his clothes on board. The parents were shocked and terribly grieved, and sought to change Harry's desire to adopt such a rough life; but he was sullen and rebellious, and told them, if they did not let him go then, he would go some day; so with many misgivings and tears, they finally consented to let him make the voyage, and fitted him out in a comfortable manner.

Harry was delighted, and showed his affection for his father and mother in so many ways, that their forebodings and heart-aches were in part assuaged. When the time came for him to leave, he felt so badly that he wished he could remain at home, but he was too proud to recede, and, taking Good-bye kisses, he choked back his sobs, pulled his hat down to hide his tears, and went on board the good ship Heron. He immediately joined the sailors in getting up anchor and making things ready for sea. He knew all the gear of a ship and made him-self so useful, that he was soon upon good terms with the sailors and officers. The sails were spread one by one, the bowsprit was pointed seaward, a lively breeze filled the snowy canvas, the noble ship sped on her course, and long before sunset, the salt sea mists had blotted out the last headland that marked the bay before Harry's native city.

Harry and another boy had a little room adjoining the cook's galley where they kept their sea-chests and slept; but they took their "grub" with the other sailors in the forecastle, in the forward part of the same deck-house. One boy was put in the port watch and the other in the starboard, and their duties were many, onerous and perilous. The highest climb-ing fell to their lot. The royals, the highest square sails upon the masts, were loosed, furled and kept in order by them. They were obliged to scrape, and grease or paint the highest spars; to ride down in a boatswain's chair and tar the highest ropes; to repair the chafings and secure mats upon the stays, in the giddiest and most inaccessible places; to accompany the other sailors in loosing, reefing and furling the heavy sails; to hold the turn or bear a hand in all pulling and hauling ropes; to help wash the decks, paint the hull, steer the ship, row the boats in harbor, and pound the iron-rust from the cables and anchors. When there was nothing else to do, blocks had to be strapped, ropes knotted and spliced, and old hemp rope picked into oakum—the latter, the usual employ-ment for rainy days and Sundays. The sailor's command-ment is different from the one in the Bible. It is,

> "Six days shalt thou labor and do all thou art able;
> The seventh day, wash down decks and scour the cable."

The merchant sailor before the mast has a laborious, un-comfortable and dangerous life. He swings through the air high above the ship upon a slender spar or rope, sometimes traversing an angle of forty-five degrees, as the ship rolls in a heavy sea, clinging with feet and one hand for life, while the other hand works for his master. He battles to secure stiff, heavy, perhaps icy sails, that are slatting around before a rising gale, in imminent danger of being knocked overboard. He holds on to rail and ropes, as the heavy seas dash over, and works in wet clothes and sleeps in a wet bunk sometimes for weeks together. He gets poor food and poor wages; he is often cursed and knocked about by the officers, and works as hard in loading and discharging cargo as a dock laborer. He is exposed to frigid, and pestilential climates; to the dangers of the sea, and to the perils of immorality that surround him whenever he sets his foot on shore.

These hardships and dangers are little considered by the sentimental landsman, who sees a beautiful ship moving over the shallow waves of a harbor, or watches her gentle rise and fall upon the puny billows of the sea-coast on a summer's day.

Rough countries and climates develop sturdy, energetic men, and none other can endure the hardships and face the dangers of the sea successfully. Harry was a product of the New England sea-coast, whence come the best and bravest sailors in the world, and he did not shirk his duty, nor suffer his moral character to be contaminated by his associates. His lessons of truth and virtue had been well taught by good parents, and he passed unscathed through fourteen months of life before the mast. The ship made several voyages during this period, nearly foundered in a gale off Newfoundland, lost a deck-load of timber in a hurricane off Bermuda, spilled a deck-load of molasses into the sea off the coast of Cuba, and was finally wrecked upon the iron-bound coast of Maine.

Harry was saved, and was greeted as a hero by his native city. He had become wiser and better, and had lost his desire to be a merchant sailor. He laid aside his blue shirt and pea-jacket, cleaned the tar stains from his calloused hands, and spent the next eight months in reading law.

A vacancy at the Naval Academy was to be filled by the Congressman of Harry's district. The Hon. Mr. About said one day to Mr. Careswell: " Your son has grit. I like his ways. He has given evidence of courage and ability. He came home after several voyages and a shipwreck, laid aside his sailor dress, and settled down to quiet pursuits. He has no bad habits, and no one would know from his manners or conversation that he had ever been a sailor. I should like to appoint him to the Naval Academy."

Mr. Careswell thanked him for the good opinion of his son and his kind offer, and said he would consult Harry upon the subject. Harry was delighted with the idea of being a midshipman, and went to call upon his Congressman.

The matter was soon arranged, and Harry prepared for examination. He received an official document, with a ponderous seal, from the Navy Department, in August, which directed him to report on a certain date to the Commandant of Midshipmen, at the Naval Academy, Annapolis, Maryland, for examination. He presented himself there before a board of naval officers, resplendent in gold lace, bronzed and gray, kind but critical, and passed the physical and mental examinations easily and successfully.

He was assigned a room in Building No. 1, with a middy from New York State; changed his civilian dress for the cadet uniform; got his books from the store-keeper, and settled down into the regular routine life of the Academy.

One day he received the following document:

"NAVY DEPARTMENT, September, 185-.

"SIR:

"You are hereby appointed an Acting Midshipman in the Navy of the United States from the 10th day of September, 185-.

"If, after the course of attendance at the Naval Academy, prescribed by the Revised Regulations, approved January 25, 1855, you shall satisfactorily pass the graduating examination, you will receive from the Academic Board the 'certificate of graduation,' referred to in the 5th section of the 6th chapter of the above Regulations, which shall entitle you to a Warrant. as a Midshipman in the United States Navy, bearing the date of the certificate. If, however, you shall fail to obtain such certificate, you will be dropped from the list.

"Enclosed is a copy of the requisite oath, which when taken and subscribed, you will transmit to the Department with your letter of acceptance, in which you will state your age.

"I am, respectfully,
"Your obedient servant,
"ISAAC TOUCEY,
"Secretary of the Navy.

"Acting Midshipman
"HARRY CARESWELL,
"From the Third Cong. Dist. of M."

Harry took the oath to support the Constitution of the United States, and became a regular officer of the Navy. The four classes of the institution were divided into sections; the professors arranged their recitations; the hours for study, drill and recreation were promulgated by the officers, and the new life began in earnest.

CHAPTER II.

THE beautiful campus of the Academy lay upon the right
bank of the Severn river and fronted upon Chesapeake Bay.
The two sides towards the water were faced by a sea-wall at
the level of the ground. The two towards the city were
limited by a high wall, pierced by a guarded iron gate. Thus
middies were kept in and civilians out. Special permission
was necessary to pass the guard. Freedom gained by the
water way depended upon the tide or a boat, and was indulged
in at considerable danger of discovery.

The buildings within the walls consisted of dwellings for
the officers; dormitories for the middies; a large recitation-
hall of many rooms, including the mess-hall and kitchen; an
astronomical observatory; a hospital; a chapel; several store-
houses; a boat-house; an armory; a laboratory; a gas manu-
factory, and several minor structures. A small fort of twelve
guns occupied the corner of the campus towards the bay, and
a wharf to its left projected out into the Severn river. The
grounds were smooth, and shaded along the walks by trees.
A beautiful monument near the observatory honored the
memory of the hero, Lieut. Herndon, who went down with
his ship, after he had given every chance of rescue to his
passengers and crew. A fleet of boats and one yacht dimpled
the waters of the Severn at the boat house, and the distant
banks of the river and bay fringed a beautiful country of valley, hill and forest.

No lovelier or more salubrious spot could be selected for a
home for students, nor one better adapted to the requirements
of a naval school. Harry was in love with it from the first,
and performed all his duties with earnestness and zeal. These
were not light by any means, and they severely taxed him
physically and mentally. In those days, the middy arose at
sunrise to the stormy music of the drum and fife, calling the
"reveille;" swept his room; made his bed; finished his toilet;
reported at roll-call on parade upon the portico in front of the

mess-hall, and marched to prayers in the chapel. He then returned to the portico and marched into the mess-hall to breakfast. Each table in the mess-hall was occupied by a gun's crew, as detailed at the fort, and the captain of the gun, a first classman, sat at the head and kept order. A half hour was allowed for the meal, and then a short time was spent in any way the cadets chose. Study and recitations began at 8 A.M., and continued till 1 P.M.—the classes assembling at the call of the bugle.

The drum and fife played the familiar tune of "roast beef" at 1 o'clock, when the students formed parade quickly and marched to dinner. Study and recitation began again at 2 and continued till 4.15 o'clock, then the drum and fife called to quarters, and there was a drill in small-sword, broad-sword, infantry or field artillery till 5.30 or 6 P.M. At 6.30, roll-call and parade were followed by a half hour supper; study began at 7 and ended at 9.30, and "taps" of the drum, at 10 P.M., warned every midshipman to extinguish his lights and go to bed. This was the regular routine every day except Saturday and Sunday.

Saturday, study ceased at 10 A.M., the drum beat to quarters at 10.15, the midshipmen manned the guns in the fort, and fired at a target of timber and canvas, a mile distant out in the bay, until 12 M. They spent the next hour in getting new books, clothes, etc., at the store-house, went to dinner at the usual time, and used the balance of the afternoon and evening in recreation—half of them going out in the city on leave alternate weeks. Saturday evening was the jolliest time of the whole week. The band played in the fencing-hall for the middies to dance with each other; leave fellows came in from town with taffy, oyster-patties, cake, wine and cigars, and inaugurated little supper-parties in out-of-the way places, and card-parties were formed and pipes lighted, while a faithful watch was kept for the officer-of-the-day, who, in many cases, be it said to his honor, kept himself in his office. Taps were not heard in the social din or were ignored; darkness reigned; but quiet stories, smothered laughter and glowing pipes, showed where the groups were shrouded in their mephitic, nicotine vapors; shadowy forms moved around the campus and sped swiftly away at the approach of a watchman, and, down upon the sea-wall, a long line of dark, lounging forms bordered the placid waters and shook their tell-tale ashes into the briny river.

The Naval Academy was officially asleep at 10 P.M., but the middies of the institution were communing with kindred spirits and the stars, and building visionary fabrics of future glory till long past midnight. Who that has been there can ever forget those hours wrenched from despotism and stolen from sleep? Who can ever forget the officers-of-the-day, who assumed the beds were all filled in the dormitories, and scorned to play sneaking detectives with their subjects? Generations of midshipmen remember and love them, and generations yet to come will have the same debts to pay, for Yankee middies change not as the world changes.

Sunday was well kept by the midshipmen. After breakfast, every one dressed in full uniform, then the whole corps was inspected by the executive lieutenant in charge, at 11 A.M., and marched to chapel, where the chaplain conducted the beautiful service of the Episcopal Church. After dinner, midshipmen, who had applied for the privilege, went out in the city for afternoon church; a study hour was kept from 3 to 4 o'clock; supper followed at the usual time, and the evening study and taps were the same as on week days. The discipline and military training of midshipmen were excellent; the course of study was varied and thorough, though there was a lamentable absence of natural history; but the crowding of meals and study hours so closely together, the severe demands made upon the minds of youths developing rapidly, and the imprudence of many, released from parental control, caused a large percentage of failures at examination and failures of health, and made an annual loss to the navy of men who would have honored her. Some of the best officers of the old navy were not remarkable for fine scholarship when students at the academy.

Harry enjoyed his new life greatly and stood well in his class. His practical knowledge of seamanship, gained in the merchant service, permitted more time for the other studies, and he needed it. Many a night he covered the windows and the door of his room with quilts to hide the light and studied till after midnight. He wrote to his father, on one occasion:

"You may imagine how we have to work, when I tell you that we went through *Davies' Bourdon's Algebra* three times in five months, and *Davies' Legendre's Geometry* four times in four months—the last time, taking a book at a lesson."

The Academy gave a technical education, and inculcated morality and a high sense of honor. The middies belonged to all parts of the United States, and were representatives of the manners, thoughts and prejudices of the sections from which they were appointed. The cool, logical humanitarian from the North roomed and associated with the passionate pro-slavery advocate from the South. Although politics were tabooed by the regulations, there was more or less political discussion among the middies, and this often led to personal difficulties. These were settled by friends or fists. Among men bred to the profession of arms, it was natural that every one should protect himself and resent insults by the only means within his power. Not to do so was a disgrace which few cared to endure, and some few timid or Christian characters were made miserable for years by taunts of cowardice, and social ostracism, because they had not vindicated their honor *vi et armis* at the critical moment of trial. Yet, there was a great deal of friendship and good feeling among the middies, and they would rally in force to resent any invasion of their rights by the boys of Annapolis, their superior officers, or even the Department at Washington.

The Commandant of midshipmen and his staff recognized the rights of students, and were not too strenuous in enforcing the law against one who had defended his honor. At general quarters on board ship, during a practice cruise, a middy, acting as second sponger, accidentally dropped the sponge upon the foot of a fastidious comrade, who was acting as train-tackleman, and immediately said, "I beg pardon."

The latter mumbled, "You are no gentleman."

"What did you say?" asked the former.

"You are no gentleman," was the reply, loud enough for the whole gun's crew to hear.

The words were hardly out of his mouth before he was knocked down by the aspersed middy. He was ordered to report to the captain for fighting at quarters—a heinous offence against discipline. The captain heard the story from the

principals and witnesses, and placed both middies under arrest.
He told one of his officers, later, that he had punished one for
striking a comrade at quarters, and the other for insulting him
and *not striking back.*

The most of the buildings of the Academy were heated by
steam, and, on cold winter days, the heat was not always
sufficient to go around. A number of midshipmen were sick
at the hospital, and appealed to the surgeon's steward to have
fire in the grates, that had been painted and closed for a long
time. He refused. They took their newspapers, broke up
several chairs, and made a brisk fire. The smell of burning
paint soon penetrated to the office below and aroused the
olfactory organs and the ire of Monsieur B. Up he came
with haste, and demanded the reason for the act and the names
of those who had destroyed Government property. Every
middy in the hospital had helped, and the honors were equally
divided. A second classman was the leader, and he defied the
steward and threatened to report the condition of the heating
apparatus to the Department. The affair was amicably settled by an agreement to pay for the property used, and the
steward promised not to report to the surgeon.

The next morning the surgeon came to visit the patients
and said to Mr. C., "Put out your tongue! Why did you
break those chairs last night?"

" To protect us all from cold," was the firm answer.

" Well, sir; I shall report you to the commandant."

" Very well, sir; I shall report you to the Department for
cruelty to sick midshipmen in freezing them in the hospital."

There was no report made upon either side, but the next
time that second classman went to the hospital with a head-
ache, Monsieur B. gave him a gobletful of a most villainous
compound of senna and salts.

The teachers of the Academy were lieutenants, lieutenant-
commanders and naval instructors—the latter in the minority.
Studies were recited in the rooms of the mess-hall. Every
Saturday noon, the bulletin-boards in the vestibule recorded
the standing of each middy in his section and class, and they
were the rallying points until each one had copied down his
averages. Here the professors were discussed freely, and approved or condemned according to their markings. Here

orders were posted and sundry epigrams and poetic effusions exhibited. One might read, " Through cramps to crown ;" " Through straits the great and grand we reach, through study touch the stars ;" " *Per ardua ad astra ;*" " *Per ardua ad augusta,*" etc.

The months flew by. The time was so filled by studies, drilling, recreation and sleep, that the June examinations and the Board of Examiners arrived too soon for the last sections of the classes. Regular order was changed, and new orders were issued.

The examinations; the inspections; the exhibition drills with swords, muskets, field-howitzers and heavy guns ; the large number of civilians and officers coming and going; the presence of beautiful ladies in squads and battalions; the graduating exercises of the first class ; the brilliant naval ball in the mess-hall, to which many persons came from Baltimore and Washington ; the disgust and grief of those middies who had " bilged " in examination; the joy of those who had passed and were getting ready to go upon a practice cruise in a real man-of-war, or upon leave to see their friends; the good-bye suppers and smokes; the hearty cheers of the send-offs ; all these, contributed to make those June days exciting and forever memorable. Discipline was relaxed in a measure, and none but the meanest of men cared to confine the middies to their quarters after " taps," or to follow a suspicious smell of smoke to its origin.

One night, the dormitories were prepared for a visitor. A bombastic, martinet lieutenant, fond of whiskey, was on duty as executive officer, and the middies knew he would come around as a smelling committee about midnight. He came, odorous and funny with wines, resplendent in a new uniform, and accompanied by one of the half-dozen academy police. He walked to the hall door of No. 1, pushed it incautiously open and stepped in ; a pail of dirty water, gathered from the rooms, had been poised upon the door, and it descended and ducked him thoroughly. He rushed through the rooms, peered into each sleeping (?) middy's face, and then went down to No. 2. Heedless and enraged, he pushed open the door and received a second baptism. He would have had others, had he not been cooled by his receptions, and ordered the policeman to make further investigations with a pole. The new uniform was ruined; the midshipmen were cross-examined unskilfully by a sympathetic commander next day, and no one was found guilty, so cunningly had the division of labor been accomplished.

The June examinations and festivities were soon over, and half the middies went upon leave and waiting orders, and the other half to sea in a regular man-of-war, for two months, to learn practical seamanship and navigation. Harry went with his class on the practice cruise, and took a high standing in nautical studies on account of his previous experience. The sloop-of-war Plymouth, a full rigged ship, carrying eight guns and a crew of about one hundred and fifty officers and men, had been sent around to Annapolis early in June, and lay in the middle of the Severn with yards squared, ropes taut, guns frowning from her port-holes, and the flag of our country floating from the spanker gaff. Two classes of midshipmen with their luggage were transferred from the wharf to the ship's spacious deck, and introduced to the steerage, where they were domiciled during the voyage. It was impossible to stow over a hundred middies in such narrow quarters for sleeping, except by swinging them in hammocks. Each middy was allotted a number and two hooks for swinging his hammock close up beneath the beams of the deck. The hooks for each sleeper were near together laterally, but the hammock slings at each end permitted one to introduce his legs between them and over the corner of his canvas, and, by lifting himself by the arms, and working his body like a corkscrew, he could finally worm himself into it. This was probably as comfortable a way of getting aboard as any.

To land securely in a hammock at sea requires an amount of dexterity that is found only in a sailor or an acrobat. If you jump for it, you crack your head against the beams and find it is not there. If you lay your body across it and wriggle your legs, it takes your breath and interferes with your neighbors. If you get a good hold and launch yourself suddenly towards its middle, it slips away from you like an eel in the grass and lands you down below. It is better to stand alongside the hammock, take hold of the head with the right hand, put the left leg over one side of the canvas, push yourself cautiously and slowly between its two sides, watch your chance, give a vigorous kick with the right leg and roll right into bed.

The ventilation of the steerage was by the hatches and wind-sails, and was not remarkably successful. There was an odor similar to that of a zoological garden about four bells in the mid-watch, but the excess of fresh air on deck fully compensated for the foul below, and no one's health suffered. Occasionally an asphyxiating middy would sling his hammock between two guns upon the gun-deck above, or stretch out on camp-stools, if the sea was quiet. This was against orders, and brought reprimand and ridicule sometimes, which did not cause much suffering. Every middy lashed up his hammock, took it upon deck, and had it stowed in the rack along the rail in the morning, and thus the steerage was left free, with its table and camp-stools, for meals, writing, studying and lounging during the day. The bull's-eyes let in enough light for all purposes during pleasant weather, and the gun-deck above was used amidships for reading and recitations. The port side of the quarter-deck and the gangway, covered by the blue sky or, in part, by an awning, furnished room for exercise and exposure to sunlight. In these spaces over a hundred midshipmen lived, moved, studied and worked during two summer months at sea.

A practice cruise in old times differed from every other kind of cruise. There were more middies to every square foot of deck than could be found anywhere else afloat, and they were obliged to perform many of the duties of the common sailor in order to familiarize themselves with everything practical pertaining to their profession. Annapolis gave a liberal education and taught theory; the practice ships taught manipulation and manœuvres, and improved the mind by experience and travel.

The midshipmen on the practice cruise were divided into watches and stationed in different parts of the ship; they did regular duty day and night, and acted now as sailors, now as officers, according to command. They knotted and spliced ropes; fitted rigging to spars; bent, unbent, loosed, reefed and furled sails; sent yards and topmasts up and down; cast the lead; threw the log; had tricks (of steering) at the wheel;

took time sights with the sextant for longitude; caught the sun at meridian for latitude; drilled in all the different manœuvres of sailing a man-of-war; exercised at fire quarters with hose and boats, and at general quarters with small arms and heavy guns. They had regular lessons in navigation; found time to read some general literature; kept their clothes in order, and attended service and Sabbath-school on Sunday. The time was fully occupied and every hour brought its duties. Many persons imagine there is little to do at sea except to trim the sails and spin yarns. There never was a greater mistake. Merchant sailors are kept busy enough upon ship work, but a man-of-war with her large crew is a perfect hive of industry.

The good sloop-of-war carried her precious freight safely to Europe and back again without serious accident. When the anchor was dropped in the Severn, and the Academy band came down on the wharf and played "Home Again," starting tears and loud hurrahs testified to the gladness of the imprisoned midshipmen at their return. This was even more manifest the next day, when they landed and took up their quarters in rooms for the third and first classes; the caterer, waiters, policemen and room servants were greeted heartily; Dorsey, Johnson, Simmons and other favorite colored men were given commissions for the town, and the first few nights ashore were celebrated merrily by music, dancing, suppers, smokes and hazing the new fourth classmen, many of whom had already arrived.

Hazing is looked upon by moralists and those who have never been to college, as outrageous, nay, almost heinous; but those who have borne and done their share of it bear no malice against any one. It is an experience of college life which few care to invite, yet most persons are glad to have passed through. It becomes sometimes cruel and illegal, and should be restrained within reasonable limits.

It was midnight at the Academy, and a fourth classman slept sweetly in his narrow iron bedstead by the wall. The door of the room was opened stealthily, and two youths walked on tiptoe, one to the foot, the other to the head of the bed. They raised the bedstead steadily from the floor, turned it rapidly over, and deposited the sleeper upon the floor, with the mattress and bedstead upon him. Shouts of laughter from a dozen witnesses, and hastily retreating footsteps, informed the buried, dazed middy of the perpetrators. He rubbed arnica upon his bruises, made up his bed and went to sleep. The next day he made no complaints, but gathered from the significant looks of several Southerners that they were the guilty hazers. He took the attack so quietly that they thought this son of New England was afraid, and so tried their game again a few weeks later. Two middies sought the ends of his bed and were about to raise it, when the sleeper arose with a broomstick, which he had hidden under the coverlet, and gave them a mighty beating as far as the outer hall door. This was the last time his bed was disturbed.

Harry went home on leave at the end of the second school year; made a short cruise along the coast as a second class-man, the next summer; graduated the following June, as one of the star members of his class, and received his commission as midshipman. He was soon after ordered to the Charles-town Navy Yard, where he was engaged some months drilling volunteer officers in smallarms and infantry tactics. He then made a cruise to Bermuda and Charleston; returned to the Brooklyn Navy Yard; was examined and promoted to Ensign, and ordered to the sloop-of-war Nautilus, fitting for sea at the Philadelphia Navy Yard.

CHAPTER III.

THE great war for the preservation of the Union had gone on with varying fortunes for several months. The Quaker City was full of strange faces and uniforms. Squads of soldiers were marching here and there. The drum and fife were heard in all parts. The Cooper Shop Refreshment Saloons were besieged daily by car-loads of soldiers, who stopped only long enough to satisfy urgent hunger with the good food provided, and then hurried onward to the front. The jokes, handkerchief flirtations, laughter, cheers and martial music of the merry, rollicking soldiers, *en route* from the North, were in strange contrast to the low sobs, the sad, earnest Good-byes and the wailing anguish of women, with children clinging to them, taking a last leave of their husbands who were under marching orders. Strong men wrung each other's hands, and parted in silence, unable to speak from emotion ; others cried noisily to keep from unseemly laughter, or laughed hysterically to restrain unmanly tears.

The bulletin boards at the newspaper offices were surrounded by crowds eagerly reading the latest news; newsboys were shouting late editions with reports of the last battle, and quietly dressed ladies, with parcels and baskets, were flitting about the hospitals and ministering to the wants of the wounded. Everywhere one was met by strange scenes for the staid city of Penn. Everybody talked war, read of battles, dreamed of desperate adventures of arms, and walked the streets with shoulders thrown back and feet keeping time with the taps of the drum. The ladies by their home firesides were scraping lint, cutting and rolling bandages, making haversacks, and fitting out sewing-cases for the soldier boys. Even the children forsook their tamer toys, donned paper cocked hats, and strutted around the rooms with mimic swords and painted guns. Never before did a Christian people lay down the arts of peace and become so thoroughly and rapidly permeated by the martial spirit.

Harry came over to Philadelphia by a morning train, and, strolling about the city in the afternoon, he realized for the first time that there was a great war in progress. He spent the evening with a family which had long been associated with others in aiding the escape of negro slaves from bondage, and found the ladies, young and old, engaged in making bandages. The lady of the house, a very intelligent woman, well read upon all the phases of politics which had precipitated the war, gave him a rapid sketch of the rise and progress of the free spirit in the North, and the selfishness, arrogance and treasonable acts of the South. Harry had not paid much attention to politics, as in *ante-bellum* times political discussions were avoided in the Government service, and he had been too busy till then studying his profession, but he acquired upon this visit and subsequent ones clear ideas of the justice of the cause for which he was expected to fight, which his reading and reflection increased. Many a time afterwards, when destroying property and attacking the soldiers of the South, did the convictions then formed satisfy his mind and strengthen his resolution against the enemies of his country.

Harry went down to the old navy yard at the foot of Federal St., the next morning after his arrival, and attempted to pass the sentinel at the gate.

"You can't go in here," said he.

"But I want to see the sloop-of-war Nautilus," said Harry.

"Stand back, sir; no admission without a permit."

"A permit, hey? Take a cigar, old fellow; I only want to look over the yard a little."

This softened the marine, but he glanced over to the guardroom, saw the conversation had been heard by the corporal, and refused with some show of anger. The corporal came over to see what was the matter.

Harry unbuttoned his light overcoat, exposed his naval buttons, and said, "This stupid fellow will not let me in, when I want to see the Nautilus and report to the Commodore."

A glimpse of the beautiful naval buttons cleared the cloud from the sentinel's brow, as the sun sometimes lifts a Newfoundland fog bank, and he said, "Why didn't you tell me you were an officer? I thought you were some blasted spy."

They all laughed. Harry gave each marine a cigar and passed in.

The Commodore endorsed Harry's orders; told him his ship would not be ready for some weeks, and he could remain in the city and report at the yard every morning until further notice.

The navy yard was thronged with busy men, fitting out gunboats, sloops-of-war and ironclads for sea service. Howitzers and heavy broadside and pivot guns, with and without carriages, were mingled with piles of solid shot and unfilled shell; timbers, coils of rope, anchors, chains, water-casks and accumulated stores, lay around everywhere, obstructing the paths and making locomotion a task. The ship-houses were full of monster vessels approaching completion; merchant ships, redolent with the spices of India, were having their bulwarks pierced for guns; pretty schooner-rigged gunboats were receiving the last touches from the carpenters and painters; two beautiful bark-rigged sloops-of-war were taking in cables, anchors, guns and heavy stores alongside the dock, and the clean, trim, old receiving-ship Princeton, full of men, lay at anchor a little way out in the stream, as if quietly surveying the scene with the feelings of an old pensioner, whose fighting days had long been past. Harry looked around with feelings of satisfaction and pride. The yard men treated him with deference; the sailors greeted him with smiles and lifted caps, and officers exchanged the naval salute with him, as they moved around the yard, important with the duties entrusted to them.

Harry found the Nautilus to be one of the bark-rigged, steam sloops-of-war before mentioned, and walked aboard by the gang-plank. He inspected her from stem to stern and was very much pleased with everything. At last he stood by the engine-room hatch and looked down upon the ponderous engines. He noticed a gentleman, with spectacles and a slouch hat, standing upon the opposite side of the hatch, and remarked, "Fine engines those."

"Yes, rather larger than I have seen before," replied his vis-à-vis.

"I like the ship, but I would not like to do duty down there," said Harry.

"Wouldn't you? Well, I shall be obliged to do it."

"You are going in the ship then?" said Harry. "So am I," and he went around to the stranger, presented his card, and received one in return. He read, "Richard Dayton, Brooklyn, N. Y."

"You are an engineer then?" said Harry.

"Yes, a third-assistant on my first cruise."

"Is it possible? You'll have a nice time being sea-sick down there among the piston-rods and crank-pins."

"Perhaps so, but I've never been sea-sick yachting around New York. My brother has a yacht, and I have often been out a hundred miles from Sandy Hook."

"Well, I hope you will not. It is disagreeable, not to say disgusting, but I've never experienced it myself."

"You go in the wardroom, I suppose?" said Dayton, glancing at the gold band upon Harry's sleeve.

"Yes, they say so. I've had my cruise in the steerage. I'd rather go in the steerage though. Steerage life is jolly. You need not be so particular about dress, what you say, and how you act there. We had lots of fun in the last ship. The steerage is a democracy. Social, ship, and government affairs can be discussed freely and fully there. We had a warm time talking down the greasers in the opposite steerage."

"The what?" said Dayton.

"I beg pardon, I said the greasers, a term sometimes applied to the engineers. I meant no offense. You see, we sometimes became excited, and, when they called us market-boys, because one of us had to go in charge of the early market-boat in port to bring off fresh provisions, we retaliated by calling them greasers, though of course they had only scientific work to do in the engine-room. One must be careful of speech and action in the wardroom, because the First Luff lives there and might take notes sometimes. They have their own sport there, I suppose, and I hear our executive is a jolly good fellow. We shall see."

Dayton looked quizzically at Harry and said,

"You graduated at Annapolis?"

"Yes."

"I graduated at the Polytechnic Institute at Troy."

"The deuce you did!—the finest civil engineering school in

the country. What can possess you to go out as third-assistant?"

"Patriotism, or a desire to be of some use to the country in
her time of need," said Dayton earnestly.

Harry smiled, but the deep brown eyes looked calmly into
his and he became grave immediately. It was a revelation to
him. He approved of patriotism, of course. He had been
bred to arms and was an officer in the line of promotion.
Patriotism was easy for him. Here was a man of his own age,
thoroughly educated in science, and occupying a good position
in life, forsaking everything pleasant and going out on rather
unremunerative, dangerous and disagreeable service for love
of country. Harry was touched. He held out his hand and
said, "My dear fellow, I am glad to know you. I am sure
we shall be friends, whether our lots are cast in the steerage or
the wardroom. I have known too many educated engineers
not to have the greatest respect for their acquirements and their
profession. We shall meet again on board ship, until then,
Good-bye."

"Good-bye," said Dayton calmly, "I shall be glad to
renew our acquaintance."

Harry hurried ashore and left him looking down upon the
monster engines of the Nautilus.

A few days after this conversation, the Nautilus was dropped
away from the dock and anchored in the stream, and the officers were notified to be on hand before meridian, on Wednes-
day, as the ship was going into commission. Harry came
down with his luggage and was taken on board by a cutter,
in charge of an officer and crew from the Receiving-ship. He
had a fine view of his future home, as he moved rapidly over
the dimpled Delaware. Never had he seen a more beautiful
vessel, and his heart swelled with pride at the thought of being
an officer of such a noble craft.

The hull was constructed of the best oak and Southern pine,
and every brace, bar and bolt, wrought of the best Pennsylvania iron, had been carefully put in place under the watchful
eyes of the master builder. The seams were well caulked to
resist the searching currents of the sea. The bow and stern
had those exquisite curves and water lines, which distinguish
a yacht from a coaster, or a clipper from a Chinese junk. The

masts and other spars had the delicate taper of a lady's finger, and the shrouds, stays, lifts and running gear, shone in the morning sun like a gossamer web spun on the dewy grass.

There were several boats hanging at the davits and a couple floated alongside. A massive anchor hung from the port cat-head, but the starboard one was at the bottom of the river at one end of the heavy chain cable, which passed into the hawse-pipe and kept the ship securely at anchor. A set of steps and landings, shining white against the jet black hull, was placed at the starboard gangway for convenience in getting on board while in port, and the officers and sailors moving about the deck showed that the crew had been already transferred from the Princeton.

Harry stepped lightly down upon the deck, touched his cap to the group of officers, and, seeking the executive officer, Lieutenant-commander Felton, reported to him for duty. "I am Ensign Careswell and I have come on board to report for duty, sir," said he. "Commodore Paulding told me this was a regular man-of-war, fitted out in the best style, and probably going on special service."

"I am glad to see you, sir," was the reply. "I know several of your family in the service, and have no doubt we shall have pleasant cruising together."

Harry bowed and then went to look over the ship. What a beauty she was! The spar-deck stretched in a gentle curve from stem to stern. Upon each side, there was a row of 56-pounder guns on their carriages, with their muzzles project-ing slightly through the gun-ports. At each extremity of the rows, there were some handsome brass 24-pounder howitzers, holding the "black dogs of war," as it were, in golden corners. Over the guns, cutlasses and boarding pikes were arranged upon the bulwarks in symmetrical figures, and a long line of snowy hammocks, snugly lashed, filled in the netting along the rail from bow to stern.

An immense 200-pounder Parrott gun rested upon its com-plicated carriage behind the foremast, and an XI-inch Dahl-gren gun and carriage occupied the space just forward of the mizzen mast. Both were supplied with brass trucks, laid in circles upon the deck, and removable sections of the bulwarks showed that they were pivot guns, capable of being pointed to

starboard or port, as the exigencies of war might demand.
Other places along the deck were occupied by hatches. Some
were for lowering and hoisting stores and ammunition; some
had steps and ladders leading to the main deck, and others
were covered by skylights and transmitted light and air to the
rooms below.

The forecastle-deck, raised about six feet above the spar-
deck, filled up the bow nearly flush with the bulwarks, and
was guarded by a chain and posts. It had the cat-heads and
knight-heads, the usual appliances for the anchors and forward
sails, and a 30-pounder Parrott gun upon a pivot carriage
amidships. The space below the deck contained numerous
lockers, or closets; a capstan amidships, and the chain-stoppers
and cables—the latter running out the hawse-pipes forward,
and backward through pipes in the deck to the chain lockers
at the foot of the foremast.

A small deck away aft, called the monkey-poop, or midshipman's quarter-deck, filled up the stern even with the bulwarks, and was surrounded by a chain. A 30-pounder Parrott
gun on pivot carriage was secured amidships. A person standing upon this deck could look down upon the spar-deck, and
have, at the same time, a comprehensive view of the outside of
the ship and the surroundings. Here the quartermaster, with
a spy-glass in hand, was constantly on the lookout for shore
signals, ship signals, and the general movements of boats and
vessels around. Upon each quarter hung the life-saving apparatus, with cork floats, coils of life lines, and a case of pyro-
technics, ready to drop into the sea and flash out its saving
light at the pulling of a lock-string. Beneath the monkey-
poop, there was a square well with hoisting gear for taking
the screw out of the water, when it was desirable to go under
sail alone. Upon each side of this box, there was a wide
passage-way, with a port opening astern—the port side being
in all ships a favorite smoking place for officers—and around
the walls were numerous lockers, containing the codes of signals, the flags of nations, rockets and signal lights, spy-glasses,
logs and other treasures of the quartermaster.

Forward of the poop-deck, a large double wheel, with its
steering gear, was covered by a tarpaulin, having painted upon
its face the U. S. coat of arms and "U. S. S. Nautilus," and

a handsome binnacle forward of it contained two large compasses and a lamp.

The whole ship was open for inspection, and Harry went down the steps of the narrow gangway into the cabin. There was a dining-room amidships, a small pantry forward of it, and a state-room with bunks, upon each side, all well carpeted, while the chairs and sofas were upholstered in blue velvet. A table, a hanging rack for glasses, a compass, a barometer, toilet requisites, bedding and curtains completed the furnishing. Beneath the floor there were places for storing provisions, etc. A door opened forwards into the wardroom, the home of the higher officers of the ship. This room was about fifteen feet square, carpeted with oil-cloth, and lighted from above by a large skylight in the deck. There was a row of state-rooms upon each side, one for each officer, and a pair of steps aft led upon deck. A door upon each side in the forward partition communicated with an intermediate space between the steerages, called the country. The state-rooms were to be occupied by the executive officer, the lieutenant, two masters, the ensign, the paymaster, chief-engineer and surgeon. Each state-room was about six feet square, and had a wide, comfortable bunk, with drawers beneath, a dead light in the outer wall, and the usual toilet appurtenances.

A long table was secured across the forward part of the wardroom, and the mizzenmast passed through the deck just aft of it. A swinging shelf with glasses, a narrow sideboard, and a few chairs and camp-stools comprised the outfit. A small room aft served as a pantry, and was filled with dishes and silver in box-like shelves. Two small hatches in the floor opened into store rooms; one contained the wardroom supplies, and the other, the powder and shell for the quarter-deck howitzers.

The country was simply a passage-way, and had a hatch above and one in the deck below, leading to a room for the officer's provisions, and the paymaster's stores of clothing and grog. A door opened forward into the engine-room; one on the right, into the midshipmen's steerage, and one on the left, into the engineers' steerage. The midshipmen's steerage contained half a dozen bunks, numerous closets, a table, two swinging shelves and some camp-stools. Several dead-lights in the side of the ship let in light and, sometimes, air. The engineers' steerage on the opposite side was an exact counterpart of the midshipmen's. The intermediate was a sort of commons for steerage and wardroom officers, in wet and cold weather, and many were the jokes and stories told there, during the relaxation of official dignity.

The space from the country to the mainmast, from the spar deck to the very bottom of the ship, was occupied by the powerful engines, the condensers, the cranks and forward end of the shaft. The shaft ran along above the kelson and underneath the wardroom and cabin to the two-bladed screw at the stern.

The fire-room, boilers and coal bunkers filled another large section of the entire hull just forward of the engine-room and mainmast. A large hatch, covered by skylight and gratings let the light and air down through the spar-deck to this fiery region. The smoke-stack and escape-pipe came up through the afterpart of this hatch, and, between these and the mainmast, a narrow foot-bridge, with bell handles for signalling to the engineer below, extended across the ship upon a level with the hammock nettings. The officer of the deck, and, at stations, an engineer, stood upon this bridge, which gave a commanding view of the whole ship and the waters around.

The space between decks, from the fire-room to beyond the foremast, contained the galley and cooking utensils for the whole ship's company, but the greater part was used by the sailors for general purposes by day, and a sleeping place at night, when the snowy hammocks were unlashed and swung to the numerous hooks in the solid beams overhead. Here they spread their mess-cloths and ate their meals in bad weather, but they were transferred to the spar-deck, when pleasant weather and ship discipline permitted. Several rooms upon each side were occupied by the boatswain, carpenter sailmaker, gunner and apothecary. A space was set apart on the starboard side next the apothecary shop for the sick-bay where the apothecary, nurses and surgeon remained during action.

A triangular space in the bow was partitioned off for prisoners undergoing punishment, and was called the brig—a sad place to visit or contemplate. A large store-room beneath his, in the very peak of the bow, was filled with oils, paints, cordage and ironwork for ship's use, and was in charge of a petty officer, called a yeoman—a very important man in his own estimation. The whole space from the fire-room to the yeoman's room, beneath the main-deck—the hold of the ship—was filled with ship's stores, ammunition and chain cables. The magazine, heavily walled, lined with zinc, and full of powder and shell, was a little distance behind the foremast, and the space around was stowed with barrels, boxes, bags, etc., containing provisions for a long cruise.

The condensers of the boilers furnished water for general use, and numerous butts of fresh water were lashed about the par-deck to supply the daily consumption.

The ship was complete and beautiful from kelson to truck, from jib-boom end to taffrail, and the hardy sailors and fine looking officers who covered her deck, this brilliant day in October, were evidence that great deeds were expected of her by the Navy Department.

Harry made his tour of inspection and reached the group of officers upon the starboard side of the quarter-deck, as Captain Prescott came up from his cabin, touched his cap to the officers, who had saluted him, and said, " Mr. Felton, you will have the crew mustered upon the port side and the officers upon the starboard side of the quarter-deck; let the quarter-master get the pennant and colors ready, and station men at the halyards to put the ship in commission."

Lieutenant-commander Felton touched his cap, said, " Aye, aye, sir!" gave his orders to the officers, and then to the quartermaster and the boatswain.

The shrill whistle of the boatswain rang through the ship and his rough voice called, " All hands muster aft on the port side of the quarter-deck!" The whistle and order were repeated by the boatswain's mates; a file of marines and the sailors gathered quietly and respectfully upon the port side of the quarter-deck and waist, and the officers, in uniform, wearing their swords, stood in a line upon the starboard side. Paymaster Horton was directed by Mr. Felton to muster the crew, and his clerk called the names of the men and officers, each responding, " Here, sir!" The names of some of the men were peculiar and often caused a smile among the auditors. It is well known that the enlisted men of the navy are from all classes of society and of all nationalities. Induced by a desire for adventure, to see the world, to serve the country, to obtain a livelihood, to gain promotion, to drown grief, to escape persecution, or to avoid punishment for criminal offences, they enter the navy under assumed names, and disappear from the terrestrial places that knew them. Such names then, as Sam Patch, Davy Crockett, Dan Rice, Napoleon Bonaparte, George Washington, Timothy Ticklepitcher, etc., were calculated to excite amusement and philological interest. The full names were called, and the given ones were often as curious as the surnames. Timothy Timpkins Ticklepitcher's name was never mentioned without a sensation, and the man who claimed it was as queer as his cognomen.

The paymaster's clerk told the paymaster the roll was finished and all were present; the paymaster reported to Mr. Felton, who reported to the captain. Captain Prescott then said to Mr. Felton, "Hoist the colors, sir!" then, as they were being run up, he stepped upon the midshipman's deck and said:

"OFFICERS AND MEN OF THE NAUTILUS—It is with pleasure that I take command of this beautiful ship. No finer or better equipped vessel sails the sea, and I expect noble deeds from such a sturdy crew and gallant set of officers. I shall exact implicit obedience from all. Naval discipline must be maintained from stem to stern, but those who do their duty faithfully will find me a kind and indulgent commander. The part of the humblest among you is important for the welfare of all, and it is only by each man doing his best that perfect work will be accomplished. Let us then pull together, each in his appointed sphere, in order that we may achieve a name and fame for the good ship Nautilus and Our Country. Now, by the power vested in me by the Navy Department, at Washington, I declare the United States Ship Nautilus in commission."

The long naval pennant had reached the main truck and floated out on the breeze, and the starry ensign curled and waved in the bright sunlight at the end of the spanker gaff. Then Mr. Felton sprang upon the steps and shouted, "Three cheers for the good ship Nautilus and her gallant captain!"

The loud hurrahs rang out across the water from over a hundred throats, and stopped the workmen in the yard by their echoes around the great ship-houses, while the naval band upon the wharf struck up "The Star Spangled Banner." The inspiriting music of the national anthem came, like the sounds of an æolian harp upon the breeze, and caused hearts to beat faster and eyes to shine brighter from the excitement of the occasion.

The crew was now divided into a port and a starboard watch; the petty officers were sent to their duties; the warrant officers were instructed to take charge of their departments; the commissioned officers were requested to see everything ready for sea service, and were appointed to the watches. Mr. Felton had already made out his "Watch, Quarter and Station Bills," and had only to fill in the names. He proceeded with the deck officer to organize the crew and instruct each man in his place in the boats, in getting under way, tacking ship, coming to anchor, putting out fire, and going into action.

Harry and the remainder of the officers busied themselves in unpacking their trunks and boxes and arranging things in their state-rooms, and introductions of one officer to another, with friendly courtesies and occasional jokes, soon established a brotherly feeling in steerages and ward-room. It was rumored that the Nautilus was to be the Flag-ship of a fleet, i. e., to have the commodore or admiral commanding a squadron on board, in addition to her full complement of officers, and that the latter had been selected with care because of the social as well as professional duties that would be demanded of them.

Though naval officers are all supposed to be gentlemen, and the best sailors are the kindest and most honorable men, there is some choice when one comes to consider social etiquette, and a flag-ship needs and generally gets the best material. Howbeit, the personnel of the Nautilus was generally excellent, though events proved that there were a few persons on board whose characters were somewhat defective. The stewards, cooks and waiters soon had their departments in good order, and dinner was the first meal served on board. The executive sat at the starboard, and the paymaster at the port end of the long table ; the senior officers were next them to the right and left, and the junior officers filled up the middle. The eight officers, who formed the wardroom mess, had the captain for a guest that day, and they discussed the viands and wines, the ship, the prospective cruise, and the different events of the war on land and sea in brotherly love, and congratulated each other upon the prospect of glory and promotion. In the port steerage, six assistant-engineers, in the starboard steerage, two midshipmen, two master's-mates, the paymaster's clerk, the captain's clerk and the apothecary, had an equally pleasant time, to judge by the laughter that occasionally came through the bulkheads. The boatswain, gunner, sailmaker and carpenter dined in their room forward, and the sailors and marines spread their square mess-cloths upon the main-deck around the galley fire, and, sitting cross-legged by their wooden and tin dishes, loaded with wholesome food, began those yarns for which they are famous.

Who can fitly describe the inauguration of a ship's company? It would require the pen of a Hugo, and that he should serve in each and every capacity. An official order, signed by the Secretary of the Navy, and transmitted through the Commandant of the navy yard to Captain Prescott, was the instrument that brought all this life together into moving, methodic system. The captain was on board, the pennant at the main truck, and, henceforth, all was to move with that beautiful precision and harmony seen on board of a well disciplined ship and in the workings of perfect machinery.

Every day at 9 A.M., the drum and fife called to quarters, and the ship's company was drilled carefully and patiently in handling the guns, boarding, repelling boarders, and in using the broadswords, pikes and muskets. At other times, the men were exercised in getting under way, tacking ship, wearing ship, making sail, taking in sail, sending up and down spars, coming to anchor, putting out imaginary fires, and getting out the boats. Each man knew his number, his position and duties ; each officer had his place and a particular routine to accomplish with the men under his charge, and everything went like clock-work.

In a few weeks the Nautilus was ready for sea ; the sailing

day was appointed; the Good-byes were said; all the private stores and knicknacks were stowed away; the casks, guns and other movable things were securely lashed; the heavy boats taken on board, and the others hoisted up to the davits.

CHAPTER IV.

It was a clear, cold December day, that steam was gotten
up; the pilot taken on board; the anchor hove up, catted and
secured, and the Nautilus steamed down the Delaware, receiving cheers and salutes from the neighboring vessels and giving
hearty ones in return. The dense blocks of buildings faded
in the distance; the scattered cottages and imposing villas
along the banks and shores became less and less distinct; the
men and officers were called from their stations; the pilot,
officer-of-the-deck and executive held possession of the bridge;
two men at the wheel steered according to orders, watched by
a quartermaster; a lookout on the forecastle and another upon
the midshipman's deck walked forwards and backwards, and
all day long there was heard the hum of active men, the sharp
orders, the shrill whistle of the boatswain's mates, and the dull
thud and whirr of the screw, driving the Nautilus towards the
open sea.

The pilot was discharged at the Breakwater; Cape Hen-
lopen light was passed during the night, and those who loved
the deep blue sea rejoiced at feeling the dancing billows beneath their feet and the saline breeze in their nostrils. When
morning dawned, a low line of sand upon the western horizon
showed that the Nautilus was running down the coast, and
even this remnant of mother earth was soon lost in the mist
and the blue haze of extreme distance.

Mr. Felton had turned in at midnight, and the watch officer
had taken to pacing the quarter-deck, glad to shield himself
behind the bulwarks from the piercing wind. The decks were
holystoned and washed down; the skylights, gratings and steps
scrubbed; the ashes hoisted overboard out of the fire-room;
the running rigging hauled taut and coiled down in circles
and figures of eight; and all hammocks piped up and stowed,
as is usual on board ship before breakfast, and, when the executive came up on deck at seven-bells, the ship looked as trim
as a bride arrayed for a wedding. The watch below was then

piped to breakfast, and, at eight-bells, came on deck to relieve the morning watch, and another wardroom officer, who had just breakfasted, relieved the deck-officer, Master Sanborn.

Mr. Sanborn was a large, strong, blonde young man, with a face as round as the sun and beaming with health and good nature. He was conscientious in his duties, slow and methodical in action, rather firm in his opinions, kind and considerate of others, and, withal, so full of good humor and a disposition to look on the bright side of every thing, that he was a favorite with both officers and men. Just as he came down the wardroom steps, the ship gave a lurch, he missed a step and came down flat on the deck, so easily, that the officers of the mess, who were still at table, knew he was not hurt.

Several laughed. Mr. Felton said, "I hope you are not hurt, Mr. Sanborn?"

"Oh, no," said he, "I only came down on a run."

"You'd better look out," said Lieut. Ashton; "the doctor hasn't unpacked his splints yet."

"I'm not afraid of either splints or splinters," was the reply, as the victim of the *faux pas* rubbed his elbow, "but I'm as hungry as a shark. If any of you poor, thin staff officers want to get an appetite, go on deck for an hour or two and you'll want a second breakfast. It's lovely up there. The wind is coming off the shore in elegant puffs, and I smell old Virginia as plain as a nosegay." With this speech, he took his place at the table and began upon his breakfast, which one of the colored wardroom boys had brought hot from the galley.

Mr. Felton said, "I think we're going to get fourteen knots out of the ship after the engine gets well greased. How is the machine working now, Mr. Lawson?"

"Very well indeed, sir. There is a little roughness here and there in the valves and bearings, but I think a week's run will make them as smooth as glass. These contract engines are never up to the mark, as they used to be before the war. I suppose the shops are too hard pushed, but it takes a little while to find out the qualities of an engine, just as it does those of a horse. A horse will make better speed one day than another, when all the circumstances and conditions seem the same, and it's just so with an engine; a man must study

4

its mechanism, its movements, its whims, so to speak, and
then, when he gets his mind into harmony and sympathy with
it, he can get better work out of it than any one else. I try
to get my assistants to consider their duty in this way, but
they listen gravely and then laugh behind my back. I know
I'm right, sir, and I'll prove it before the cruise is over."
Having delivered this speech with an earnest voice, the chief-
engineer's face flushed and his eyes shone brilliantly as he
looked around the table.

"You are perhaps right," said Mr. Felton, approvingly.
"Study and experience can accomplish great things in the
world. Steam has properties that command respect. Watt
and Fulton would be astounded to go into our engine-room
and see the improvements there exhibited in the application of
steam as a motor."

Just then there was a loud report; Lawson turned pale and
rushed through the country to the engine-room, followed as
far as the door by the executive, while the officer-of-the-deck
leaned over the hatch coamings above and asked, "What's the
matter down there?"

No steam was heard escaping, and the screw kept up its
steady action. The chief soon returned and reported to the
officer-of-the-deck, the executive, the captain and others, that
little damage had been done—only one of the condenser bon-
nets had burst. After general quarters and some drill with
the guns, the wardroom officers assembled below, reading,
writing and talking.

"I wonder where we are bound," said Mr. Ashton, with a
significant glance at Mr. Felton.

The executive looked up a moment, but said nothing. He
was intently studying a chart of the West Indies spread out
upon the table. He was a man of medium size and delicate
build; his face was of a pure Grecian type; wavy black hair
clustered around his high forehead and prominent temples; a
long moustache curled over the corners of his sensitive mouth,
and his eyes were of that soft, deep black, which tells of ardent
affections and passions. His graceful bearing, finished cour-
tesy, superior education and just discrimination, marked him
as one of nature's noblemen, who would be generous and just

to those who did right, and unfriendly, perhaps, to no one but himself.

"The captain has sealed orders," said he at last. "They will be opened when we get in the latitude of Cape Charles."

"I hope it will be a roving commission," said Sanborn. "I would like to get a crack with our heavy Parrott at some of those long, low, rakish privateers, that are picking up so many of our merchantmen. My brother's ship was captured off Bermuda, on her return voyage from Brazil, last month, and the whole crew was set afloat in a long-boat and reached St. Georges after much suffering."

"What vessel captured her?" asked Mr. Ashton.

"I did not learn her name; I suppose it was the Florida or Alabama," was the reply.

"Well, you'll have to catch them in a trap to get them within range," spoke up Surgeon Willett. "We sighted them several times last voyage, but they showed clean heels and ran us out of sight in no time. It's my opinion they can steam twenty knots an hour when they are pressed."

"Those English engines are the finest in the world," said Mr. Lawson. "It is perfectly astonishing what work can be gotten out of them month after month. They seldom need repairs, last a long time, and produce a uniform and high rate of speed. It's mortifying to chase one of the English blockade-runners, with even one of our best steamships, and have them get hull down in a few hours. It is my opinion our Government ought either to remodel and improve our marine engines, or else buy a few across the water."

Lawson's face flushed, as he delivered this speech and noticed the earnest eyes of the executive fixed upon him. It was not patriotic to talk in this manner, but all who had been in service during the war felt the truth of his remarks.

Mr. Lawson was a remarkable man. His features were regular; his eyes deep blue; his face was that pure pink and white seen only in perfect blondes, and his fine yellow-brown hair and whiskers clustered around his face and served to partly hide the tell-tale expressions which were constantly flitting over it from his lively thoughts. When he spoke, he generally communicated something worth knowing, and all were glad to listen to him.

"What can politicians know about marine engines?" said Ashton sneeringly. "The men who rule our destinies come from counters, warehouses and law offices, and know nothing about the exigencies of a Navy Department. I heard the other day, that our Honorable Secretary was walking through one of the navy yards and stumbled over a bale of oakum. 'What is that?' said he, to the officer who was showing him around.

"'A bale of oakum, sir.'

"'A bale of oakum? Where does that stuff grow?'

"The officer explained that it was made from old hemp rope."

Some of the officers laughed. Mr. Felton looked grave and said, "Mr. Ashton, you will not forget that the Honorable Secretary is your superior officer."

"No, sir, I will not forget it," said he, biting his lips to keep from laughing.

Ashton was a brunette, with an unpleasant countenance. The expression of his eyes was restless and snaky. The lines about his mouth, partly hidden by a thin moustache, showed that sneering had been very frequent. He was insinuating, servile and hypocritical to superiors; haughty, arrogant and severe to inferiors. He was quiet, uncommunicative and often morose; he seemed to be always on the watch for something, and as sly and mysterious as a cat; he did a great deal of thinking, but rarely let any one know what he was thinking about. A single incident will throw some light upon his character. Careswell was stationed upon the forecastle, at general quarters, and had charge of the Parrott gun. It was found in exercising and pivoting the gun from side to side, that the shifting tackles were not necessary, and a rope, with a hook in one end to catch into a side eye-bolt, enabled the gun's crew to handle the gun with great rapidity. Harry reported the fact to Ashton, who was ordnance officer, and he said, "Work the gun as you please, and take the tackles off." Harry told one of the men to remove the tackles and to deliver them to the yeoman. This was done and, a day or two afterwards, Harry was surprised to learn that Ashton had reported him to the executive for "giving two gun-tackles to the boatswain." Mr. Felton asked Harry about the tackles, and was satisfied with the explanation. The technical mistake was in not turning them over to the gunner.

Ashton was guilty of little meannesses like this very frequently, as much from his desire to harass others, as to advance his own importance in the minds of his superiors, and, it is needless to say, was held in general contempt.

Harry had been so busy since coming on board, that he had not had much time to talk to Dayton, who was in the port steerage, but he visited both steerages one evening and made the acquaintance of all the officers. He found Dayton and Webster discussing the proper translation of a phrase in Cæsar. Dayton took it apart, gave the declension of this and the conjugation of that word, and the relations of all the parts of the sentences so clearly and rapidly, as to excite the surprise of all. He repeated considerable of the first page of Cæsar's Commentaries verbatim, and exhibited great familiarity with the writings of Cicero, Virgil and Horace. This was done in the course of conversation with the different gentlemen, some of whom aired their knowledge of the classics by referring to one or the other of the authors named. It was developed later, that Webster, who was a third-assistant engineer, was secretly preparing for college, and Dayton helped him greatly, not only in Latin, but in Greek, of which language he had, also, a very considerable knowledge. This evening, however, the conversation drifted on to the modern languages. Several of the engineers and midshipmen spoke French and Spanish, and one of the former, named Hanson, French and German. Dayton knew the French better than most of them, and talked German with Hanson, a native of Prussia, with the fluency and ease of a Hanoverian.

Gardner was one of the best educated of the engineers, and he expressed the opinion of all by saying, " Dayton, you are a philological curiosity. How in the world have you ever acquired these languages so well, and, yet, had time to master the technical education required of a graduate of the Polytechnic ?"

" How? By beginning early, and by persistent digging. I got my Greek, Latin and myopia before I was seventeen, and took my moderns at Troy. I keep up a little reading in all of the languages every week, so as to hold what I have and make further progress. That is the secret of knowledge—

hold and get.   Any intelligent person can become a fair linguist by persistent study."

Dayton became an authority in the steerage, and, by his modest efforts, infused a desire for culture there which bore rich fruits.

The next morning the ship was headed westward, and it was soon known that the Nautilus was ordered to Norfolk. Hampton Roads were reached in the afternoon, the anchor was dropped, Captain Prescott reported to the Captain of the Minnesota, and then went on shore and paid his respects to the General in command of Fortress Monroe.

There was news that the Confederates were giving the soldiers plenty of work at Suffolk and threatening an advance upon Norfolk, and the naval force was needed for the defence of the city.

How beautiful the land looked after the short voyage! The shores and trees still held their summer green, tinged here and there by the brown footsteps of autumn.   Fort Monroe stood silent and sullen upon the right; sentinels paced its parapet; the flag of the Union upon its staff snapped sharply in the wind, and great black guns frowned upon every side.   The light-house, the wharf and the great Union and Floyd guns upon a heap of sand on the shore, relieved the eye glancing seaward.   Midway in the Roads stood the unfinished, yet, formidable Rip Raps Fort, garrisoned by soldiers and crowded by laborers, who were busy working the huge derricks and ponderous stones to complete the massive walls. Just above, two English men-of-war and several wooden and iron-clad U. S. vessels swung at their anchors, and a few small craft were flitting across the haven.   The little village of Hampton lay in the cove above Monroe, and, upon the wooded bluff, far up the shore, one could see the rude shanties and tents and the long line of army wagons of an encampment, with a little wharf and a transport-steamer in front.

The James river stretched away like a great bay beyond, and the eye took up the misty outlines of the opposite shore and traced them outwards past the entrance of Elizabeth river and Norfolk, until it rested upon the wooded bluff of Sewell's Point.

This was the scene of two of the most thrilling naval battles of the war.   Here the Congress and Cumberland were de-

stroyed by the Merrimac.   Here the little Monitor fought a
fierce battle with that celebrated ironclad, and drove her,
shattered and defeated, back to her lair.

Mark you there near the shore that rough, charred line of
oaken ribs projecting a few feet above the tide?   Those are
the remains of the funeral pyre of brave men—the vestige of
the U. S. frigate Congress.   Out beyond in deeper water lies
the sloop-of-war Cumberland, with only her tops and a little
of the lower masts above the surface—melancholy monuments
to the heroes, who fought her batteries until the hungry sea
lapped up her decks and swallowed all.

The Nautilus was much admired by army men, and there
were a great many visitors on board whom it was necessary to
entertain.   This interfered somewhat with discipline, but a
great deal of drilling was done daily.   It was reported by a
dispatch-boat, that there were six Confederate ironclads below
the obstructions in James river.   The small arms and heavy
guns were loaded; a buoy was placed for slipping the cable;
steam was kept up, and a most vigilant watch was maintained.
During the day, only one boat at a time was permitted to go
ashore, and her officer had to look out for instant recall.   The
English ships had music on board every night, and, on one
occasion, the crews sang the "Bonnie Blue Flag."   The next
day some of the singers were soundly thrashed in Hampton
by a Nautilus boat's crew.   Ashton was in charge of the boat
and said he could not prevent the fight.   He said, "the
English officer was a dandy and had a light cane.   I asked
him why he carried it.   He replied, 'Oh, it's so jolly, you
know.'   That made me sick, and I left him in disgust."

No one was favorably impressed with the scions of nobility
belonging to the English navy, perhaps, because of their
known sympathy for the Southern cause; but the discipline
on board their vessels was fine, showing the advantage of
shipping men for a long term of service.

During the war, our naval vessels were manned partly by
farmer-boys, mechanics and longshore-men, all good men
after they had been trained, but it tried the patience of the
officers much to get them into fighting order.

Several times during the period the Nautilus lay in the
Roads, suspicious craft were seen in the James, and all hands

were called to quarters, only to be dismissed again, when it
was found that no enemy was approaching. The Nautilus
went up to Norfolk in a few days, anchored off the city, took
out a kedge-anchor and cable astern, swung round broadside
to the railroad bridge, and trained her guns upon it.

A council was held with the General commanding, and
instructions were received to destroy the bridge, if the enemy
approached, and, under certain circumstances, to bombard the
city. The dull boom of heavy guns day and night in the
direction of Suffolk; the departure of gunboats, and their
return, riddled by shot and shell, and bringing wounded and
dead to the Marine Hospital below Portsmouth; the reports of
Longstreet's attempt to erect batteries upon the Nansemond,
in order to drive supply vessels and gunboats out of the river;
the sentinels all around the city; the couriers riding hastily
over the hills, and the frequent communications with the fleet
below; all indicated that it was war times, and kept the
officers and men of the Nautilus alert and anxious.

Though the occasion would have been deprecated, there
was a desire upon the part of many to try the guns upon the
bridge and to knock down a few houses, to repay the inhabitants of Norfolk for their insulting and hostile conduct.

Portsmouth and Norfolk were in great contrast to the clean
and thriving cities of the North. War had paralyzed their
commerce; emptied their docks; taken away all the able-
bodied men, and left the women, the negroes and the crippled,
infirm, and sneaking white men behind.

Longstreet was finally repulsed at Suffolk; the crisis passed,
and free communication was permitted with the shore.

The Gosport Navy Yard was a sad sight—a ruin of blackened timbers, charred and sunken ships, piles of bricks and
stone and ghostly, windowless walls. The sloop-of-war Plymouth, dear to the hearts of midshipmen, showed only a line
of blackened ribs above the water. Patriotic hands had
burned and sunk her, and saved her from profanation. Would
they had been as completely successful with the Merrimac,
then she would not have been so formidable in the defence of
Norfolk, and, finally, laid her shattered frame upon the sand
beach below, like the skeleton of a warrior who has not
deserved burial.

CHAPTER V.

THE buildings upon both sides of Elizabeth river had an antiquated, substantial, quiet appearance, that reminded one of the Wm. Penn district of Philadelphia. They seemed to have been built for utility rather than show, and ornamentation, even upon the churches and public buildings, was reduced to a minimum. Granby and Freemason streets, in Norfolk, contained numerous portly mansions, belonging to the wealthier people, and markedly in contrast with their surroundings, but they could not be considered fine buildings. Throughout the city a Sabbath quiet prevailed. Very many of the houses had the curtains down, the shutters closed, the door-steps dusty, and the yards full of dirty paths and untrimmed bushes, showing the absence of care-takers, the lack of interest in present things, the hopelessness of a conquered city. Some residents let their property get in this unattractive state, so that not a verdant shrub or tender flower should gladden the hearts of the enemy patrolling the streets. Many persons, if they had followed their inclinations, would have planted nettles and wormwood, only they were afraid there might be some personal application made to themselves.

Here and there throughout the city of Norfolk, clean walks and grounds, open shutters, drawn lace curtains and, sometimes, smiling faces, indicated the homes of Union families, and such oases in the desert of rebel indifference were exceedingly pleasant to the hearts of Northern men. It is a peculiar and decidedly unpleasant feeling that one experiences, when surrounded by even helpless enemies.

Away from the main streets, very few people were seen, and those mostly negroes, slouching along with bundles or baskets. In the heart of the city, at the markets and stores, there was a motley crowd of negroes, bilious, lank-faced white men, and blue-coated soldiers of the U. S. army. The latter came and went, saying little, but keeping sharp eyes upon the loungers.

The principal business of the others seemed to be to chew tobacco, tell stories, and sleep in the shadows of the buildings.

Three-quarters of the stores were closed and their walls and
windows covered by posters of concerts, theaters and regiments. The open stores did a poor business with the soldiers,
sailors and the few residents who had any money to spend.
There were several distinct castes noticeable in the streets at
all times. The negroes were most numerous and amusing.
They were dressed in all kinds of garments, the cast-off clothes
of the higher classes. The men were partial to highly-colored,
variegated vests and broad-brimmed hats; the women, to bright
calico and red bandanna handkerchiefs. Here and there, a
soldier's cast-off cap, pants or overcoat helped out the civilian
rags. The great lips and pouchy cheeks, broad noses, densely-
curled, woolly hair, dirty bodies and lazy attitudes of these
contrabands, made them a striking contrast to the clean, intelligent negroes of the North and to the colored men of the
Nautilus.

Joshua, one of the wardroom boys, said, "Dem niggers
ashore is no good—all animals. I saw seberal ob dem wid de
teeth sharp like a shark's. I specs dey was cannibals 'fore dey
com'd here. I wouldn't like to be alone wid dem in de dark,
if dey was hungry. Dey'd eat a fellar shuar!" This was
acute criticism upon the lowest of his race.

The poor white men, holding up the corners of the city, and
telling stories of their experience, formed a distinct class.
They were not much better dressed than the negroes, but wore
many garments of butternut, gray and blue colors, having brass
buttons and other unmistakable marks of the soldier. They
were not prepossessing in countenance; their faces were lank
and sallow; the whiskers and moustache were thin, long and
wiry; the hair swept over low foreheads and behind the ears;
the necks craned forwards; the shoulders were stooped, and
the limbs were flung out from the spare trunk, as if the muscles were not developed sufficiently to handle them with precision. The wives of these men were very much like them in
build and attractiveness, and seemed always hard-worked and
disconsolate.

The men never cared for the future, worked only when it
was necessary, were said not to respect the rights of property

in country districts, and considered it the height of felicity
to tell stories, drink whiskey, and consume tobacco. They
were ignorant, and knew almost nothing of the world outside
of their own county; were miserably poor, having only the
fewest household goods, a gun and a dog, and depended upon
hunting, fishing, odd jobs and charity for a living. They had
little patriotism or love for the chivalry; were hard to keep
in the army, and were looked upon with suspicion by the
planters and with contempt by the negroes.

The "po' white trash" was fastened upon this class of hu-
manity by the latter, with whom they often came in conflict,
years ago, and seemed so appropriate that it has remained to
distinguish a distinct class in the Southern States to this day.

The groups around the market-place of Norfolk had some
of the genuine sort, as one could determine by listening a
short time to the story telling and profanity, but mingled with
them were the longshore-men and laborers of the city who had
escaped enrollment into the Confederate army or had deserted
afterwards.

The negroes were always full of smiles and bows, when
U. S. officers passed them, and invariably took off their hats
and said, "Good mornin', Massa Captain," or "Good ebenin',
Massa Colonel." The white loungers generally cleared the
walks and a few touched their hats, but other salutations were
rare. The storekeepers were barely polite, and could not be
drawn into any war talk. One could not blame them. They
were in the power of the United States; the guns at Suffolk
and upon the Nansemond had been making sweet music in the
ears of every friend of the Confederacy, telling them *their*
army was near. Perhaps within a week, the stars and bars
of *their* country would wave over them again. Conservatism
under such circumstances was eminently wise.

Occasionally one would meet old men, with silvery hair
and moustache, erect and stately form, and that dignified cour-
tesy that distinguishes a gentleman. They invariably bowed
slightly to all officers, though they knew them as enemies, and
passed on in reflective mood. The girls and young ladies
about the city could not restrain their curiosity to get good
views of the naval officers, and, though they would dodge
from the doors and windows, hide behind fences and corners,

get entirely off the walk, turn their faces away and even hold their dresses back, so that no touch of the North should pollute them, they would relax their vigilance, when they thought they were not observed, and look with the greatest eagerness.

Master Bloss was a large man, with brilliant black eyes, black hair and moustache, and clean-cut lips that could roll out the most exquisite English. He was an active and faithful officer; always up in professional studies and general literature, and exceedingly fond of a cigar, a bottle of wine, and a good story. He averted threatening quarrels among his messmates by a flash of wit or an apropos quotation, and was a great favorite on board ship. Such men are the salt of sea-life.

Ashton and Lawson had been ashore one afternoon, and came on board just before supper not in pleasant mood.

"What's the matter, Mr. Ashton; did you meet with any mishap ashore?" asked Sanborn.

"Mishap! No; we were insulted repeatedly by the people along the street. I don't see why the Provost Marshal allows U. S. officers to be abused in his department. I'd blow the place up first."

"Why, how was it?" asked several.

"Well, we were going along to look at the crib, and three or four females yelled out of a window, 'See those nasty Yankee officers!' We lifted our caps and went on."

"Nothing but giddy girls, I suppose," said Careswell.

> "A little rosebud set in wilful thorns,
> And sweet as English air could make her,"

chimed in Bloss.

"Yes, sweet and dirty," replied Lawson.

"We went up the hill, and a lot of street loafers cried, 'See them Lincolnites, nigger lovers, abolitionists!' I swear I would have killed some of them, if I'd had a revolver along," said Ashton, and his eyes flashed wickedly.

"To cap the climax," said Lawson, "we met a very beautiful young lady, handsomely dressed, near the Baptist church; she could not get off the walk into the dirty street, and so stepped inside the walk near the fence, drew her skirts closely around her legs, so as not to touch us, and when we went by hissed at us like a venomous reptile."

"Well, you were particularly unfortunate; you must have had the appearance of conquering heroes, or you would not have awakened so much rebellion," remarked Felton.

"Mr. Dayton and I had some adventures last Sunday which were almost as bad," said Careswell. "Several ladies held their dresses away and got off the walk, as if we were bales of small-pox. Some girls at the church entrance called us 'Lincoln's hirelings,' 'Yankee abolitionists,' 'Nigger lovers.' When we went into church, no one would give us a seat. We marched well up front and took a pew, with an aristocratic name on the door-plate, elegant cushions and finely gilded and clasped prayer-books, and the congregation, mostly women and old men, nearly all dressed in black, scowled upon us from all sides. That's war Christianity. The minister prayed covertly for the success of the South, exhorted slaves to obey their masters, and preached a moderate doctrinal sermon. He spoke of 'a barrier of steel dividing kindred,' and gave out the hymn, 'When foes assail and tyrants frown.'"

"He meant foes of the Union, of course," said Paymaster Horton.

"Not a bit," continued Careswell; "he looked significantly at our pew, and so did the congregation."

"The observed of all observers," remarked Bloss, "How happy you must have been!"

"Well, we were not unhappy," replied Careswell, "we paid more attention to the service than the rest of them. It was a little funny to hear ourselves prayed against, but one must get used to everything these times. These people are not changing our principles by their mockery and insults, only drying up little by little the human sympathy which every Northern man has for the unfortunate and distressed. The masses are grossly ignorant of the character of Northern people; the newspaper men, orators and leaders paint us in the blackest characters, in order to excite the greatest opposition, and to keep the slaves from fleeing to us. One dollar in greenbacks is worth one dollar and sixty-two cents in Virginia scrip. The goods are marked in the two currencies in the stores. Now, that's a fair estimate of the relative value of a Northern and Southern man. In education, ability, integrity and moral worth, one Northerner is worth about one Southerner plus sixty-two one-hundredths of another one, and these deluded people and chivalric humbugs will find it out before many years." Having delivered this speech, which evoked hearty laughter, Careswell took a drink of claret and said no more.

Lawson took up the thread of conversation as the supper went on, and said, "We met several old gentlemen, whom we knew to be rebels, and they bowed to us with cool politeness. Gentlemen always bow to each other, in the South, whether they have been introduced or not. We passed an old gentleman with his lovely daughter, on Freemason street; both bowed and said 'Good morning' so heartily, and smiled so pleasantly that we knew they must belong to the Union side. It was awfully refreshing to meet the loyal and true after the experience of the morning, and when we met some of Gen. Vielé's staff-officers, and talked over matters, we felt relieved."

"They said 'the citizens of Norfolk were bitter secessionists; had lost many relatives in late battles, and were greatly disappointed at Longstreet's failing to retake Norfolk, and this last fact accounted for the evidence of animosity, which had slumbered quietly for some months. We have passed through the same experience here. We have been cognizant of these petty insults to officers of all grades in the services, and have arrested some persons for their misbehavior, then let them go, because it is not our duty to teach the people of Norfolk good manners. There are some people here, who are ardent secessionists, yet are as polite and considerate as one could wish. The educated, traveled people know us better than the middle class, and respect us, though they believe us to be fighting upon the wrong side in this 'Second American Revolution,' as they like to call it.'"

"It is all owing to a fellow's bringing up, I suppose," said Sanborn. "A city fellow don't know a squash from a pumpkin, nor a countryman a brigadier-general from a New York policeman."

This sally caused a laugh around the table, and made the injured members of the mess feel more comfortable. Soon after a few army officers came on board and spent the evening, and the talk about the relations with the South was resumed.

"I have brought you gentlemen some choice rebel literature, which we get through the lines occasionally by deserters and captures," said Captain Brush. "You will see how the Northern people are held up to execration in the most abominable language. Hear what this fellow says of us:

"'We have captured, in serviceable condition, seven of the most formidable engines of war the enemy had afloat, which are now being turned to account in a good cause, serving in the 'Confederate States' navy against God-defying infidelity and hell-deserving abolitionists, who, actuated by the basest instincts of brute nature, confront us with lustful designs of fiends incarnate.'"

"That fellow must have been chewing soap," said Bloss, referring to a burlesque Othello, who chewed soap in order to foam at the mouth with an appearance of rage, during the smothering scene.

The captain read on:

"'Let us put our hope and trust in the God of hosts, for He hath set us apart as His chosen people, hence the scourging we are now receiving by the visitation of revolution and war, which has deluged our fair land in blood and anguish. If there is a people upon the face of the earth that cannot be made slaves, but which He has appointed as His own people and agents to perpetuate the work of civilization, it is the people of the Confederate States of America, the descendants of the Caucassian and Jewish races, who are entrusted with the fostering care and protection of the African race as an institution of servitude to civilization. We are commanded to foster and perpetuate this institution for the benefit of future ages. God has commanded us to buy our servants from the heathen nations to be an inheritance to our children and our children's children.'"

The captain paused.

"This is rather peculiar reasoning," remarked Mr. Felton. "It must be comforting to believe the Lord chose the Southerners in order that they might be thrashed, but I think we ought to have the credit of doing it. These chosen people, who can not be made slaves, are God's agents to perpetuate civilization by perpetuating slavery. That is simply blasphemy according to my ideas."

"Do you remember the syllogism?" asked Sanborn, with a twinkle in his eyes.

"I have heard of it," replied Felton smiling.

"One might apply it here," said Sanborn.

"All people who are scourged are the chosen people of God.

The Southerners are scourged by the Yankees.

Therefore, the Southerners are the chosen people of God.

"Again,

"The chosen people of God always promote the highest civilization.

But the Southerners seek to injure civilization by perpetuating slavery.

Therefore, the Southerners are not the chosen people."

This diversion caused much merriment and Careswell said, "That's enough tripods. We will take a dissertation upon the nineteen moods of the syllogism some other time."

"Captain Brush, has that fellow anything else interesting?" asked Lawson.

"Yes, I'll read you a little more," said the captain. "'The majority of our enemies . . . . are now being informed, by the force of circumstances, by unaccustomed intercourse and association with the negro, of their error in the course and policy they have adopted with regard to the whole African race, finding they can do nothing and accomplish less with such as have been captured and others who were induced to leave their good and kind masters and mistresses, they are now being prepared, drilled and armed for service and to be placed in the front lines of battle (finding them an unwieldy mass of helplessness and inferiority for the accomplishment of any other purpose). First being placed in the front lines of battle the negro will serve as a breastwork to shield the bodies and preserve the lives of degraded and polluted Yankees. Second having served such purpose and being slain upon the field of battle, the Yankees have no more trouble with Cuffee, and say he has been turned to good account.

"'Thus it will be seen that the poor and deluded African is to serve a two-fold purpose to the Abolition Yankees of the East, whose principles must be corrupting to the most depraved and demoniac fiends of hell.

"'Permit me, kind reader, to ask does not a contemplation of the Yankee character excite in you a feeling of condemnation and scorn mingled with alternate pity and contempt for our demented enemy whose every existence, *being* and *to be* (now and forever) is qualified by the epithet Yankee, a term comprehensively expressive of all that is impure, inhuman, uncharitable, unchristian and uncivilized (barbarian and heathen is scarcely applicable in the case), demons of hell in the guise of men.

"'I have not done yet. If, indeed, there should be a discrepancy it will be found in favor of language not containing words of sufficient force to express the baseness of the character and nature of the Yankees and the perverting influence of their self established creed, which has given birth to all the demoralizing, degrading, and hellish isms, including (the last though not the least) equalityism or negrophilism.'"

The captain ceased reading and looked around with a smile. The expressions of the different faces were studies for an artist. They gave evidence of amusement, curiosity, deep thought, and indignation. There was a moment's silence, then Ashton broke out, "The impudent scalawag! The diaphanous shallow-pate! The prognathous liar! Who is this fellow, who slings such foul ink from a safe distance?"

"His name is—fiddlesticks—what matter what his name is?" replied Brush. "He would only be too proud to have it mentioned. Here, you can read it yourself. A man who would use such language and tell such falsehoods is beneath contempt. He hails from Georgia, far enough away from the lines of battle to be perfectly safe, or he would not write such bathos. For my part, I should be inclined to question his loyalty to the Southern cause, he tries to be *so very* virulent. I am sure that the better people of the South have little sympathy with this sort of jaw-bone warfare, but it serves to give many, who do not know better, very erroneous opinions of our character, which accounts in part for our treatment in Norfolk."

"I am of your opinion," said Mr. Felton, quietly pulling his moustache between his fingers. "I know so many good fellows, who have gone with the South in this unpleasantness, that I cannot believe they hold such opinions as are expressed by this blackguard. The most pronounced abolitionists and the most rabid pro-slavery men formed a band of brothers at Annapolis. When the Academy was broken up and the Southern students left, they were cheered by the loyal middies. When the fortunes of war have thrown naval officers of one side into the power of the other, there has generally been an interchange of friendly courtesies, though the officers of the Cumberland refused to shake hands with their captors. ,I feel towards these rebels, as I should towards an erring brother, who has sinned greatly, but whom I am ready to forgive."

"Human nature is human nature," said Careswell sententiously. "These people are our enemies and we are theirs, and we need not waste any sentiment upon them until they deserve it. Peace and war make different feelings in people, and we may expect the most treacherous and deadly enmity from former acquaintances in the South. There will be exceptions now and then, but it behooves us all to be on our guard and to keep our side-arms ready."

"That is so!" said Ashton. "If I had only had my revolver to-day!"

"You'd have shot one of those girls in the window, wouldn't you?" asked Bloss, humming in a low tone,

> "I have a tress of silken hair,
>   That was severed from thy brow;
> A truant curl most beautiful,
>   I'm gazing on it now."

Ashton scowled, and said, "No; a loafer whom the city would not have missed."

"Would you have shot a defenseless man?"

"Well, no, but I would have arrested him and turned him over to the army."

"*Tres-bien, avez soin, vous n'êtes pas le roi.* Hello! what have we here?" continued Bloss, separating the *Chattanooga Rebel* from the pile of Southern literature that Captain Brush had brought on board. He then said, "Hearken to this:

"'A CONFEDERATE ALPHABET.'"

"'A is for Anderson, foremost and least;
B is for Bethel, or Butler the Beast;
C is for Chase and also for Cheat,
D is for Darkies, Disaster, Defeat;
E is for Eagle, transformed to a crow,
F is the Flag spreading ruin and woe;
G is for Gibbet on which we will hang,
Hunter the Hound and all of his gang;
I is the infamy of which they are proud,
J Johnson the Jackall, the worst of the crowd;
K is the Kalendar of accidents dire,
L is for Lincoln, the Long Legged Liar;
M's for McClellan who Richmond would see,
N is for Never, when his it shall be;
O shows what Yankees will make by the war,
Q is for Query, "what is it all for?"
P, which was passed, stands for Puppy and Pope,
R is for Rosecrans, Rascal and Rope;
S stands for Seward, well surnamed the Snake,
T, the three months, the Rebellion will take;
U's for the Union of all that is base,
V for the Victories that never took place;
W for Winfield, whose victories great,
Xerxes-like ended in shameful defeat;
Y stands for Yankees that self-esteemed nation,
Z is for zero, their true valuation.'"

"There, gentlemen," said Bloss, "if that is not enough to turn the milk of human kindness sour, I don't know what would. I feel the gall rising in my throat now. When a leading journal vilifies some of our best men in that scandalous manner, we can readily understand what they think of the rest of us. I'm going to have my sword ground to morrow."

"Come and join our cavalry, Lieutenant; we'll give you a longer blade," said Lieut. Hart. "You could not do much in a hand to hand fight with your naval toad-sticker."

"Is this the fruit of war," asked Sanborn, "that one side must abuse the other so shamefully? History is full of atrocities perpetrated by armed men upon their enemies, but she is silent about these personal outrages upon character. We think the Southerners are chivalric and brave; ardent in love of their section; wrong in their support of state rights and human slavery, and deficient in that finer sense of morality that permeates society at the North. Bad as we know them

to be in some sections, you may search the entire press of the
North and you will not find as much misrepresentation and
billingsgate about them, as is condensed about us in this miserable article."

"These are the utterances of policy and spitefulness," spoke
up Surgeon Willett. "They are welcome to the masses, because they feel impotent to avenge their fancied wrongs, but
passion past, the educated people of the South will repudiate
such stuff. I am sure the action of Major Anderson commands the respect of the civilized world, and the other names
mentioned will stand high upon the pages of history. We
must fight these people into subjection; educate them to an
understanding of moral purity, and prove that we are actuated
by principles of justice, not blinded by the mad partisanship
of the hour."

"Have another glass of sherry, gentlemen," said Lawson,
as the doctor ceased speaking.

The doctor was as calm as a May morning. He was a me-
dium-sized, solidly-framed man, about twenty-five years of
age. His features were regular and expressive; his dark eyes
had a depth and steadiness in them which attracted attention,
and his brown hair and moustache and the poise of his head
gave him an aristocratic bearing. He was rather reticent, but
always expressed practical common sense when he spoke, to
which every one was glad to listen.

"I've had enough sherry to give me gout for a week," said
Lieut. Hart.

"Good wine don't give soldiers the gout," said Willett.

"That's because they seldom get it," said Brush. "We
poor devils have to put up with Commissary whiskey. I
sometimes think it's a fraud for us to drink your fine wines
and then set out army stuff when you visit us. Here's confusion to our enemies and damnation to the man who wrote
that doggerel" said he, as he tossed off his glass of sherry with
the others. "Lieutenant Felton and gentlemen, we shall be
glad to see you at Headquarters any time." '

"Come often, gentlemen," said Lieut. Hart, "we shall not
have these pleasant opportunities long."

"We shall all be glad to see you aboard any time," said
Mr. Felton. "Boy, tell the deck-officer to order the second

cutter, with a midshipman in charge, to take the gentlemen ashore."

The boat was ordered ; the officers shook hands all around, said "Good-night," were accompanied to the gangway by Felton and Willett, and then taken ashore. At ten o'clock, the lights were put out, and all was quiet except the steady tramp of the officers and men on deck, keeping the first watch of the night.

The conversation of this evening and the rebel literature made a deep impression upon the officers of the Nautilus, and did much to strengthen their opinions upon the justice of their cause, and the necessity for punishing those in rebellion against the Government. Henceforth, things were named correctly ; rebels were rebels, and Southern seceders from the army and navy were called traitors.

The immediate danger of attack from the enemy having passed, a little more liberty was permitted, and a boat could be obtained for excursions up the river, across to the Marine Hospital, and down to Hampton. The surroundings of Norfolk were not very attractive, and, late in the season as it was, there was a peculiar stuffy smell along the river, which was anything but agreeable. The doctor said the atmosphere was full of malaria, and he cautioned everybody to be careful of exposure after sunset.

The Marine Hospital was clean and comfortable, but had the admixture of odors which indicated suppurating wounds and savage sufferings. Many of the pretty white beds contained men badly shattered by bullets and grape-shot, and, though all that was possible was being done by skilful surgeons, the death damp rested upon many a brow and shocked visitors into a remembrance of the frailty of man and the horrors of war.

The visits to Newport News, Hampton, Fortress Monroe, and the naval vessels in the Roads, were very enjoyable, and full reports of the incidents of a trip furnished topics of conversation in the evening and kept the mess lively. A vessel arrived from the North nearly every day and brought letters and late journals, so that everybody was kept informed of the progress of the war, as papers were passed from officer to officer and from man to man, until the smallest boy in the ship had read their soiled and worn-out columns.

It was amusing to see the reports of affairs in the immediate vicinity, and to read the misspelled names of those who deserved and coveted fame. A *N. Y. Tribune* correspondent came on board one day and was taken to task for his reports, but he threw all the blame upon the compositors and proof-readers, and claimed that he wrote a hand a thousand per cent. better than Greeley's. He then began a direct, indirect, circumlocutory style of quizzing for facts, which was so persistent and searching, that the officers were glad to fill him up with sardines, cheese, hard-tack, sherry, &c. and to get rid of him, feeling as exhausted and empty after he had gone, as he must have felt replete and comfortable. Several had supposed prior to this experience, that any one could be a newspaper correspondent, but this indefatigable fellow caused a complete revolution of opinion.

The next morning Bloss came down to breakfast " mad clear through." He cursed the engineers because they would not do their duty, in sending men from their department to hoist up the ashes early and to wash and scour the engine-room skylights and gratings, and ended by reporting one of the assistant-engineers to Mr. Felton for disobedience of orders. Felton had a talk with the chief, and he disciplined the refractory officer by an extra watch. There is frequent trouble between the engineers and officers-of-the-deck from this cause; the former hinder the morning work and make themselves obnoxious, because, having a special department, they do not like to acknowledge the supremacy of the deck-officer, and because they forget the golden rule. If the engineers of a ship are not held in esteem by the wardroom officers, it is because they are guilty of petty meanness unbecoming officers and gentlemen. In conflicts of authority, the deck-officer is supreme, because, while on duty, he has full charge of the ship, is responsible for her condition, discipline and safety, and represents the captain. The executive enforces his just and often his unjust orders, because orders must be obeyed first and considered afterwards.

The morning watch from 4 to 8 A.M. is full of the miseries of dashing water, wet decks, wet feet, wet clothes, flying buckets, grinding holystones, flourishing brooms, dirty swabs, and scrapers. Women clean house once or twice a year, but Jack Tar cleans the ship every morning, in port or out, from kelson to truck, from water line to midships. Then the running rigging must be hauled taut, yards braced, sails snugged or trimmed, ropes coiled down, guns cleaned, brasswork scoured bright, hammocks lashed and stowed, and the watch below piped to breakfast. The steady grind of the holystones and sand upon the deck, the rattle of buckets and other paraphernalia, the shuffling footsteps, the sharp orders, and the frequent ze-ze-ing of the boatswain's mate's whistle, make a racket that awakens those unaccustomed to man-of-war life, and causes considerable growling below and upon deck. The officer-of-the-deck growls at the petty officers, the petty officers at the men, the men at the boys, and the boys start a grumble that goes back along the line, growing milder and milder until it reaches the quarter-deck. The bulk of the work is done at four-bells, or six o'clock; the ship's cook gives the men coffee; a wardroom boy brings a cup of coffee and some hardtack to the deck-officer, and the respite and refreshments generally restore good humor.

Sailors are great growlers, and ominous muttering can be heard in some part of the ship at all times of day and night. Jack will curse the calm, the wind, the sky, the sea, the ship, the shore, the officers, and the Government, but he don't mean anything by it. He could not be hired to stay ashore, and will defend the very things he has just maligned with the first one who answers him. He is at one time misanthropic and miserable; at another, the jolliest dog afloat; he is careless of self, fearless of danger, fond of adventure and full of generosity; he is proud of his ship and his sweetheart; faithful to his flag and country, and regardless of the value of money, often dissipating the wages of a two or three years' cruise in the riotous debauchery of a month. Then he is ready for another cruise, and goes cheerfully to work again.

CHAPTER VI.

EVERYBODY on board the Nantilus had seen enough of
Norfolk and vicinity, and was glad when a dispatch-boat
brought orders from Washington, countersigned by the flag-
officer of the station, to go to sea. The kedge was taken
aboard; the anchor weighed; the fleet passed with the customary cheers, and at meridian the gallant ship was breasting
the billows of the restless ocean, with the course directed
southward. The screw was hoisted up, the fires were banked,
all sail was made, and for several days the good bark went
bowling along at the rate of ten knots an hour, with a strong
southwest breeze. The sailors were kept busy setting up the
stays and shrouds, as they stretched in the warm sunlight;
the men of the watch off duty sought snug spots between the
guns and, sheltered from the wind, opened their bags, overhauled their clothing, and stitched, mended and talked the
hours away; the steerage officers chatted in the lee gangway
and read papers and books in cosy places, and the wardroom
officers brought up camp-stools and sat under the midshipman's
deck, smoking, reading and talking, as they watched through
the open gun-port the rapid race of waters astern.

The conversation one forenoon was upon the destruction
caused by the rebel ironclad Merrimac, and the splendid services rendered the country by Capt. Werden and the little
Monitor, in driving her back shattered and demoralized.

"It was not a fight between the Merrimac and Monitor at
all," said Careswell, "but between the Virginia and Monitor."

"You are mistaken," said Ashton; "it was the old Merrimac that had been burned by us when we destroyed the navy
yard; her upper works only were damaged; the rebs built
her up, plated her with boiler-iron, and then knocked spots
out of our wooden vessels."

"You are correct," replied Careswell, "but she was renamed
the Virginia, and so figures in the *Confederate Naval Register*."

"That is true," said the doctor; "that's the way history'

gets falsified. While we remember her as the old Merrimac, the Southerners know her as the Virginia." No one doubted any longer, for the doctor had a phenomenal memory upon which his messmates had learned to rely.

"I don't wish to go to sea in any such iron coffins as the Monitors," said Careswell. "They pitch their noses under and lift great seas upon them, which break around the turret and rush off the sharp stern like Niagara. The seas roll right across the deck, dash over the obstructions, and run in at every opening. The hatches are all closed solidly at sea, the dead-light holes on deck are full of water, and the only openings from below are up through the smoke-stack and the turret. The only escape in a heavy seaway is by a two feet by four hatch in the grating-like, iron deck of the turret; it would be impossible to get at the boats, if they had not been swept away, and next to impossible for any boats to approach for rescue without being dashed to pieces. I don't see how the Monitor's crew ever escaped. The heat from the furnaces and the foul air accumulated below deck, owing to the imperfect ventilation, are almost unendurable, and the duties and discipline are more comparable to those of a machine-shop than to a man-of-war."

"You are right," said Ashton. "I had a dose off Charleston last fall. I couldn't stand it to live like a hot-house plant and went home sick."

"Have you read the rebel account of the first fight?" Careswell asked the doctor.

"No," said he; "but I suppose it is greatly exaggerated."

"Yes; I have it down below in the *Illustrated News*. I will get it and read the article."

Careswell got the paper and read as follows:

"'On the 19th of April, when the Massachusetts troops were attacked on their passage through Baltimore city, Capt. Buchanan was in command of the navy yard at Washington. He immediately resigned his commission, and, in a short time thereafter, tendered his services to the Southern Confederacy, which were promptly accepted, and he drew his sword in defence of Southern independence. He was assigned to duty as Chief of Orders and Detail, in the Confederate navy, then in its infancy, and in February, 1862, hoisted his flag at Norfolk on board the iron-clad frigate Virginia, such being the name given by the Confederate Navy Department to the United States frigate Merrimac, partially burnt and sunk by Commodore Paulding, when the Federal forces evacuated the Norfolk navy yard on the secession of Virginia, and on Saturday, the 8th of March, 1862, engaged the enemy off Newport's News. It may not be uninteresting to the readers of our paper to give here a short description of this the greatest naval engagement that ever took place in American waters.

" 'The Virginia had been cut loose from her moorings, and was on her way down the harbor, when Commodore Buchanan, calling "all hands to muster," delivered the following brief but spirited address to the crew:

" 'Men, the eyes of your country are upon you. You are fighting for your rights—your liberties—your wives and children. You must not be content with only doing your duty; but *do more than your duty!* Those ships (pointing to the Yankee vessels) *must* be taken, and you shall not complain that I do not take you close enough. Go to your guns!"

" 'How well the officers and the gallant crew of that "monster of the deep" performed their whole duty, we let an eye-witness of that memorable engagement tell:

" 'The morning was still as that of a Sabbath. The two Yankee frigates lay with their boats at the boom, and wash-clothes in the rigging. Did they see the long, dark hull? Had they made her out? Was it ignorance, apathy, or composure? These were the questions we discussed as we steamed across the flats to the south of the frigates with the two gallant little gun-boats well on our starboard beam heading up for the enemy. Our doubts were solved by the heavy boom of a gun from beyond Sewell's Point. The reverberation rolled across the sun-lit water and died away, but still the clothes hung in the rigging, still the boats lay at the booms. Another gun (21 minutes past 1) broke on the air, and a tug started for Newport's News, while at the same time two others left Old Point, taking the channel inside Hampton bar. Steadily, with a grim and ominous silence, the Virginia glides through the water, steadily and with defiant valor the Beaufort and Raleigh followed where she led. At ten minutes to two, a rifle gun from one of these little vessels rang out, then a white puff from her consort. Still the clothes in the rigging, still the boats at the boom! Was this confidence? It could not be ignorance. Did it mean torpedoes, submarine batteries, infernal machines? The gun-boats have fired again, and lo! here away to the eastward were the Roanoke and Minnesota rising like prodigious castles above the placid water, the first under steam, the second in tow. Other puffs of smoke, other sharp reports from the gun-boats, but the Virginia goes on steadily, silently to do her work. Now the inshore frigate, the Cumberland, fires; now the Virginia close aboard; now Sewell's Point battery; now the Minnesota; now the Roanoke; now the air trembles with the cannonade. Now the Virginia delivers both broadsides; now she runs full against the Cumberland's starboard bow; now the smoke clears away, and she appears heading up James River. This at twenty-two minutes to two. The Congress now lets fall foretopsail, and then the main, and so with a tug alongside, starts down the North channel, where the Minnesota has grounded, and presently runs plump ashore. Meanwhile the Virginia opens fire upon the Yankee fort, slowly she steams back, and the Cumberland, sunk now to her white-streak, opens upon her again. A gallant man fought that ship—a man worthy to have maintained a better cause. Gun after gun he fired, lower and lower sunk his ship, his last discharge comes from his pivot-gun, the ship lurches to starboard, now to port, his flag streams out wildly, and now the Cumberland goes down on her beam ends, at once a monument and an epitaph of the gallant man who fought her. The Virginia stops. Is she aground? And the gunboat? Raleigh and Beaufort! glorious Parker! glorious Alexander! there they are on the quarters of the Congress hammering away, and creeping up closer and closer all the time. At ten minutes to four the Congress struck. Parker hauled down the ensign, run up his own battle-flag in its place, there the heroic Taylor, who fought the Fanny at Roanoke Island and Elizabeth City, got his wound —there the gallant young Hutter fell, all shot by the dastards who fired from the ship and shore when the white flag was flying at the main and mizzen of the Congress! Here too, and in the same way, Flag Officer Buchanan and Flag Lieut. R. D. Minor, were wounded. Now the James River gunboats, whose dark smoke had been seen against the blue distance ever since three o'clock, came dashing along past the shore batteries. Tucker, the courtly and chivalrous, leading the van with the Jamestown, Lieutenant-Commanding Barney, close aboard, and the little Teaser, Lieut. Webb, in her wake —like a bow-legged bulldog in chase of the long, lean, staghound. It was a gallant dash, and once past the batteries, the two heavy vessels took position in line of battle, while the Teaser dashed at the Minnesota, looking no larger than a cock boat. And right well she maintained the honor of her flag and the appropriateness of her name. Now the Roanoke puts her helm up and declines the battle. Now the Virginia is thundering away again. The Teaser is still closer in. We are closer in—sizz comes a shell ahead, presently another astern, finally a third with a clear, sharp whizz, just overhead, to the great delight of the Commodore, who appreciated the compliment of these good shots, which were the last of six shots directed at the Harmony. Now the schooner Reindeer comes foaming along, cut out from under the shore batteries; she reports, and is sent up in charge of Acting Master Gibbs.

"'And next the gallant Beaufort runs down. Parker steps and brings on board the great piece of bunting we saw hauled down just now. He brings also some thirty prisoners and some wounded men—men wounded under that white flag yonder desecrated by the Yankees. One of these lies stretched out, decently covered over, gasping out his life on the deck— a Yankee shot through the head, all bloody and ghastly, killed by the inhuman fire of his own people. Another pale and stern, the Captain of the Beaufort's gun, lies there too, a noble specimen of a man, who has since gone where the weary are at rest. A gallant man, a brave seaman!

"'We shake hands with Parker; he gets back to his vessel slightly wounded, as is Alexander, and steams back gallantly to the fight. The Patrick Henry, the Jamestown, the Teaser, the Beaufort, the Raleigh, and the grand old Virginia, are all thundering away. We steam down and speak the first. We hear a report of casualties, we shake hands with friends, we shove off, cheer and steam towards the Swash channel. Presently through the thickening gloom we see a red glare, it grows larger, and brighter, and redder. It creeps higher and higher, and now gun after gun booming on the still night as the fire reaches them, the batteries of the Congress are discharged across the water in harmless thunder. It was a grand sight to see, and by the light of the burning ship, we made our way back to Norfolk. At half-past eleven the act of retribution was complete, for at that hour, with a great noise, she blew up.

" ' When Commodore Buchanan was wounded and taken below, a feeling of deep sadness pervaded the entire crew, but they soon rallied when Flag Lieutenant Minor, himself wounded and sent below, appeared on deck, and delivered to them the following message from the noble flag officer :

" ' Tell Mr. Jones to fight the ship to the last—tell the men that I am not mortally wounded and hope to be with them again very soon.'

"The cheers that greeted the delivery of this message resounded far above the cannon's roar, and every man was again quickly at his post, dealing death and destruction with their heavy guns.

" ' Congress was in session when the engagement took place and shortly thereafter passed a bill creating the grade of Admiral in the Navy, to which position Buchanan was nominated by the President and confirmed by the Senate.

" ' The news of the great naval victory fled over the country with electric speed, and was received with wonder and astonishment by the people of the South, who regarded it as the turning point in our fortunes, then under a cloud from recent disasters to our arms at Donaldson and other places.

" ' England and France, with all their powerful resources, for two years had been endeavoring to solve the problem of iron-clad ships, but it remained for the Southern Confederacy, the youngest sister in the family of nations, to demonstrate conclusively, by actual trial in battle, their great efficiency, and thus to radically revolutionize the old system of naval warfare, a fact still more wonderful when we consider that the Virginia was cut down, mailed, armed, manned and fought with unprecedented success, all within the brief space of six months, by a people heretofore entirely dependent upon the Yankee States for all commercial advantages.' "

The gentlemen smoked on in silence for a few moments, then Ashton spoke up excitedly :

"It was a gallant fight and I wish I had been there. This report is loose and unsatisfactory. It is easy to see that it is not an official one. In a general fight, the surrender of one vessel don't compel the rest of the fleet to cease firing. It was very natural that some random shots should fly around the Congress, and some persons should get hurt, even with the white flag flying. The shots were not from under the flag of truce, but from an infantry regiment on shore. Parker and Buchanan knew the Congress was not responsible, yet they opened fire upon her maimed heroes.

"The disaster to our fleet was unavoidable, because there was no suspicion that the rebels had an ironclad that could cope with the heavy guns and splendid ships we had in the Roads," said Mr. Felton. "I am sorry that Buchanan and Minor cast their lot with the enemy, and considered their fealty to states more binding than to the Nation which they had sworn to serve. They were good, brave fellows; it was a pity to lose them and all the rest whom we knew so well."

"That states' rights question is a difficult one," said the doctor. "It is my opinion, if a man were influenced by sentiment, he would go with his state, if by reason, with the Nation. I have no doubt many officers left the United States' service in haste and now repent at leisure; believing then they were simply choosing between two Nations, whereas, they simply allied themselves with a rebellious faction which can never succeed."

"It is what might have been expected from the passionate and illogical Southerners," said Careswell. "It is hard, however, to fight against one's blood relations. I am not so sure we would all be here, had our states seceded. We should have thought over the matter long, however, and probably have most of us remained true to the central Government. The funny thing about Buchanan's action is, that neither his native, nor his adopted state, seceded, though he probably thought the former would."

"Well," broke in Bloss, "the most of the naval officers who went South have sea-ceded, that is, given up sea for land service, for we know they have no navy."

"What vessels they have are mighty fast, though," said the doctor. "There's the Florida, the"—

"Sail ho!" rang out sharply from the lookout up in the foretop-mast cross-trees.

"Where away?" hailed Sanborn, who was officer-of-the-deck.

"One point on the port bow, sir!" came the answer.

"Very well. Keep a sharp lookout!" said the officer, who went up on the poop-deck with the quartermaster and took a good look with a spy-glass at the speck of ship and smoke ahead.

The executive looked at her awhile, and summoned the captain, who remarked, "It is probably the British mail-steamer from the West Indies."

The group of officers scattered; some went below, others got private glasses and looked at the stranger, and soon after dinner was served. Careswell took the deck at meridian, and, about four-bells, informed Mr. Felton that 'he thought the stranger had changed her course more to the north'ard.' The course of the Nautilus was altered a little more to the east-ward, so as gradually to draw nearer to the steamer, which was now about four miles away, steaming rapidly, and leaving a long trail of characteristic, bituminous, black smoke behind her. The flag of the Nautilus was hoisted, and the stranger ran up the British ensign.

The officers and men were looking at the craft and specu-lating upon her character. None of them had seen a blockade-runner or a rebel cruiser at sea, and the captain seemed satis-fied the vessel was a British steamer. At last Careswell said 'Sanborn had chased the Florida during a flying cruise.'

"Where is Mr. Sanborn?" asked the executive.

"Down below, asleep," said several.

"Mr. Ashton, tell Mr. Sanborn I want to see him on deck immediately," said Felton.

Sanborn soon came up, rubbing his eyes, and looked rather sheepishly at the group of officers. He touched his cap to the executive, who told him he wanted his opinion upon a sus-picious sail.

"Where is she?" asked he.

"There, on the port bow," was the answer.

He looked at the vessel, started, grasped a glass quickly and looked again a moment, then uttered an oath and exclaimed, "That's the Florida, sir, as sure as I'm a sinner. I chased her last voyage. We almost caught her, and had a good long spell looking at her during the chase, but she gave us the slip after dark."

The captain's face flushed, and he ordered Mr. Felton to make chase with all steam and sail. All was excitement now. The executive took charge of the deck; "All hands make sail!" rang through the ship from the boatswain's mate; the course was changed directly for the Florida; the royals and several staysails were set; the sails were trimmed carefully; the screw was lowered; the fires were unbanked, coaled, and stirred up, and the Nautilus flew through the water about twelve knots an hour.

The instant the course of the Nautilus was changed, the bow of the Florida swung around to the southeast, and her smoke-stack began to belch forth great volumes of dense, black smoke, showing that the fires were being fed freely, and she sped over the water like a flying-fish.

The sails of the Nautilus drew beautifully, and the screw revolved fast enough to add something to the speed, yet, it was apparent, the first half hour of the chase, that the Florida was drawing away from her. No. 1 gun's crew was called to quarters and the executive said, "Mr. Careswell, take charge of your gun and see if you can't reach her with a shell!"

"Aye, aye, sir!" was the reply.

Careswell and the crew soon had the 30-pounder rifled Parrott on the forecastle cast loose and ready for action, and reported, "All ready, sir!"

"Give her extreme elevation and fire as the ship goes off a point!"

"Aye, aye, sir!"

"Quartermaster, keep her off one point and steady!" ordered Felton.

"Aye, aye, sir! Off one point and steady it is, sir!"

All hands watched the discharge with anxiety. Careswell aimed the pivot gun himself with great care and pulled the lockstring. There was a flash, a puff of smoke, a sharp report, a whizzing sound, and the shell flew high in the air, then curved downwards, struck the water, ricochetted a few rods, and exploded within a hundred yards of the enemy's stern.

"Well done, sir," said Felton. "Load with a heavy charge and try her again."

The interest among the initiated and the excitement of the green hands were intense. All were watching the stranger, and noticed that she altered her course a little more to the southward. The gun was loaded and another shell exploded, as it seemed to the lookers-on, just under the stern of the Florida. This caused a murmur of applause from the men.

"You are doing well, sir," said Felton. "Load and fire as fast as you can!"

The ship was pointed for the Florida, during the intervals of the discharges, and steered off a point when the gun was ready. The Nautilus was shooting through the water; the Florida was going like a bird, with her black smoke clouding the sky; the shells were bursting just in her wake every few minutes, and every one was hopeful of coming to close quarters, when there was suddenly an ominous flapping overhead, and the royals were quivering along their weather luffs. Every sailor's hopes sank, for it was evident the ship was running close to the wind which was changing, and the courses the vessels were running would soon render the square sails useless.

In another half hour, the topgallant sails and topsails were flapping against the masts, and orders were reluctantly given to take in the square sails, which was accordingly done. The Florida was slowly drawing away, and the officers and men were frantic. The engines were driven at their fullest speed; several howitzers were moved from the forward spar-deck to the quarter-deck, and many of the men were crowded aft to keep the stern of the ship down and steady, so that the screw might do its best, but the Nautilus could not keep up her former speed. The Florida rapidly increased the distance from her pursuer; the Parrott gun stopped talking and was secured; the men stood around and cursed their luck, and the officers listened to a lecture from Lawson upon the respective merits of American contract and English engines. Everybody was ill-humored and disgusted, and, when night fell and hid the distant speck from sight, there was a sullen gloom about the ship that showed the bitter disappointment of all hands.

Cape Hatteras and Cape Lookout were far behind, and those stormy regions had smiled with beautiful weather. The sailors say,

"If Cape Lookout lets you pass,
Then look out for Hatteras."

There was a delicious aroma in the breeze all night, a fruity, flowery smell, most delicious in the nostrils of a brine-soaked sailor, which told of land not far away. Early in the morning, the lighthouse and pretty island of Abaco were made out; the Nautilus steamed up Northwest Channel, past Stirrup Key and the Hens and Chickens, and away southeast from Carrysfort light-house. The water was clear and shallow, showing grayish green from the light sands of the Great Bahama Banks below; the deep-sea lead was frequently thrown to mark the depth of water, and to bring up the sand and tiny shells to confirm the vessel's position upon the chart.

The next night was foggy, and the sea was as smooth as glass; the ship rocked gently upon the lazy billows, and steamed onward slowly. Suddenly in the still night came a cry from the forecastle lookout, "Sail ho! Hard a starboard! A schooner, sir, dead ahead!"

Careswell was deck-officer and upon the bridge. He immediately yelled, "Hard a starboard, Quartermaster!" and, at the same moment, pulled the bell to the engineer to "stop," and another to "back," and the Nautilus almost touched the schooner's side.

It was dead calm and the small vessel was helpless. The Nautilus was turned around and run back near the schooner.

"Schooner ahoy! What schooner is that?" shouted Careswell.

"Schooner Harcourt, of Wilton, S. C.!" was the answer.

"Where are you from and where bound?"

"From South Edisto, bound to Nassau!"

"What is your cargo?"

"Eighty-four bales of sea-island cotton!"

"Very well; I will send a boat on board!"

The second cutter was piped away by the boatswain's mate

the boat was manned with armed men, and Mr. Sanborn was sent to board. He soon returned with the captain, the owner, and first mate of the schooner, which he had seized as a prize, and he had brought her papers and a Confederate and an English flag.

Capt. Prescott and Mr. Felton had been called, in the mean time, and were ready to receive the prisoners and to hear their story. The captain had run the blockade successfully, and expected to reach Nassau easily, but he had only coasted along shore, did not understand navigation well, had lost his reckoning, owing to squally weather and strange currents, and was glad to be captured and saved from shipwreck and danger. The owner of the vessel and cargo, who had never been to sea before, was equally rejoiced at his rescue from a watery grave, but he thought he paid rather dear for the ransom. The officers and owner were messed with the warrant officers forwards, and the sailors of the schooner were divided between the watches, under the surveillance of the petty officers.

The Nautilus lay by the prize nearly all night, putting provisions, water, luggage, instruments, charts, etc., on board, and the senior midshipman, Mr. Osborne, and a crew of eight good sailors were transferred to her, with orders to proceed to Philadelphia and report to the Commandant of the Navy Yard. A breeze sprang up towards morning, the schooner sailed away to the northward, with hearty cheers from both crews, and arrived home safely.

The fog had not lifted yet, and twice during the night the flapping of sails and the voices of men indicated the presence of vessels, which, when pursued by the Nautilus, vanished in the darkness like phantom ships. The escaping steam warned them in time of the presence of a steamer lying-to—a suspicious circumstance in those waters—and they changed their courses luckily in directions which the Nautilus did not happen to strike. It was presumed they were blockade runners on the way to or from Nassau, although they may have belonged to the merchant marine of the North.

After the prize had cleared away, the Nautilus proceeded on her course at a moderate rate of speed, and the officers and men of the watch below, who had all been on deck assisting in the work, turned in to their bunks and dream-bags. Hardly had they fallen asleep, before they were awakened by a shrill cry of " Breakers ahead! Hard a port !" and the violent ringing of the signal bells in the engine-room. The officers and men rushed upon deck, clothes in hand, and forward upon the forecastle to see the threatening reef.

Here they saw, not jagged rocks, lashed by foaming, roaring surf, but an enormous turtle, probably *Sphargis coriacea*, fully ten feet in length, throwing out its enormous flippers and sporting upon the surface of the rippled ocean. He seemed for a time unconscious of any intruders upon his domain, but the engine was started, the screw began to churn up the water and drive the ship ahead, and this king of the Chelonia paddled lazily away, and sank gradually below the surface and out of sight.

Everybody had a good laugh at the scare, though it had been so severe to a few that they felt more like crying—so near are laughter and tears. Such a night of excitement had not before been experienced on board; there was little slumber in the ship the remainder of the night, and everybody was glad to turn out early and get a cup of matutinal coffee with hardtack.

The next day was warm and sultry and the men were ordered into straw hats and white shirts. Their black hat-bands bore the name Nautilus in golden letters; the corners of their shirt collars were embroidered with blue stars; the shirt bosoms of some of the petty officers bore the national coat-of-arms, the sleeves, the typical anchor, and the heavy shoes were replaced by light slippers. The officers off duty donned straw hats and white pants, and the whole ship appeared lively, cheerful and summery. A sudden squall, with heavy thunder, sharp lightning and cold rain, forced a change back to the habiliments of winter, in the afternoon, and the wind hauled around to the northward and increased to a gale.

A schooner under close reefs was sighted, overhauled, and ordered to heave to, but either the captain did not hear, or was too much frightened to give the proper orders, and a blank cartridge was fired. This seemed to frighten him much, and he paid off sheets and tried to run away. Then a 30-pounder Parrott shell was fired through his mainsail and exploded beyond, and he hove to the wind, shivering upon the quarter-

deck, as much as his mainsail aloft.   An officer was sent on
board the supposed prize, and great was the disgust of all to
learn, when he returned, that it was a Boston vessel, loaded
with molasses, having papers all right, just out of Matanzas
and bound to New York.   The captain supposed the Nautilus
to be the Alabama, hence his perturbation.   The vessels exchanged salutes by dipping colors and sped on their way, one
to the icy north, the other towards the region of perpetual
summer.

The next morning the sky was cloudy and angry; the wind
was singing and roaring through the rigging; the great waves
were jumping up the sides of the ship like a lap-dog for
caresses; the spray was flying over the forecastle with each
plunge of the rolling, struggling ship; the upper yards were
sent down and everything lashed securely; the men were
dressed in oil-jackets and sou'westers, and gathered in little
knots under the bulwarks, holding on by rail-pins and gun
tackles; the two helmsmen and the quartermaster held the
wheel and glanced occasionally from the compass in the binnacle to the bow of the uneasy vessel; the officer-of-the-deck
had left the bridge and was walking up and down the quarter-
deck in the lee of the rail; the Mother Carey's chickens were
darting and chirping astern; the gulls were sailing around and
screaming sharply, and everything about was dismal and
threatening.

Down below it was not much more agreeable.   The bunks,
tables and shelves were creaking and cracking; the chairs and
camp-stools made sudden and noisy excursions around the
rooms, when they worked loose from their lashings; the
crockery, china, glass and silver ware rattled, jingled and rang,
as it moved about in the pocketed shelves prepared for it; the
wardroom boys tumbled about, as they put the guards and
rails upon the table for breakfast, and the officers steadied
themselves by doors and partitions, put on their clothes with
difficulty, then ventured to show their faces above the companion way, and shrank shivering back from the cold pelting
rain.

The Norther had come suddenly; the thermometer had
fallen from temperate to frigid; the bodies and hopes of those,
who the day before had rejoiced in balmy, summer air, were

chilled, and the storm necessitated slower speed towards the coast of Cuba.

The Norther is well known and dreaded by the citizens and sailors of the South. It drives the enervated to shelter; it nips the tender buds of the orange and vine; it prostrates poorly built houses and stately trees; it splits sails, breaks off topmasts, and strews the shores with wrecks.

Sailors like storms. There is something majestic in a furious gale. The spirit rises with the wind and waves. The force and energy increase with the elemental war and the necessity for action. A sailor is obliged to exert his power, his skill, his nautical knowledge to save himself and vessel from destruction, and the very exercise of these makes him feel proud that he can conquer often in the most adverse circumstances. He passes through manifold dangers; he has hundreds of hairbreadth escapes in a lifetime, and thinks no more of them than he would of the ordinary incidents of life in a metropolis. He loves to talk about them. His mind is full of oft repeated experiences. His tongue is ever ready to tell them to listeners. They are his literature, his library of useful knowledge; they are so strange, so startling, so extravagant to the dwellers upon *terra firma*, that they are disbelieved by the ignorant, the unimaginative and the untravelled. Jack is said to spin yarns. He does sometimes draw upon his imagination; but he tells not the half of what he might tell, in truth, of his voyage of life, far surpassing in thrilling interest that to which objection is made. Jack is a specialist, and none who have not pursued a parallel course with him can be fit judges of his character. Landsmen should not presume to sit in judgment, or they may be as ridiculous as the old lady whose son had made a voyage to the West Indies. He told her that "out to sea, one night, he hung a lantern up in the rigging, and so many flying-fish came on board that the crew had enough for breakfast; and, down in Cuba, there were hills of sugar and rivers of rum."

"I may well believe there are hills of sugar and rivers of rum," said the wise old lady, "but fish that fly the good Lord never did see."

"Tell that to marines" is an old saying, because they, of all a ship's company, are generally the freshest and greenest.

Jack ought to be credited with a fair presentation of facts, except when he is talking to marines. It is undeniable that he does sometimes lie to these unsophisticated and credulous individuals.

Jack glories in a rousing gale off Hatteras or Cape Clear, but he hates the sneaking, chilling, savage Norther, that comes plunging into the pleasures of a warm, tropic day, like a drunken loafer into an assembly of refined ladies, and any one who has experienced one of these cruel blasts will feel as he does.

Old Brenneman, one of the boatswain's mates, was particularly grumpy upon this disagreeable day, and, if the men did not jump quickly to obey orders when he blew his shrill whistle, he would swear like a pirate. He was sixty-three years old; his hair and whiskers were as white as snow; he had only two teeth left, and was obliged to soak his hard-tack in coffee or tea before eating it. He was broad shouldered, gaunt and thin; scarred by accidents and battered by long service, and a fit subject for an easy chair and a chimney corner, but woe to any one who hinted at his senility or scoffed at his waning prowess.

Twenty-one years' service in the Navy entitles a man to a snug and comfortable home the remainder of his days in a Naval Asylum. This brave old man had been in constant service for thirty-two years, and still preferred "a life on the ocean wave," to repose in the sailor's snug harbor.

He said he had never been married—no soldier or sailor had any right to marry. He had given a landsman brother $1300 out of his savings and asked no interest or repayment. Uncle Sam was a good enough relation for him, and some day, when he became old, he intended to retire and write a book. He had a firm belief that the good Lord would not be hard on poor Jack, but judge him according to his opportunities. He said one day, "the fellows who doubt the existence of Deity always have badly shaped heads," and then quoted,

> " No God! the simplest flower,
> That on the earth is found ;
> Shrinks as it drinks its cup of dew,
> And trembles at the sound."

He would talk in the sweetest and most touching manner of
the Saviour's sacrifice for man, and say,

> "There's a sweet little cherub sits way up aloft,
>   To keep watch o'er the life of poor Jack."

and, a few moments afterwards, get in a furious passion because some clumsy sailor would not do what was wanted
promptly, say "the —— landlubbers can't climb," and swear
in a way to make one shudder. Jack's sins are numerous,
and he is hardly capable of works of supererogation. May
his faith be strong and his good deeds count well up aloft.

The Norther was full of misery. Smoking and talking
upon deck were reduced to a minimum, owing to the wind
and rain. Writing at the mess-table was out of the question,
on account of the violent movements of the vessel. Some
officers lay in their bunks and slept or read; others gathered
with camp-stools in the country, which was warmed by the
heat that came through the open engine-room door, and discussed physics with the engineers, and told stories with the
middies; all were glad when the meals were served, as the
efforts to keep one's balance and to save the dishes and rations
from disaster led to misadventure and hilarity.

The storm abated somewhat in the afternoon, and a brig
was sighted and made to heave to. A boat was lowered and
Mr. Sanborn and a crew attempted to man her, but she nearly
swamped alongside, the officer lost his cap, and, as the vessel
hoisted French colors and looked like a Johnny Crapaud, she
was allowed to proceed and the boat was hoisted up. The
night was dark and threatening and many felt dismal forebodings as they turned in to sleep.

CHAPTER VII.

THE next morning the sun was shining brightly, the wind was blowing soft and warm from the southwest, the sea was going down, and the Nautilus was steaming rapidly to the southward. Just after quarters, the lookout aloft shouted, " Land ho! Dead ahead, sir!" and the Pan y Matanzas and high, bold coast of Cuba soon after broke through the mist and gladdened the hearts of everybody. The light-houses of Santa Cruz and Moro Castle, the line of fortifications upon the shore, and the narrow entrance to the haven, were soon in plain view, and the Nautilus steamed boldly in among the numerous sail, which always flit in and out among the buoys that mark the channels of a great harbor, until a gun from Moro Castle warned her to stop and submit to a visit from the Health officers.

The engines were stopped, a boat flying the Spanish flag pulled out from a pier and came alongside, two Spanish officers in full uniform, wearing their swords, were received at the gangway by the officer-of-the-deck and Mr. Felton and conducted below. A glass of sherry all around; a few questions and answers between the strangers and Mr. Felton and Surgeon Willett, and they all appeared upon deck again, shook hands, touched their caps, and the visitors departed. The engines were started, " All hands come to anchor!" was called for the men to take their stations, the vessel moved slowly through the channel into the basin, and dropped her anchor near several men-of-war at the upper part of the harbor of Havana.

The narrow channel seaward and the nearly circular harbor, surrounded by sloping hills, resembled a frying pan in shape, and the stillness of the air and the heat of the afternoon sun seemed to make frying a possibility. The green hillsides, winding roads, little white-walled gardens and houses, foreign architecture and green, feathery palm trees, made a picture fair to look upon.

Vessels of many nationalities lay along the docks or were anchored around, and rowboats, sailboats and little steamers were shooting across the harbor in every direction. A man-of-war boat, flying the Spanish ensign, came alongside; a Spanish lieutenant came on board, presented the compliments of the Spanish Admiral in command of the West India Squadron, and offered Captain Prescott the hospitality of the port and any assistance that might be needed. Lieutenant-commander Felton and the deck-officer received him, his card was sent down to Captain Prescott, Mr. Felton conducted him below and introduced him, and he delivered his message again, after the trio had discussed a bottle of sherry. The captain returned his compliments and thanks, and announced his intention of paying his respects to the admiral upon the morrow, then adieux were said and the officer was shown over the side with the same punctilious regard to naval etiquette as upon his arrival.

The awnings were spread, the windsails hoisted in the hatchways, the crew was ordered into summer clothing, and the ship cleared up fore and aft. Then there was a call to quarters, the Spanish flag was run up to the fore truck, the magazine was opened, and an admiral's salute of thirteen guns was fired from the 24-pounder howitzers. About an hour later, the Spanish flag-ship returned the salute gun for gun, with the American flag flying from her fore truck. This customary etiquette being over, the captain ordered his gig, took the doctor along, went ashore to pay his respects to the Consul General of the United States and to the Governor General of Cuba, and returned after dark with a small mail-bag and some news.

"Yellow fever is bad among the merchantmen and quite prevalent on shore," said the doctor, after the few letters had been read, some fine Havana Principe cigars had been distributed, and the wardroom mess had assembled in the accustomed place on the port side for an evening smoke. "You must take frequent baths, put on your merino underclothes, drink little water and wine, eat little meat, beware of unripe fruit, keep out of the sun as much as possible, and avoid getting wet and then sitting around in the night air."

"All right, Doctor," said Careswell; "I don't want to

leave my bones upon this island, beautiful as it is. I was
shocked by a merchant ship's boat passing near us this evening,
having six poor fellows laid out in the stern. They were covered with a tarpaulin, but it was not large enough and the
feet and heads could be plainly seen. They went across the
harbor to an out of the way cemetery, I suppose the potter's
field, where their friends will never be able to find them,
even if they can bear the expense of removal. They put
people out of the way here with short prayers and little cere-
mony, when they die of yellow fever, just as they do the pau-
pers in Paris."

"Bah! you make me shudder," said Ashton. "Do you
think we are in danger, Doctor?"

"We are always in danger," said the doctor gravely.
"Every naval man takes his life in his hand, when he goes
cruising about the world. The coast of Africa is our most
dangerous station. The vessels are not allowed up the rivers
unless absolutely necessary; do not communicate with the
shore between sunset and sunrise, and must anchor as far off
shore as possible to avoid the terrible malaria, which is deadly
to every foreigner. The native Kroomen are employed to do
all the boating necessary, and the crews of our vessels are often
sent to the Canaries or home to recuperate."

"I think this place is nearly as dangerous; it is much
worse than Rio de Janeiro for Yellow Jack, because of its
situation. Here we lie in the bottom of a tub; the wind cannot blow much, owing to the surrounding hills; the water is
foul with the sewage of the city, and the tides and sea cannot
replace and purify it on account of the narrow channel inwards. We are floating upon a bay of filth; the fish in it
are not fit to eat, and the vessels that wash decks are sure to
get the fever. We shall not wash our decks here, and not a
bucket of water should be drawn by the men for any purpose."

"Will we have to stay aboard all the time?" asked Bloss.

"No. You can go ashore after five or six o'clock, but must
take care not to get overheated, nor to get wet by the sudden
showers."

"What's the news from home?" asked the paymaster.

"Oh, very little. The war goes on all right. We have

won a few battles, and every one thinks the war will soon be
ended."

" Yes? So everybody thought in '61, but we are in for a
long struggle, I think."

" Did you see the Governor General?"

" No; he was away, but an aid-de-camp was very hospitable."

" Did you meet our Consul General?"

" Yes, and he will be aboard to-morrow. He says there is
great curiosity to see the Nautilus. She has been the talk of
the place for weeks. The blockade-runners are here in force
and they are especially anxious."

" I saw half a dozen of them across the harbor, flying the
stars and bars," said Careswell. " The impudent scoundrels!
One of them pulled down a small flag and hoisted a large one
just for our benefit, soon after we came to anchor. I'd like
to go over and scuttle her, if the captain would give me
leave."

" You'd have a nice time of it before you finished," said
Ashton. " We could read a newspaper through you in the
morning. You'd be riddled with bullets before you had bored
two auger holes."

" Well, I would try it anyway," said Careswell doggedly.

" The English are to blame for this state of affairs," said
Mr. Felton. " If they had not granted the South belligerent
rights, these vessels would be seized as pirates."

" The blockade-runners are swaggering around the city
every night and frequently attack American sailors," said
Willett. " The captain said to-night that every officer must
wear his side-arms ashore. The North is in high favor among
the Cuban merchants, but the slave-holders and the grandees
sympathize with the South. My greenbacks were taken for
only fifty cents on the dollar, however, which don't show much
respect for Northern finances."

" Is the Confederate money worth anything?" asked Bloss.

" No; the blockade-runners all pay with gold. The crews
are made up of English, Irish and Southerners, and they don't
like shinplasters. Money is advanced here on cotton, which
is to be delivered by the vessels in England, though some of
it is unloaded here and sent to Europe by regular European

st·amers. All the cotton brought in here by small vessels is sold outright, and the money invested in supplies for the return cargoes."

Night had fallen and the lights twinkled like stars among the shipping and in the city and away over the surrounding hills. A gentle breeze, perfumed by many flowers, came over the placid bay and entered the gun-ports. The sounds of dipping oars, the ship's bells striking the hours, the hum of the city streets, and the tinkle of a guitar in a little *casa* upon the hillside, invited to repose and revery. Nowhere in the world does one experience such calm, delicious, soothing influences, as in the tropics after the fervent heat of the day is passed. No pleasure on board ship can compare to swinging in a hammock beneath the awning upon the quarter-deck of a man-of-war, in Havana, and adding perfume to the soft, sweet, evening air from a prime Principe.

The contrast between the stormy night at sea and the following night in port was great and impressive, and every one felt that it was almost like a transition from purgatory to paradise. Tattoo had been sounded by the different men-of-war in port, and all the wardroom lights had been extinguished, long before the officers turned in to dream of orange groves and señoritas.

The next day the ship was cleaned up with extra care, an early boat was sent to market for fresh vegetables and fruit, the broad pennant and the large ensign were hoisted at nine o'clock, the side steps were shipped at the gangway and draped with bunting, and everything took on a holiday appearance.

At ten o'clock the Consul General of the United States came on board and was received at the gangway by Capt. Prescott and the officers of the ship, in full dress uniform, and a salute of nine guns was fired in his honor. He was delighted with the Nautilus, and enjoyed, as heartily as did the officers, the running conversation of home and the social amenities of the occasion. He extended the hospitalities of his establishment to all, and proved that he was a noble representative of his country.

He had no sooner gone, than a beautiful barge, flying the Imperial flag of Spain, was reported approaching the ship, and the Governor General of Cuba, with a brilliant staff, came

alongside and up the gangway. He was received by the captain and some of the officers; the marines were in line upon
the port side of the quarter-deck; the men were stationed at
quarters, and the Spanish ensign was run up to the fore truck.
As the visitors stepped upon deck, three ruffles of the drum
were heard, the officers and men raised their caps, the marines
presented arms, and a salute of fifteen guns was fired. The
gentlemen were conducted over the ship; spent half an hour
in the cabin and wardroom, conversing in passable English
and excellent French, and departed with many thanks, profuse offers of friendship and hospitality, and the customary
honors. One of the visitors gave Careswell his card bearing
the following, "Juan Montalvo, No. 49 Calle dela Perse-
verancia. *Una casa y un amigo a su disposicion.*" The
gentleman meant all he said and was a firm friend as long as
the Nautilus remained in the squadron.

After dinner the Spanish Admiral came on board to pay his
respects and was received like the Governor General, except
that two ruffles of the drum were given, and only thirteen
guns were fired. He was entertained royally by Capt. Prescott, and was greatly interested in a critical survey of the
ship.

"That fellow knows a belaying-pin from a marlin-spike,"
said old Brenneman. "He'll go and copy all our Yankee in-
ventions in his old tub over there. "

The admiral departed with the usual formalities and every
one felt relieved. The official visits were over, and the officers
and crew were tired of full dress and naval parade. Visitors,
military and civil, foreign and native, handsome and hideous,
kept coming on board till supper time, and they had to be
shown about, wined, and talked to in different languages,
until every part of the ship resounded with polyglots, and
one might have thought a school of Philology had been established, or the Babylonic confusion was being rehearsed by
amateurs. Tongues and legs were so tired after the exodus
of sight-seers, that not an officer asked to go ashore; the evening smoke and conversation were interrupted by yawns and
cat-naps, and one after another took his camp-stool and went
silently to bed.

The next morning there was exercise sending up and down

the yards and topmasts, and, later, barges came alongside and
the men were put to work coaling ship. Scores of visitors,
including some American and Cuban ladies, came aboard, and
the officers were busy entertaining them till the shades of evening fell. After supper several officers from the steerage and
wardroom went ashore in the second cutter and the captain
followed in his gig.

There is an excellent macadamized road leading through
pretty gardens and broad estates away from the city and over
the hills around the harbor. It is well shaded by palm,
mango and avacada trees, and is deliciously cool in the early
evening. It is a favorite resort of the *élite* of the city after
dinner, and is crowded for hours with the peculiar Cuban carriages, called volantes. A volante is a covered chaise with
extremely long shafts, and the driver, in top boots and livery,
rides the horse. He is about ten feet ahead of the occupants
of the carriage and can not hear the conversation behind, which
has its advantages. The chaise is lined with silk of a color to
harmonize with the complexions of the ladies, and their costumes are in harmony with it, so that a very agreeable *tout
ensemble* is produced. A blonde has a blue lining to the
chaise and wears a white dress; a brunette, a lining of crim-
son and wears pink; a blonde and brunette in the same carriage would have a lining of black and wear blue and buff.
The ladies generally have nothing upon the head except their
luxuriant hair in massive braids, but they carry a lace man-
tilla to throw over the head and shoulders when the air becomes cool. Gentlemen accompany their ladies on horseback,
and the long lines of carriages and gallant riders present a
fashionable procession of exceeding interest to natives and foreigners.

After the evening ride, the volantes are arranged around
the *Plaza da Armaz*, a park, full of beautiful flowers and
noble orange and palm trees situated in the heart of the city,
in front of the Governor General's palace and the Louvre and
Dominica restaurants, where the band plays all the evening,
and the people assemble to sip wines and eat ices and cakes.

The officers of the Nautilus arrived at the Plaza just in time
to see the volantes and their attendants returning from their
evening ride. The drivers dismounted and held the horses of

the carriages and their attendants. Some of the ladies remained in their seats, partook of refreshments, and held sweet converse with the attentive gentlemen. Others were escorted around or through the walks of the park to the Dominica. The seats, paths and restaurants were full of well dressed, happy people, eating, drinking, smoking and gossiping, while the military band in the middle of the Plaza played exquisite music for two hours. Here and there could be seen naval officers of Denmark, Germany, France, England and the United States; soldiers of the garrison, of different grades and uniforms; sailors from the merchant ships and blockade-runners, and ladies and gentlemen of the city, often accompanied by negro servants.

The soft evening breeze, the murmuring trees, the hum of conversation, the rippling laughter and the strains of music, were pleasant to the storm-tossed mariners, and they lingered about the place until the band departed, and then went into the Dominica. They took seats at one of the tables by an open casement overlooking the park and ordered ices and wines. While resting and discussing the events of the evening with several resident Americans, half a dozen roughly dressed blockade-runners took seats at a table upon the other side of the room and began to talk in a boisterous tone of the American war. Their remarks became pointed and offensive to the Union men present, and their nods and scowling glances towards them indicated plainly their desire to precipitate an encounter. As it grew later, the wit went out as the wine went down, and the whole party broke out into song and sang "The Bonnie Blue Flag" with a great deal of enthusiasm, clinking their glasses and pounding on the table in unison. Then three cheers were given for Jeff. Davis and the Southern Confederacy, and loud talk and boisterous oaths attracted the attention of every one around the Dominica, but no attempt was made by the proprietor or servants to restrain the ribald folly.

The officers of the Nautilus were quiet and apparently unconcerned, but they felt exceedingly comfortable that they had their side-arms. The leader of the crowd, a ferocious looking Southerner, rose from his chair, walked rapidly over to the table of the Union officers and spat at Ashton, who quick as thought dashed a glass of claret in his face and, before the ruffian had recovered, drew his sword and gave him a blow over the head with the back of it that caused him to stagger and retreat.

The groups at both tables sprang to their feet, and the rebels advanced a few steps, but when they saw a determined front and the muzzles of several revolvers, they halted, and several police appearing upon the scene, they left the restaurant, sending back all kinds of vile epithets and horrible curses. The Union officers left soon after, proceeded cautiously through the streets to the boats, and arrived on board ship in safety.

Every boat's crew went ashore armed after this adventure, and the men were particularly careful to keep in groups and not to get intoxicated. There was a native of Mississippi in the crew, an ardent Union man, and in some way the blockade-runners learned his history and watched for him. One night, in company with two shipmates, he went into one of those small, suspicious-looking drinking-houses near the dock, and soon after four blockade-runners came in behind them. The men fraternized, had several drinks together, and then got into a discussion upon the war. They exchanged experiences and grew quite confidential, then became excited and angry, and, finally, the identity of the man from "Natchez under the hill" was betrayed. The Southerners had sworn they would capture him and send him back to the South in a blockade-runner, and the opportunity was theirs.

Two of them seized him and the others each attacked his man. The fight was a fierce one. The keeper of the place ran out for the police. The Natchez man kept his assailants busy, and the Yankee sailors were fast conquering their adversaries, when several police appeared upon the scene and marched the whole party off to the calaboose. The man-of-war's men had left their arms in the boat, and the Southerners did not attempt to use any they may have had. They were all liberated the next day through the intervention of their officers, after the payment of light fines, and the Natchez man never ventured on shore again in Havana.

The streets of Havana are narrow and paved with square blocks of stone. The houses are built of white stone and plaster; have small rooms and small barred windows, and the

7

main entrance is a carriage way leading to an inner court-yard and garden. The stores are much like the houses and have an inner court where the employés lounge and smoke cigarettes when there are no customers about. Meals are generally served in the court or garden behind, and the *siesta* is spent there in bamboo chairs and hammocks.

Many of the public buildings are of white marble, and the churches are rich in stained glass and interior decorations. The low buildings, tiled roofs, narrow streets and peculiar architecture, are essentially European in character, and the city is in as marked contrast to one in the United States as any in continental Europe.

The people do business in the cool of the morning and evening, and abandon all exertion for several hours in the middle of the day. Even the slaves are permitted to be lazy then, partly because their masters are too indolent to look after them. Coffee and bread is served early; fruit, fish, yams, meat and wine compose the breakfast, at 9 or 10 o'clock, and a hearty dinner of many courses is enjoyed at any time from 4 to 7 P.M. Then a ride; a visit to the theatre, opera, plaza or ball, and social calls and gossiping, consume the time till midnight and bedtime.

Colored and white women of the lower classes may be seen in the streets at all hours, but ladies seldom go out till evening, and never without a duenna or some member of the family. A man must do his courting in the presence of a third person, or through the grated windows, or surreptitiously, during the evening ride and rest at the plaza.

One evening at seven, a handsome man, wearing a broad sombrero, light cloak and sword, stood under a window and clasped a lady's hand pushed through the bars. He looked languishing, mysterious, cavalier-like, and the lady, dressed in white, seemed a vision of loveliness in the dim shadow of the casement. Three hours later the lady and gentleman occupied the same respective places. The former had the same beautiful arm protruding, the latter was standing on the same leg. He was left there in the shadows and may be standing there yet. It would have been too fatiguing to have watched and waited for the dénouement.

The slaves dress in coffee bags; the coolies and poor whites, in whatever they can get; and the well-to-do men, in Panama hats and white or gray suits. The latter carry white umbrellas. An umbrella in Cuba is a sign of pecuniary plethora. All men and some women carry a cigarette or cigar in the mouth. They are offered freely to acquaintances. No one is ever expected to accept. Politeness thus costs very little. A colored mother smokes a long cheroot, her three year old child, a six for a cent. The white women wear an immense comb in the back hair; the colored ones replace it with a toothpick. A negress with a cheroot and a toothpick is inspiring to look upon.

The right hand side of the entrance to Havana is a low, sandy beach, stretching away to the westward and rising a little southward to elevate the city above the tides. The broken timbers of many a luckless vessel protrude along the shore beyond the light-house, as the skeletons of animals and men lie half buried in the desert.

The left side of the entrance is a solid wall of shelving and perpendicular rock, rising several hundred feet, and covered by gardens and lawns, a light-house and the massive towers and bastions of Moro Castle. Against the shelving rock a frigate was dashed to splinters and not a soul was saved. A cave runs inwards from the water's edge, makes a sharp turn upwards and opens out upon the hill—a spouting horn it is called. In heavy storms, the sea dashes inwards and upwards upon the greensward with a melancholy roar.

Moro Castle is a vast fortification, heavily armed and garrisoned, and overlooking the city by the sea. It could only be taken from the land side—its water approaches are so steep and difficult. It frowns over the narrow entrance to the harbor, as many a robber's castle does above the lovely Rhine, and demands a tribute of respect from every passing vessel. An iron-clad would not be impregnable there, because shot and shell could be pitched by hand down upon her thinly armored deck.

An American man-of-war was detained in the channel awhile, when trying to go to sea in chase of a blockade-runner that had recently sailed. She got away too late to catch the fleeing craft, and her captain and officers were angry. After dark all lights were extinguished, and the man-of-war was

turned about and run back until Moro was barely visible
through the mist. Then the 11-inch pivot was loaded with
solid shot, the gun given extreme elevation, and the pointed
mass of iron fired directly at the offending fortification. There
was a flashing of lights, a roll of drums, and a manning of
the batteries, but the ship's helm was put to starboard and she
was soon far away to the eastward. The shot went entirely
over Moro and ploughed up the hill beyond, narrowly missing a human habitation. The garrison and the authorities
were very much surprised and exercised over the occurrence,
but no plausible explanation was reached. Some thought a
gun had gone off accidentally; others, that a shot had been
fired at a vessel and gone astray.

The fruit of Cuba is delicious; the oranges are finer than
the apples of Hesperides ; the plums are delicate and luscious;
the bananas melt in the mouth like rich custard, and the cocoa-
nuts furnish a refreshing drink and snowy food. A couple of
oranges, a banana, a piece of bread and a cup of coffee, make
an excellent breakfast. It is not considered safe to partake of
fruit and distilled liquor together. They do not agree in the
fervid climate. A banana and a glass of brandy have sent
many a sailor to Davy Jones' locker, i. e., to the place where
dead sailors are supposed to go.

The leather-skinned, moustached cavaliers of Cuba have
exquisite manners, and are hospitable and generous. They
are fearless and graceful riders, and would form a grand cru-
sading party to rescue Jerusalem from the Mohammedans.
The young ladies are beautiful and generally dress with excellent taste, but the middle aged and old present few traces of
early good looks.

The people of Cuba are religious in externals, at least, and
the churches are full upon the Sabbath day. It causes some
astonishment and awakens thought in an American Protestant
to find that the Roman Catholic church is there *the church*,
where all the fashion and wealth attend, and that the numerous sects with which he is familiar at home are not represented.

A dozen negresses came on board the Nautilus one day.
Their hair was curled so tightly upon the head, it seemed, if
one could only cut a kink and get hold of an end, he might
unravel the whole coiffure like a yarn stocking. Some of them

had teeth filed to a point, probably to eat human beings in their former home. All were as black as polished ebony, and had noses flat enough and lips thick enough to delight an ethnologist. They wanted the officers' washing, and they received a pile of dirty clothes almost as high as the turret of a monitor. It was a month's accumulation.

Two important duties must be performed in port, to coal ship and get the washing done. Enlisted men wash their clothes themselves, either in a bucket, or towing at the end of a line overboard out to sea. Officers are obliged to depend upon the washwomen of the seaports for the purity of their linen. Strange as it may seem to yachtmen and others who rough it in colored shirts along the coast in summer, naval officers invariably wear starched white shirts all the time. It is considered *infra dignitate* to do otherwise.

The coal was all aboard; the deficiency in stores was made good; the washing was returned; the officers and men had seen Havana; half the population of the city had seen the Nautilus, and ship and officers were ready for sea. Not a case of yellow fever had occurred on the Nautilus, though there had been some deaths ashore and many on board the merchant vessels. There was no fear, only an anxious watchfulness of every morbid feeling by everybody. No one knew when the dread scourge might make an attack. It was like being in front of a threatening enemy without power of advance or retreat, and no one liked it. Everybody was happy, therefore, when Mr. Felton gave out the news that the ship would go to sea in the afternoon. It was apparent soon after dinner that one of the six blockade-runners was getting ready for sea. It had been learned on shore that she was bound for Mobile. Capt. Prescott was informed that the Nautilus would not be permitted to pass Moro in chase until an hour after she had sailed. Thus safe escape was in a measure guaranteed by the Cuban authorities, because it was hardly possible for the American man-of-war to steam as fast as the fleet Clyde-built steamer, and, besides, a stern chase is a long one, and darkness would soon hide her from view.

All of the blockade-runners carrying valuable cargoes were of this class of steamers. They were long, low, narrow, iron vessels, painted lead color or black, and had sharp bows, short spars, large screws and powerful engines. They were captured occasionally by running them ashore, catching them in a corner or narrow channel, or getting them within gunshot range by their own miscalculations; but they were seldom caught by a stern chase, when they had a few miles the start, because they could outrun nearly all of the seagoing vessels of the United States Navy. After a few of them had been captured and turned into Yankee gunboats, luck changed, and blockade running became so perilous and unprofitable that few men would longer engage in it.

The blockade-runners were all covered with bunting this afternoon, and some of the vessels had three and even four Confederate flags flying, partly to cheer the departing vessels, partly to signify their contempt for American men-of-war. The Victoria hove up her anchor to the songs of "Dixie," and "The Bonnie Blue Flag," in which her crew was joined by the whole rebel fleet, and steamed out of the harbor, while her men cheered and received cheers from the crews of sympathizing vessels around. She had chosen her time for sailing well. It was only about an hour to sunset, and no vessel was allowed to go to sea after sunset.

CHAPTER VIII.

THE Nautilus had been quietly preparing to sail; the fires had been started, the boats hoisted up, the anchor hove short, and everything made ready. Finally, the order was received with a glad shout from the men, " All hands up anchor !" and, in a few moments, the anchor was up and catted, and the ship was moving slowly through the shipping towards the open sea. Great crowds had gathered all along the shore to see her go out, and they sent up shout after shout of approbation and admiration, as the noble craft spurned the waters with her screw and moved like a living thing along. A lieutenant came on board in a customs boat, in the channel near Moro, and forbade the captain's going to sea until an hour had elapsed since the Victoria had passed. Capt. Prescott and the officers compared watches, talked, argued, drank a bottle of champagne and smoked, but it was no use; the order was peremptory, and must be obeyed.

Everybody felt like pitching the lieutenant overboard, defying Moro and the whole Spanish fleet, and going after the steamer that was flying away to the northwest. Somebody knew, however, that port regulations must be respected and International laws observed. It was not any fear of Moro's batteries or the Spanish frigates inside, that deterred Capt. Prescott from proceeding. It was the knowledge that he must answer to his own government for disobedience of plain instructions.

The Nautilus was kept backing and going ahead in the channel for half an hour, waiting for minutes to pass which seemed days, and blowing off steam like the roaring of an enraged tiger robbed of its prey, while the officers and crew were fretting, cursing and walking the decks, and wishing the Island of Cuba would sink, and the magazine in Moro might blow the whole garrison to kingdom come.

Permission was finally given to go ahead, the officer departed, the ship sprang onwards under a full head of steam and passed out to sea just as the setting sun tinged the walls of Moro with rose color and the sunset gun was fired.

Then a small schooner, flying the stars and bars, and loaded clear up to the booms with bales of cotton, was seen creeping along close to the shore to the left hand, and then going straight into Havana in spite of Moro. She may have been boarded, but she did not stop for it. The regulation of the port was, that no vessel should pass either into or out of the harbor of Havana after the sunset gun had been fired. The Nautilus escaped outwards by a few minutes only; the blockade-runner entered some ten minutes afterwards. There was evidently one law for vessels on Government service, and another for blockade-runners.

Freebooters always were favored in the West Indies. The islands are full of lurking places and easily defensible passages, and the inhabitants recruited pirate crews and protected them not many years ago. There is a feeling of sympathy with pirates still existing there, and plenty of men can be found, who, scorning labor upon a merchant vessel or a man-of-war, would jump at a chance to rob honest people on the high seas.

It is contrary to International law for one vessel to capture another within a marine league of the shore. The schooner was inside of the arbitrary line, and the men of the Nautilus could only grind their teeth and curse their luck.

The wind was easterly outside; the sea was rising; the stars were hanging low and bright; the gulls were shrieking, like a lot of hoydenish girls just out of school, and storm clouds were gathering in the orient. All sail was made on the Nautilus; the engine was driven at its greatest speed, and the course was shaped to the westward in order to intercept the Victoria near Tortugas. All lights that could be seen outside the ship were extinguished; the bow-chaser Parrott gun was freshly loaded with shell, and double lookouts were stationed in all parts of the ship. The log was thrown just before eight-bells of the second dog watch, and the quartermaster reported the ship was going fourteen knots. This speed was increased another knot during the next watch, and all night long the vessel flew before the wind and sea and rapidly revolving screw. Several sailing vessels were passed without questioning them, appearing and vanishing like bats in a dismal cave, and the "Sail ho!" of the lookouts was barely answered from the quarter-deck before the vessels were too far away to give a definite report of their direction.

At daybreak the course was altered more to the northward, and, about two-bells in the morning watch, another cry of "Sail ho! a steamer on the starboard bow, sir!" attracted universal attention. When the sun had scattered the mists of morning and good glasses were used, the sail was made out to be a low, black steamer, showing black smoke, and heading about northwest. All· sea-going United States steamers used anthracite coal, giving off grayish smoke in moderate quantities. When dense black smoke trailed along the sky from a steamer, she was almost certain to be English or a blockade-runner. These vessels were supplied with bituminous coal, which burned like grease and smoked like a Pittsburgh furnace. The course the stranger was steering made it reasonably certain that she was not an English vessel—they had nothing to do in those waters at that time. She was probably a blockade-runner and, perhaps, the good ship Victoria. Another fact was apparent—the Nautilus was outsailing her, and she was becoming larger and more distinct every hour. Such was the gossip all around the decks, and the men could hardly go on with the work of the ship from their desire to watch the chase. Even the cooks slipped up the step-ladders and neglected their boiling coppers to pass judgment upon the situation.

Captain Prescott determined to keep the wind behind him this time, and not lose its influence by having to brace sharp up, as in chasing the Florida, so the course was altered directly for the strange steamer, and a sharp lookout kept upon her by the quartermaster and the officer-of-the-deck. The steamer was distant about three miles at noon; the crew of the forecastle gun was called to quarters, the ship kept off a point, and a blank cartridge fired towards her. She hoisted the English flag in answer to this compliment, but did not slacken speed; she appeared rather to increase it by piling the coal under her boilers, as indicated by the greater volume of smoke that poured out of her smoke-stack. A shell was then sent after her, but it fell short, and she sped onwards over the quieter

waters of the Gulf, with square sails hardly drawing and the
hull almost hidden by the clouds of smoke. Another shell
burst under her stern, but still she flew. The next shell produced a commotion on board both vessels. It caused the
Victoria, for she could now be plainly made out, to swing
around a little and the smoke to clear away, revealing a hole
through her smoke-stack. The movement was only momentary,
and she kept her course bravely, exciting the admiration of
every one on board the Nautilus. The gun was now loaded
with solid shot, that lives might not be sacrificed, and with the
hope that the vessel might be crippled and saved from fire.
Shot flew to the right and left several times, but, at last, one
entered her stern, there was a great cloud of escaping steam,
the vessel slowed perceptibly, the sails were clewed up, and the
British flag was hauled down.

The Nautilus was soon within hail, the men manned the
broadside guns for fear of treachery, and Mr. Felton shouted,
" Ship ahoy! What ship is that?"

" The British steamer Victoria!" was the answer.

" Where are you from, and where bound?"

" From Havana, bound to Vera Cruz!"

" Very well! Lay by and I will send a boat aboard!"

The second cutter was piped away by the boatswain's mate,
the boat was lowered, the crew armed, and Master Sanborn
went on board. He returned soon with a set of informal
ship's papers, a British and several Confederate flags, the captain, mates and chief-engineer of the vessel, and the information that the cargo consisted of arms, ammunition, provisions
and clothing. The vessel was therefore seized as a lawful
prize of the United States; part of her crew, including six
wounded men, were transferred to the Nautilus, and part left
on board; Mr. Sanborn, with an engineer and a picked crew,
was sent aboard to take command, and a careful examination
was made of the hull and machinery. The shell that pierced
the smoke-stack had knocked down the men at the wheel and
exploded in the bow of the vessel. The shot that struck the
stern had gone through the cabin, traversed the hull beneath
the deck, cut a steam pipe, twisted and broken the engine in
such a way as to stop it instantly, and lodged in the cargo.

Had it been a shell, it would undoubtedly have set the ship on fire.

It was learned later, that the men had been kept at their posts by the officers with loaded revolvers, and their zeal and courage were accounted for by the fact that they owned considerable of the cargo. They made a brave attempt to save their property, in great contrast to the conduct of officers of some prize vessels, who gave up at the first fire. These men were mostly citizens of the South, and they were respected for their brave conduct. The wardroom officers were delighted to find them the same persons who had acted so shamefully in the Dominica at Havana, and Ashton and the rebel captain exchanged scowls on more than one occasion. Revenge is sweet, especially in war times.

It was notorious during the war that Southerners always did their best to save their vessels, and incurred great personal peril running the blockade, while foreigners were scared at the first crack of a Yankee gun, and surrendered valuable ships and cargoes pusillanimously.

The Victoria's machinery was too badly damaged to be repaired at sea, and a hawser was taken to her bow from the stern of the Nautilus and she was towed into Key West.

Considerable excitement was created by the procession of these two vessels through the coral reefs into the snug little roadstead at the Key, and the shore and wharves were covered with cheering spectators, as they passed by Fort Taylor and dropped anchor near the naval headquarters. The captain had his gig called away ; made an official visit to the Admiral of the Squadron, and formally transferred the Victoria to the Prize Court and the prisoners to the Colonel in command of Fort Taylor.

There is no more remarkable or sudden transition in geographical characteristics in the world, than from those of the West Indies to those of the Florida group of islands. The West India islands are fertile, wooded, rugged and mountainous. They are founded upon the azoic rock, that has been raised by volcanic fury from the deep sea depths. Their shores are precipitous ; their channels deep, and their bordering reefs few. They spring up suddenly, like pyramids from the desert plain, and follow the trend of the northwest system.

The Florida group, on the contrary, is composed of infertile sand banks, sparsely wooded, flat and low lying. They rest upon the ruined houses of coral polyps, that have died after raising them to the level of the tide. Their shores are low and shelving; their channels are shallow gaps in the reefs, and their fringing and barrier reefs are numerous. They rise slowly above the surface, mere oases in the waste of waters, and follow the trend of the northeast system.

From the southern end of the peninsula of Florida to the Tortugas, a distance of 120 miles, a long, curving coral reef extends. Narrow, shallow channels occur occasionally, and there is a wide, deep passage between Key West and the Tortugas. All along the reef small coral islands are scattered, only a little above the sea level. They are sparsely covered by tufts of grass and herbs, hardy shrubs, and palmetto and mangrove trees. The mangrove is King of the Key. It drops down limbs from its branches, which take root and develop into trunks nearly as large as the parent stem; these secondary trees increase and multiply in the same way, until the family of one individual covers a great space, and makes a living lattice-work through which nothing much larger than a coon can pass.

The coral islands have no springs or streams of fresh water. Surface pools and artificial wells contain brackish water, and rain water is collected in casks and cisterns by the inhabitants. The shores of the keys and the sea bottom for miles around are covered by the snowy sand of comminuted corals, and, from the shore outwards to a depth of 100 feet, many varieties of coral polyps, with varying forms and exquisite colors, grow from their limestone beds.

The water is of a temperature above 66° F.; it is clear and shallow, and permits a good view of the shining bottom, where the living corals grow in separate groups or thickly set like a garden bed. The corallum, or solid limestone body, with the polyps imbedded in its surface, presents different forms similar to terrestrial vegetation, strongly reminding one of the varieties of cactus, though algae and shrubs have their representatives. The polyps extend and expand their delicate pink and purple tentacles, like the petals of a flower, all over the corallum, covering it with bloom.

Shells of every shape, size and color lie around in profusion. Sponges grow here and there between the corals, making dark thickets for the shuffling crabs. Fish of curious forms and brilliant colors float quietly or dart quickly over the subaqueous garden. Lazy turtles, green and brown, paddle around, safe in their imbricated armor, and sharks sneak warily like a detective from coral caves to shallow banks in search of prey. It is a beautiful and interesting sight to look down upon this panorama of nature, and to mark the variety of animated forms in the actual enjoyment of living. It excites wonder in the mind of the spectator; impresses the thoughtful with a fuller sense of the mystery of the universe, and awakens greater veneration for the Almighty.

The coral islands rise so little above the sea, that they are never seen as land until they are close aboard, and, were it not for their vegetation, they would even be found with difficulty. A heavy roller might pass entirely across some of them, if it were not hindered by the trees and the fringing and barrier reefs. The fringing reef forms the shore line and flings back the lazy seas, which have been shattered and broken into glittering foam upon the outer barrier reef. Between the two reefs, there is usually a sound of comparatively smooth water, where vessels find safe anchorage, but it is necessary to know where to find the gap in the barrier reef and to know the channel well, or the pretty coral banks, jagged, sharp and vengeful as the teeth in a shark's mouth, may crunch the timbers like an eggshell and let in the treacherous sea. High lands have deep water near shore, and give warning of their presence by odorous breezes, sudden squalls, and bold outlines that penetrate across the darkness of a tropic night made glorious by stars. These low lands, with their outlying reefs, are under the bow almost as soon as they are seen by the lookout, and the cry of "Breakers ahead!" is often followed in coral seas by the terrible crashing and crunching of timbers and coral.

Coral polyps die as soon as they are exposed to the sun; therefore, the coral growths do not reach above the low tide level. This is favorable to small crafts at high tide in still water, but the stormy seas break off great masses of living coral, hurl them hither and thither, grind some into shining sands to sprinkle the shore and the bottom, and pile pieces higher and higher till the summer seas cannot cover them and they remain ghostly stockades around the green islets. The approaches to these coral islands are, therefore, often tortuous and dangerous, and the danger is greatly increased by rapid currents, which sweep around Tortugas, through between it and Key West, along and between the keys and reefs from that key to Florida, and go to join the waters of the Gulf Stream.

Coral islands present unique types of civilization. The houses of Key West are built of wood or of white limestone cut out of the consolidated coral sand; the streets are white sand, darkened by the débris of adventitious seas and the remains of vegetation; the soil is a grayish sandy loam, and the trees above the influence of percolating sea water, and removed from surface accumulations, are dry and sickly, like aged mendicants struggling to hold upon life to protect the feebler life below them. The streets, the vegetation, the animals and the inhabitants are all dry most of the time at Key West, and still dryer at the Dry Tortugas.

The population of Key West was somewhat mixed. The lowest class was considerably increased by white refugees and runaway negroes from the main land. The native whites were mostly engaged in fishing, turtling and piloting. A few adventurers from the States kept shops, manufactured cigars, and exported coral, shells, sponges and turtles. There was a host of resident officials, with their families, clerks and servants, connected with the army, the customs and the courts. The streets presented a busy spectacle at night, and the crowds were augmented by the soldiers and sailors out for a frolic, and by the officers of the fort and fleet.

The ladies of the city kept open house for the officers and accredited civilians, and inaugurated picnics, sails, card parties and balls. A Naval Club was established in a pretty villa overlooking the harbor, and the officers at Headquarters and on board the vessels were very hospitable. There was no disloyalty to the United States apparent on the Key. Any first thoughts of rebellion had been stamped out early, and the isolated people were only too happy to have the opportunity to increase their worldly stores by the influx of strangers with full pockets.

The Admiral of the East Gulf Squadron made an official visit; was received with the customary honors, and dined with Captain Prescott. Then for many days there was a stream of naval officers, some of whom were old acquaintances, of army officers from the garrison, and citizens, including many ladies, to entertain, making it a task for the officers aboard to show them about, to answer numerous questions, and to furnish refreshments. Many pleasant acquaintances were made, however, among the shore people, who were afterwards lavish of their hospitality, and returned the favors that had been shown them ten fold. The officers of the Nautilus were soon acquainted with all the better families ashore, and received numerous invitations to land and water excursions, and to tea, card and dancing parties, of which they availed themselves frequently.

The crew of the Nautilus enjoyed themselves swimming, fishing and boat-racing in the harbor, and entered into all the enjoyments of the shore in the way peculiar to sailors. Every night some boats were ashore till nearly midnight, and the men came aboard laughing and singing, full of happiness and rum. The officers remained long upon deck, smoked their cigars, and discussed the last rubber at whist, the singing of Miss A., or the grace and beauty of Señora Z.

"How we are suffering for our country!" said Careswell one evening after supper, when several officers had gathered on deck for a smoke.

"Terribly!" answered Bloss. "I have not been in my bunk a night before one o'clock for a week. Our vessels ought to be quarantined here, or these festivities will be the death of brave men after awhile."

"Are you going to join the club?"

"No; I can't stand the racket."

"Neither can I. Mackey wants me to join, but I can't stand stimulants. I became nearly intoxicated on six *demi tasses* of Mocha at the 'Café Francais,' at Rio de Janeiro, last cruise. I did not take the *café royal* with brandy and sugar either—merely coffee with a little milk and sugar and some *gateaux*. The other fellows followed the fashion, and we had a queer time getting down to the boat landing. I had to pull them up off of door-steps, push them away from convenient

walls, and keep them moving. Five times I took the bearings and started out for the boat. Three times we ran against
hills and the streets ended abruptly. Once we climbed a hill
and brought up against a high double gate, iron-clad and firm
as the hills. My friends wanted to climb it, batter it down,
blow it up, anything to remove this unjustifiable impediment
to progress towards the ship. I looked inside through a chink
and saw sentinels marching to and fro, just as my coffee topers
kicked against the gate. There was a quick call, a rattle of
chains and bolts and a little side gate opened, as we retreated
in good order around the next corner down the hill. This
livened up the party, we filed by a gen d'arm with bold front
and a military salute, started anew, and reached the boat at 3
A.M., after three hours' marching.

"Talk of the seven hills of Rome, I believe Rio has seventeen. If you get off of Rua Dirieta or Rua Imperatriz, you
are lost, and every time you think you have found the way,
you'll run against an unclimbable hill. I looked at those hills
in the day time and found the natives couldn't climb them
except by running a system of parallels, as soldiers do when
they advance to take a formidable fortification. I would
rather climb a jury-mast. It would be much easier."

"I am glad you are such a good observer," said Bloss.
Shakespeare says,

> "All places that the eye of heaven visits
> Are to a wise man ports and happy havens."

"You need not drink at the club unless you want to do so,"
said Ashton.

"That is true," replied Bloss; "but you know what a wet
blanket a fellow would be who wouldn't. 'When you are in
Rome you must do as the Romans do.' The water here is so
abominable that a fellow would have to drink in self defence."

"Well, take claret, and sip it as parsimoniously as a German. Then you can smoke; enjoy the cards, papers, maga-
zines and books; have a pleasant time, and no harm done. I
am satisfied the club is doing a good work, keeping the best of
everything, preventing our patronizing the rapacious shop-
keepers, and promoting good fellowship among the officers of
the squadron."

"Well, you ought to know."

"The club is all right," said the doctor. "You'll always find a few imprudent men in every club."

"The club is all wrong!" spoke up Paymaster Horton, who had been leaning quietly against the rail and listening. "They ought not to have liquors in the place at all. They are destructive to health and morals, and are at the bottom of all mischief. The water here is not pleasant, but it is not injurious. Liquors are the curse of the service; 'Wine is a mocker, strong drink is raging, and whosoever is deceived thereby is not wise.'"

"That's dogmatic enough," said the doctor. "Liquors have their place; they should be used, not abused. In certain conditions they contribute to the nourishment of the body."

"Keep them for the sick then. Don't let well men poison themselves."

"Ah, you are too hard on us, Pay. You never knew the goodly fellowship in a glass of old Madeira. You never experienced the delicious reverie in a fine cigar. Poor fellow, you haven't half tasted life yet."

"I don't want to taste it, if it will make my mouth like a smoked ham and my brain and stomach like a distillery."

The paymaster was one of those good men so rarely found in the navy. He was a strong, handsome fellow, a little above the average in stature, with regular features, a scholarly brow, a moustache and goatee, and a strong, bold chin. He was known to be a church member at his New England home, and that fact, aside from his uniform kindness and conscientiousness, made all respect him. A church member on a man-of-war was considered a *rara avis*—a sort of unique specimen of the *genus homo*. He was quiet and unassuming generally, but did not hesitate to administer restraining advice and moral reproof when he saw an opportunity. He was rather vain, it was thought, of his personal appearance, and rather susceptible to the charms of ladies' society, but he shrank from the appearance of evil, as from a pestilence.

The starboard steerage was amusing itself one day in a thoughtless way with a little negro boy named George Washington. George was fond of play as a kitten; he had a hard head, and was eager for quarter dollars. The middies slung

8

a cannon ball in a piece of canvas, suspended it by a rope to a beam in the steerage, and got George to see how far he could butt it for a quarter.   He had already knocked over a barrel of bread and burst several closet doors with his head, and was therefore somewhat seasoned.   George butted the ball bravely and swung it out a yard.   The middies shouted and clapped their hands, and told him, if he would butt it so it would strike the beam, he should have a dollar.   He butted it again heavily, and, as the ball came back towards him, struck it with head down a terrific blow, and then fell limp and apparently lifeless upon the deck.   There was great consternation; he was put upon the table; some dashed him with water, others douched him with vinegar, hartshorn and whiskey; several ran for the doctor, and all the steerage fellows were terribly frightened.

The doctor and paymaster came, the lad had concussion of the brain, and was carried to the sick-bay.   The paymaster seized the opportunity and administered to those pale, demoralized youths a reproof and a moral tongue lashing, which kept them spellbound for some minutes.   Not till he was in the wardroom, did they breathe easily; then some of them went up on deck to smoke and think, others got in their bunks sorrowfully and went to sleep, and there was nothing but routine and gloom in their mess till George came back safe and sound to wait upon them.   George did no more butting; he looked askance at the split closet doors, and told the wardroom privately, " them midshipmuns is a wicked set."

CHAPTER IX.

ONE day a shore boat brought off notes of invitation to a ball at Madam Fontana's. The note to Bloss was accompanied by a bouquet. The lady was a wealthy Spaniard's widow, and she had taken quite a fancy to Mr. Bloss. Bloss placed the flowers upon the wardroom table, with an appended card, containing:

> " He who does these flowers displace,
> Must meet the owner face to face.".

There was a great overhauling, brushing up, and repairing of uniforms. Gold bands had to be sewed on sleeves, shoulder-straps required fastening at the ends, white pants demanded repair of seams and buttons, and kid gloves needed cleaning from dirt and mildew. The officers got out their sewing cases and boxes, provided by loving hands at home, and set to work in their rooms to refurbish and beautify their wardrobes. They went about it as handy as journeymen tailors. Every seafaring man makes a virtue of necessity and learns a little of back stitching and setting on buttons. If he did not, he would soon be as dilapidated as a ship after a storm, as it is impossible to get men about the ship to repair damages to clothing in an emergency.

After supper the dressing began, and one would have thought the mess was going *en masse* to a royal reception at the court of the Russian Emperor, so much time and care were expended in personal adornment. Several practical jokes were played during the mêlée. One man found his boots chalked; another had mucilage in his hair-oil bottle, and another discovered that somebody had put a few drops of carbolic acid in his cologne. At last Sanborn had his hair parted and brushed to perfection; Horton had his moustache and goatee pointed sharply; Lawson had chalked the iron rust from his shirt front; Careswell had borrowed a more becoming necktie, and Bloss had succeeded in crowding his corpulence inside his outgrown frock coat to the imminent danger of buttons.   Then occurred a magnanimous act, only equalled by Diocletian's division of the Roman Empire.   Bloss took the bouquet, his souvenir of affection, deliberately cut it apart, and gave each of his messmates a boutonnière, retaining the red rose for his own lappel.

The officer-of-the-deck was notified; a cutter was called away, and the gallant band was soon carried ashore.   It was nine o'clock; the moon shone brightly over the white beach and the whiter walls of Fort Taylor; the small vessels and the ponderous men-of-war were pictured upon a bay of dappled silver, and a soft breeze rustled the trees and cooled the brows of the animated officers.   They made their way through groups of noisy, picturesque negroes, slouching, broad-hatted sailors and quiet, well-clad citizens, to the farther suburb of the town; entered a garden along a shell walk; mounted the steps of a brilliantly illuminated mansion; gave their cards to a negro servant, and were escorted to the dressing-room. Then they descended to the parlors and were presented to Madam Fontana and the guests by Colonel Gordon.

The rooms were large and modern; the carpets and lace curtains were costly and beautiful; the furniture was heavy mahogany and cane-work in peculiar patterns; the walls were covered with engravings, paintings and pieces of shell work ; a Spanish and an American flag draped a large mirror, and exquisitely tinted shells, magnificent bunches of snowy coral, and stuffed birds of brilliant plumage, were placed upon the mantels, brackets and tables.   The windows were open, and the soft breeze lifted the lace curtains gently and mingled with the sweet music of violins, flutes and guitars, which floated through the rooms from unseen quarters in the hall.

A merry company of fair women and brave men filled the rooms, the windows, and the piazza around the house.   The gentlemen included the best citizens of the place, Government officials and army and navy officers.   The ladies were some of them wives of the gentlemen present, but the larger number were young, single ladies belonging to Key West.   The civilians were in evening dress, and the officers were in full uniform.   To have appeared otherwise, would have been to have made a *faux pas*, even upon that little dry key in the gulf. Many of the ladies were dressed in white, especially those "native to the manor born;" a few, however, rivalled their Northern sisters in silks of delicate shades of pink, buff, pearl and blue.

Madame Fontana was dressed in gray silk and wore a 'tiara of diamonds. She was about twenty-five years of age, and had lost little of the beauty which had made her a belle in her Cuban home at Matanzas. She greeted the officers of the Nautilus with particular warmth of manner, and introduced them with delicate compliments to some of her favorite lady friends. They were soon engaged walking about the piazza or strolling through the garden. The main parlors were full, and many were dancing, while others, who had just finished a quadrille or a polka, had sought the moonlit walks and the evening air for conversation. Careswell soon tired of dancing, and walked up and down the front piazza with his partner, a Miss Good, who was one of the most beautiful and graceful young ladies of the company, and whom he thought just then good enough for any one.

"It is a lovely night," said he. "How softly the wind murmurs through the trees."

"Yes," she replied, "it is very soft."

"How delicately the moonlight tints the wavelets of the Gulf and paints the winding shore with bands of snowy whiteness."

"Yes, it looks delicate."

"Do not the massive walls of Fort Taylor look beautiful, with the lights and shades so harmoniously blended?"

"Yes, it looks beautiful."

"It stands there with its guns frowning upon the harbor, a representative of the dignity and power of the United States, and a menace to her foes."

"Yes."

"Do you like the officers of the fort?"

"Oh, yes! Colonel Gordon is such a gallant man; and Lieutenant Long is so good looking."

"Do you think him handsome?"

"Oh, yes; his moustache is so pretty."

"It's taffy color, isn't it?"

"No, it—it is sort of yellowish auburn."

"Do you like to live in Key West?"

"Yes."

"It is a delightful home, isn't it?"

"Yes, I think it the best place I know."

"Have you ever travelled?"

"Yes."

"Have you been North?"

"No."

"Where have you travelled?"

"I have been to Habana."

"Ah! that's a long journey; a hundred miles, isn't it?"

"Yes."

"Did you like Habana?"

"Only a little—it is too hot."

"Did you go into the interior of Cuba?"

"No."

"What particularly impressed you in the ancient city?"

"Nothing. The ladies wear very high combs, and the gentlemen smoke all the time. Papa bought me a comb, but I never would wear it."

"Do you like parties and balls?"

"Oh, ever so much!"

"You find society different here now from what it was before the war?"

"Yes."

"Do you like to visit the men-of-war?"

"Yes, indeed!"

"You must come aboard the Nautilus some day."

"Yes, thank you."

Miss Good opened and shut her fan several times and looked through the window at the dancers. Careswell was exhausted. He had tried hard to awaken interest and enthusiasm, and had met with poor success. He could not do all the talking. He did not want to cross-question like a prosecuting attorney, and his efforts in some directions had not produced pleasant results. Miss Good was charming to look upon, and several officers had been presented to her, who looked with envious eyes upon his monopolizing her so long. Just then Madam Fontana came along with Mr. Bloss. "You naughty girl," she said to

Miss Good, "to keep Mr. Careswell so long to yourself. I have been watching you. Lieutenant Long has been talking in monosyllables to the Misses Garver, and I believe he has pulled half his moustache out by the roots."

"Let him pull," said Careswell coolly; "its yellowish auburn luxuriance will soon return."

"Now, no sarcasm, Lieutenant," said Madam; "no rivalry. You ought to be very happy for the favor that has been shown you to-night. Come with me, I have something to say to you. Laura take Mr. Bloss' arm."

Careswell said "Au revoir, Señorita," and walked down a garden path with Madam.

"You find her charming, don't you now, Lieutenant?" said she. Naval officers were all lieutenants or captains to the ladies.

"Very charming."

"She's a sweet girl, Lieutenant, and belongs to one of our best families."

"Does she?"

"Yes, and her father is rich."

"How much is he worth?"

"Oh, many thousands."

"What is his business?"

"He owns turtlers."

"Turtlers! What are turtlers?"

"Don't you know? Turtlers are vessels that go along the keys and catch turtles."

"What does he do with them?"

"He sells them to the market men, and ships them to Habana and New York."

"He is a sort of fisherman then?"

"No, indeed! Fishermen go out in boats, and fish with lines and draw seines. He never does that."

"Does he go in a vessel?"

"Yes, but he owns parts of vessels that go without him."

"Do the parts of vessels go?"

"No; how foolish! You know better than that."

"Do turtles coo?"

"Not that I know of."

"The Bible says they do in Palestine."

" Does it ?"

" Do they bite ?"

" No."

" I have seen them bite."

" Have you? They don't bite hooks. The men find a turtle in shallow water, and throw a long pole pointed with iron at him; the iron sticks into his shell, and they draw him in by a line fastened to the iron."

" Oh, I understand. Mr. Good is a turtler and catches and deals in turtles. I thought some one was at the business. We have had turtle souped, boiled, fried and roasted, aboard the Nautilus, till I begin to feel like a Testudo."

" What is that?"

" A stuffed and animated carapax."

" What *do* you mean, Lieutenant?"

" I mean I am sick of turtle meat. It may do for intoxicated aldermen and isolated islanders, but I prefer beef."

" Yes, beef is very good, but it is all jerked down here."

" Well, jerked beef is very good as they cook it in Havana."

" Mr. Bloss seems to be a favorite with the ladies to-night."

" Yes, he is a favorite everywhere. He is the life of the ship."

" How is that ?"

" Why, he is so jolly. He always has a kind word for every one. He smooths over our differences; keeps all his messmates in good humor by his jokes and stories, and is as full of poetry as the sea is full of fish. He is a talented fellow. I don't know how he will like the smell of powder, he has never been under fire."

" Are you going into danger, Lieutenant? Do you expect to go into battle soon ?"

" Not at present that I know of. You know we must go where duty calls us, and we may be ordered against the enemy's forts any day."

" Oh, I think war is terrible. It is awful to have men shot, and I should be sorry to have any of my friends on the Nautilus hurt."

" Thank you. So should I."

They walked along the piazza and met Col. Gordon.

" Ah! Careswell, my boy," said he, " beware of bright eyes

and the moonbeams. The Key West ladies are great heart-breakers."

"Has any one broken yours, Colonel?" asked Madam.

"Oh, no; only battered it a little," said he, laughing.

Dr. Willett came along just then with the regimental surgeon's wife, and joined in the conversation. Careswell was introduced to one of the Misses Garver and danced awhile, then supper was announced and he escorted her to the table.

The supper consisted of all the delicacies obtainable there. The waiters served the party rapidly and skilfully, showing that they had been well trained at many similar entertainments. Madam sat at the head of the table with Bloss upon her right. Paymaster Horton was upon her left, with Miss Lizzie Garver, to whom he had been very attentive, and Careswell and his lady were near the middle of the table opposite Lieut. Long and Miss Good.

Colonel Gordon graced the foot of the table by his commanding presence, having civilians and officers with their ladies upon either hand.

The Misses Garver were different from the other Key West ladies. They were large, strong, red cheeked girls, rather self assertive in manner, and dressed with an extravagant display of ribbons and colors. The quiet and pious paymaster was quite subdued by the manner and tone of his companion, and listened to her volubility amazed and uneasy. Careswell sat demurely attentive to the communications of his lady, and, when she showed signs of stopping talking, encouraged her by an appropriate show of interest and well considered questions. He anticipated her every want, had her plate kept full of good things and her wine glass replenished, noted her extraordinary appetite, and wondered at the difference between her and Miss Good, who spoke little, kept her eyes cast down, and nibbled at the feast as if merely to keep up appearances.

There was a wide social chasm between the young ladies. Miss Good had been born into her set, the highest upon the island. Miss Garver had gradually worked herself into it through her manœuvering and dash, and by means of entertainments which she had lately been able to give, owing to her father's accumulations in the pilotage business. Capt. Garver was a kind, generous, honest, hard-working man, ignorant of book knowledge, and he fully appreciated his deficiencies. After he had accumulated some money, he said 'his darters should have an edication;' so he sent them to the North, where they were duly instructed in a flimsy boarding school, from which they returned with a smattering of French and music to delight the declining years of their parents. The old gentleman kept open house for all the officers at the Key, supplied excellent wines and genuine Havana cigars to his guests, presented his daughters, and had them exhibit their accomplishments, and tried to use their large words with becoming gravity and most nonsensical consequences. His house was much frequented by naval officers, and there are few who served in the East Gulf Squadron who do not remember his kindness, his daughters, and his *mal-apropos* use of English.

Miss Garver rattled on quite careless of all around her, casting a glance of impudent defiance at Miss Good occasionally, while the latter lady curled her lip disdainfully and watched Careswell stealthily. If Careswell had found in Miss Good an intellectual desert, he had now struck a perfect oasis of richness.

"Lieutenant," said Miss Garver, "you don't know how to eat an orange. Here, give it to me, I'll show you, and you can introduce the fashion up North. Take the orange by the ends between your forefinger and thumb, then cut it this way clear across, now put the halves in your plate so, sweep out all the seeds, sprinkle it with sugar, if you want to, and eat with a spoon or gnaw out the pulp with your upper teeth—your little moustache won't hurt.

"Some people quarter an orange peel as if they wanted a pattern to cover a ball. That's no way. Just peel it round and round like you would an apple, then you don't get your finger-nails full and can cut it across as before. I can always tell a Yankee by the way he eats an orange, unless he has been educated by some of us."

"Well, that is an improvement," said Careswell. "Did you know Señor Fontana?"

"Yes, a little. He was a proud, haughty man, and claimed to belong to one of the best families of Spain. He held a Government appointment in Habana, and used to come over here in his yacht. He took his American wife to Europe, established a home in a pretty villa back of Matanzas on his return, and soon after died of yellow fever. Madam did not like her adopted country, so she gathered up her piasters and moved over here."

"Do you think she loved him?"

"I suppose so; she was respectful, obedient and all that."

"She doesn't seem very unhappy to-night."

"She is not; she is as gay as any of us. Who is that officer next to Miss Mixon?"

"That is Lieut. Ashton."

"Well, I hope he doesn't belong to your ship. I don't like his looks. He and that engineer seem determined to get jolly."

Careswell glanced around uneasily. Horton was fingering a full glass and drinking nothing; Willett was pledging the health of Surgeon Edwards, and the army officers and civilians were engaged in an animated discussion upon the Mason and Slidell affair. Conversation became more general with the fruits and ices, a few patriotic toasts were drunk and the party arose and sauntered about the garden.

Careswell had seen quite enough of Miss Garver by this time, and soon managed to drop her and get into the vicinity of Laura, who excused herself to Lieut. Long and took his arm for a promenade.

"Miss Garver wants an escort," said Careswell to Long lightly. Long turned red, scowled and walked away.

"How did you enjoy your supper and your companion?" was Careswell's first question.

"Very well," answered Laura. "How *can* you fancy Miss Garver?"

"Who said I fancied her? She is lively, intelligent and kind hearted. That's more than one can say of some Key Westers."

"She's a Conch!"

"A what?"

"A Conch. Don't you know what that is?"

"Yes; a conch is a shell of the genus *Strombus*. Conchology, the science of shells, is derived from it. Did you ever study conchology?"

"No, but Key West conchs are not shells."

"What are they?" asked Careswell with a puzzled air.

"A class in society. Society is rather mixed here, but there are three distinct sets, called Kingfishers, Conchs, and Sponges."

"Why, that is as bad as the Brahminical castes in India."

"Is it? Have you been to India?"

"No."

"How do you know about them then?"

"I have read about them in history."

"Oh, have you? Well, we have these castes here. The Kingfishers are all fine people with plenty of money, and are the true aristocracy. They dress well, live well, have nice houses, give parties and balls, and do very little work. Madam Fontana is the Queen of the Kingfishers, and many of the ladies here to-night are her subjects."

"I suppose you are a Kingfisher?"

"Oh, yes; I always was. The Conchs are not educated, they dress in bad taste, rarely give parties, and are obliged to work all the time. They are always trying to become Kingfishers and to get into our society. There are so few ladies on the island that some of them are occasionally invited into our set. Miss Garver is a conch, so is her sister, and that tall woman in buff—she is the Queen of the Conchs."

Careswell and Laura moved nearer to the window to have a good look at the queen. Just then Mr. Lawson appeared, looking rather flushed and excited, spoke to Miss Sanders, the queen, and they were soon whirling around the room in a waltz. The music was fast and their movements rapid, and everybody hastened to see their grace and skill. Suddenly Lawson turned pale, let go of his partner, staggered and sank into a chair. Dr. Willett was at his side in a moment, had him taken into the air outside, and announced that it was merely an attack of vertigo.

The music, dancing, promenading and gossiping went on as before, and few thought anything more of the accident.

"I want to hear about the Sponges," said Careswell. "You finished your description of the Conchs, didn't you?"

"Yes," said Laura. "The Sponges are the lowest and poorest class upon the Key, and include the laborers, the sailors and the negroes. A few of them sometimes get to be Conchs, but never Kingfishers."

"Some of the negroes?"

"No; they never bleach as some of the others do. Now you know all about us and will be able to understand, that, if you associate with Conchs, you will not have many friends among the Kingfishers."

"All right, Miss Kingfisher, I understand. Shall we go in and dance that polka?"

"If you please."

Careswell and Laura went into the parlor and were soon moving around the room to the delicious music. Madam Fontana was the centre of a group of ladies and gentlemen near a window.

"How graceful she is!"

"What pretty nut-brown hair and eyes!"

"What delicate hands and feet!"

"How well they dance!"

"They are a fine looking couple."

"Who is she?"

"Where does she live?"

"Who is he?"

"What vessel does he belong to?"

These exclamations and questions were addressed to Madam, who took pleasure in giving the party all the information desired and joined in their admiration.

Soon after this the dancing ceased, the musicians went to supper, and the guests began to depart. Careswell stood upon the piazza cap in hand among the ladies, when Lieut. Long brushed rudely by, went up to Laura and said, "Shall I have the pleasure of escorting you home?"

"No, thank you; I stay with Madam," said she icily.

Long bowed his adieux and departed.

Laura held out her hand to Careswell and said, "Good night; I hope we shall see you soon again."

"Good night," said he, kissing her hand, which action caused her to shrink within the door.

"Á Dios, Señor," said Madam; "we shall always be glad to see you when you come ashore."

"Thank you. Good night," said he, bowing and going away.

Bloss was the last officer of the Nautilus to leave, and he came away in company with Col. Gordon. The officers were all waiting at the boat-landing when he came down and had many jokes at his long tarrying. He laughed heartily at the sallies of wit at his expense, and had his rose still safe in his lappel.

"It took you a long time to say adieu, Bloss. What did you have to talk about?" asked the paymaster.

"Nothing. I remarked,

'The stars their early vigils keep,
 The silent hours are near.'"

"Always poetic. Did that take you half an hour?"

"Three-quarters, you mean," said the doctor. "I have no doubt he hung by the eyelids and talked sweet till Madam grew sleepy."

"I did not rush down here like a locomotive. Great bodies move slowly. I came with the ease and dignity of an officer on half-pay."

"Did you kiss her hand and vow eternal fidelity?" asked Careswell.

"No, but I saw you do it to another lady."

Everybody laughed and Careswell said no more.

"I might have said," continued Bloss,

'I must leave thee lady sweet!
 Months shall waste before we meet;
 Winds are fair and sails are spread,
 Anchors leave their ocean bed;'—

but I did not, because I expect to see her again to-morrow afternoon and we are not going to sea just yet."

"Will you gentlemen get into the boat?" growled the sleepy midshipman in the stern sheets of the cutter.

"When we get ready, sir," replied Felton.

"Very well, sir; I've been waiting here an hour already, and I protest against any longer delay."

"Well, protest you may, but wait you must, my son of Neptune. This is your share of the party, and it would be a pity to rob you of it."

"Let's go aboard, Felton," said the doctor persuasively.

"All right; let's get aboard, gentlemen," he answered.

The party got into the boat; the bow oarsman pushed off; the men let their oars fall, and they were soon on board ship. Ashton was rather lively and explained over and over again how Long happened to get "half seas over," and Lawson kept asking, "Did you know I danced with the Queen of the Conchs?"

The tired officers sought their bunks, but occasionally they could hear the words, sung to a popular air,

> "I danced with the Queen of the Conchs, Conchs, Conchs;
> I danced with the Queen of the Conchs."

Thus ended one of the most enjoyable entertainments at Key West.

There was queer work going on aboard the Nautilus. The hull was given another coat of black paint; the topgallant masts were sent down and replaced by thicker ones, with short stubby poles; covers were made for the lower masts and smoke-stack and painted yellow, and barrels of tar were stored in the coal-bunkers to burn in the furnaces and make black smoke. Thus the vessel could be changed into the semblance of an English steamer at short notice, and blockade-runners perhaps enticed within gun-shot. The ship was coaled to her full capacity and a good supply of stores was stowed below.

The men worked very hard, and were permitted to enjoy themselves after supper, during the second dog-watch, between six and eight o'clock, which is regarded as sailor's holiday. They went in swimming, and had foot-races on the beach and rowing races in the cutters. They had concertinas, accordions, violins, banjos, guitars, flutes, harmonicas, jewsharps and bones, which they played with a good deal of skill and taste. Quite a number formed a vocal club and sang all the nautical and popular songs with animation and spirit. They danced many of the shuffles peculiar to the stage, and formed sets and went through reels, quadrilles and hornpipes vigorously. They rehearsed condensed comedies and tragedies, and gave excellent representations, dressed in such costumes as they could improvise from their clothing. They held civil and

military courts and punished their criminals in comical ways
that caused boisterous laughter.   The space between two guns
served for a dressing-room and stage; a gun-carriage made a
judge's bench, a parlor sofa or a royal throne; the ship's pikes
and cutlasses were used to arm a band of robbers or an imperial guard; the tarpaulins and swabs were fashioned into
jackasses, camels and elephants, and ropes were stretched to
divide the deck into boxes, parquet and gallery, where the
officers and men gathered as spectators.   Every pleasant evening something was prepared for the amusement, if not for the
instruction, of the audience, and visitors from other vessels
were glad to join the company, to enjoy the entertainment, and
to add to the merriment.   The officers liked the sport almost as
well as the sailors, and the latter preferred generally to remain
aboard ship and take part in the fun, rather than to wander·
around the grog shops and waste their money ashore.   The
evenings were so refreshing after the hot days, that everybody
remained on deck far into the night, and the sailors were permitted to follow their sports till nine and sometimes ten o'clock.
There never was a more generous and liberal executive than
Mr. Felton, nor a happier or better contented ship's crew than
that of the Nautilus.

CHAPTER X.

THESE pleasant times could not go on forever, and one day the news spread through the ship that she would sail the following morning. The officers made haste ashore to bid adieu to their friends, and letters were written by many to leave by the next mail North. The U. S. supply steamer Union arrived and delivered her mail and fresh provisions to the fleet, just in time, and then departed for stations up the coast.

The next morning at eight o'clock, steam was gotten up; a rough-looking pilot came aboard and took charge of the bridge, with Mr. Felton alongside of him; the anchor was weighed, and the Nautilus steamed out of the reef-guarded anchorage of the Key and shaped her course for the west end of Cuba. She went all day under a full head of steam and slowed down during the night, keeping a sharp lookout for all suspicious sail. The next forenoon a steamer was seen, heading to the westward, and chase was made. After a sharp run of several hours, a gun brought her to, and she proved to be the Mississippi, bound from New York to New Orleans. The persons on board were badly frightened, as the Nautilus had put on her disguise and looked every bit like an English vessel. They thought she was the Alabama, and were so delighted at finding their mistake that they sent several hampers of wine aboard, which Captain Prescott shared very liberally with the wardroom and steerage. It was a great gratification to the captain and his crew, that the Nautilus had been able to overhaul, in a fair race, so fine a merchant steamer as the Mississippi, and hearty cheers were given on both vessels as they separated.

The course of the Nautilus was altered more to the southward, and, in the afternoon, the high, bold coast of Cuba was seen; then the vessel was turned to the eastward and she steamed slowly along towards Havana.

Towards evening a small schooner was reported upon the port bow, standing to the northward. As soon as the men aboard of her spied the Nautilus, they turned about and made all haste towards Cuban waters. The Nautilus was headed more in shore and put at full speed, while the forecastle gun was cleared for action, but, before she could get within gun-shot range, the little craft had crossed the bow and was fast getting into shoal water. A blank cartridge did not stop her, and a shell was sent whizzing over her, then she lowered her foresail and hove to. A boat was being made ready to board her, when a sudden squall of wind and rain hid her from sight. The forecastle was crowded with officers, the Parrott gun loaded and trained, the wind howling, the rain coming down in torrents, and the water shoaling rapidly, making it danger-ous for the Nautilus to proceed in shore much farther. Sud-denly the wind diminished, the rain ceased, the mist lifted, the sun shone brightly, and there, three miles away, the little schooner was scudding directly for the beach and not two miles away from it, with the stars and bars flying from her main peak. A shell was sent after her and burst in her wake, and the Nautilus was headed more in shore, while leadsmen were placed in the chains to report the soundings. The next shell burst nearer to her and had the effect of bringing her to again.

"She is in neutral waters and thinks herself safe," said Ashton; "we shall get into trouble with the Spanish authori-ties if we take her now."

"She is more than a league off shore," said Sanborn. "I would capture her anyhow just for her impudence; there are no inhabitants along here to know the difference."

"She looks to me about eight miles out," said Careswell, looking through the large end of his marine glasses.

"The shore is bold and the hills high inland, which makes the island seem nearer. I think she is outside neutrality," said the captain. "What do you think, Mr. Felton?"

"I think we should have the benefit of the doubt and take her," was the answer.

A boat was lowered, manned, armed, and sent on board the schooner, in charge of Mr. Bloss. He met with no resistance, took the prize, ran her off near the Nautilus, left some of his men on board, and returned with the vessel's papers and five prisoners. She was the blockade-runner Fanchon, of Mobile, bound home, one day out from Havana, with a cargo of salt, soda-ash, dry goods and aguardiente, and the very craft that had so impudently hoisted the Confederate flag over her deck-load of cotton, as she sailed jauntily into Havana, when the Nautilus came out. Revenge again was sweet.

Mr. Bloss reported that the prize was well supplied with provisions, water, instruments and charts, and there was no necessity of taking anything aboard except bedding. It was getting squally and dark, so Careswell and a crew of five men, well armed and equipped, with the rebel captain and mate as prisoners, were hastily transferred to the schooner. Orders to take her into Key West and report to the Prize Commissioners and the Admiral were handed to Careswell by Captain Prescott, as he passed through the gangway and down into the cutter. In a few minutes he was on board the schooner, surrounded by the crew, the unwelcome prisoners, the bedding, the carbines and their accoutrements. The men in charge were quickly embarked in the cutter; the officer said "Good night! Bon voyage!" and returned to the Nautilus. Before Careswell had an opportunity to make a single observation of the condition of the craft and her outfit, his ship had disappeared in the darkness, and he found himself forsaken upon a little vessel of untried qualities, in the midst of rising, threatening seas and violent squalls of wind and rain. His heart sank, and he stood irresolute upon the spray-washed deck, looking out into the darkness where the Nautilus had vanished.

Squall succeeded squall all night, and the rain-drops rushed in regiments and battalions against the faces and forms of those who kept watch aboard the Nautilus, until the morning sun shamed Neptune out of countenance and stilled the angry tumult. The ship had buffeted the seas and rolled heavily all night, and the uneasy sleepers awoke to the rushing sounds of the storm and shuddered, when they thought of the fate of the Fanchon and of those who had been so hastily abandoned. The course was changed in the morning, and an attempt was made to find the little schooner, but no trace of her could be discovered, and, in the afternoon, the ship turned around and pursued her course along the coast to the eastward, while the

officers and men talked in sorrowful tones of the good qualities of their messmates who had gone to Davy Jones' locker.

During the next few days, a French frigate was spoken,
bound for Vera Cruz; a small schooner was overhauled, which
hoisted the Sardinian flag and proved her right to its protection, and several American vessels, with proper clearance papers, were boarded and allowed to proceed upon their voyages.
The Nautilus then ran into Havana and dropped anchor in
her former anchorage; a little Spanish midshipman, with a
star upon his cap front, came aboard and presented the compliments of the Spanish admiral and offers of assistance; the
American consul sent off a bag of letters, and Captain Prescott received an order to return to Key West. The anchor
was immediately weighed and the ship put to sea in the afternoon, and, the next day, five days from the separation from
the Fanchon, she arrived at Key West and anchored near
Fort Taylor. The prize was not to be seen; she had not been
heard from, and all gave her up for lost.

A strong breeze was blowing from the southwest, the white-
capped waves were chasing each other madly across the harbor,
the pilot-boats were scudding under bonnetless jibs and single
reefed mainsails in the offing, and boats had trouble in landing
at the wharves. Away in the northwest channel near the
light-house, four or five miles from the Key, a small vessel
lay at anchor waiting for high tide. Several vessels were anchored near her, fishing or waiting for deeper water, and there
was nothing about her to attract particular attention. At
noon her anchor was weighed, her sails were set one by one,
and she began to beat up the channel. Nearer and nearer she
came, all her sails recklessly spread, her rail under the waves
half the time, and the water foaming under her bow from
her great speed.

The contrast between her broad spread of canvas, and the
snugly reefed vessels around her, attracted attention to her
from persons afloat and ashore, and the quartermaster and
some of the officers of the Nautilus watched her closely with
glasses, but could not make out who was on board, because
she had cleared the channel and was bearing down head on for
the Nautilus. She came onwards rapidly, rounded the stern
of the Nautilus, came up head to wind with everything shiver-

ing, and dropped anchor near the shore, before those on board the man-of-war had seen the stars and stripes above the stars and bars, floating from the main peak, and Careswell at the helm. When surprise had turned to exultation, the crew of the Nautilus crowded the hammock nettings and rigging and gave three rousing cheers, which were repeated by the men of the other U. S. vessels and answered by the crew of the Fanchon. Then a great crowd gathered upon the shore and cheered; the news of the safe arrival spread like fire through the town, and the whole population came down and took a look at the little craft that had weathered such a wild storm.

Careswell delivered the Fanchon to the Prize Court, transferred his prisoners to Colonel Gordon, in Fort Taylor, and returned with his men to the Nautilus, where they were received with the greatest enthusiasm and demonstrations of affection. After a day's rest and recuperation, he related his adventures. He said:

"I never felt so desolate and homesick as I did when the Nautilus disappeared in the darkness, but the feeling was only momentary, for the movements of the vessel and the rushing of the storm told me I must work, if I wished ever to see dry land again. I ordered the bedding and arms put below in the little cabin, took the helm myself, gave orders for shortening sail, and kept the vessel in the wind and head to the sea. The bonnet was taken out of the jib, the foresail furled, and a close reef put in the mainsail. The men worked lively, as there were several Cape Cod sailors aboard who knew all about schooners, but the running gear was out of order, there was trouble in finding things in the darkness, and the seas were sweeping right across the forward part of the vessel. In the emergency, the prisoners offered their services with an appearance of good will, though actuated by sinister motives, and the captain said, 'I will look after the main reef-earing, as it is not in its proper place.' It was necessary for him to pass behind me, where I stood at the helm, in order to reach over the rail out upon the boom, and he stepped back and began to fumble at the rope. Suddenly I felt a strong tug at my Colt's revolver, which was strapped in its frog on my sword-belt and hanging over the back part of my right hip. Fortunately the strap held, I grasped the handle of the pistol, struck the cap-

tain's hand, and turned around upon him. He busied himself
again with the reef-earing, apparently not noticing me. I
drew my revolver, cocked it, ordered him and his mate forward of the foremast in the drenching seas and kept them
there.

" I called Sylvester, the young man whom you remember
as the first one to go aloft to secure the foretopsail yard, when
it broke loose from the mast, in the gale we had near the Ba-
hamas, in whom I had implicit confidence, and told him what
had happened. He said he had noticed the two prisoners
talking together in a low voice, and had his suspicions that
they had some sort of an understanding with the Dago, the
Portuguese half-breed, whom we had taken along for cook.
I concluded the attempt to seize my pistol had been premedi-
tated; that, had it been accomplished, the captain was to give
a signal, perhaps, by shooting me and others; the other two
men were to rush into the cabin and seize the arms, and then
the remainder of the crew were to be driven overboard or
shot. In the darkness and disorder aboard, the plan could
have been executed easily, because, if Sylvester and I had
been shot, the other men, without a leader, would have fallen
easy victims to the pirates. The plot failed by the holding of
a narrow leather strap and button.

" I told Sylvester that he and I must remain aft and take
turn about in steering, watching and sleeping. I informed the
three other American sailors, that the prisoners and the Dago
could not be trusted; that they should keep a sharp lookout
upon their actions day and night, have their revolvers ready
for instant use, and remain upon the top of the cabin aft as
much as possible, particularly at night. I took the revolvers
of the Dago and the young sailor, Gardner; kept one myself,
and gave the other to Sylvester. I instructed Gardner to
attend the forecastle, to keep his eyes upon the Dago, especially when he was cooking the meals, and to prevent by his
presence, as much as possible, any private conversation between
him and the prisoners. I told the crew that Sylvester was to
act as executive, and his orders must be obeyed, and instructed
him not to allow any one to go down into the cabin where the
arms were upon any pretense. Sylvester and the three other
sailors were all Northern men, who perceived the gravity of

the situation, appreciated the confidence I reposed in them, and relieved me of much anxiety by their vigilance and hearty co-operation.

"The gangway to the cabin served as a binnacle; a cheap box-compass was placed upon one of the steps, and a lantern was hung on a nail opposite to illumine it. The little craft pitched fearfully; the seas knocked her about like a feather and half buried her occasionally; the rain came down heavily, and all I could do was to keep her head to the seas to ease her, and as close to the wind as she would lie. During a heavy lurch, the compass and lantern broke loose, tumbled down upon the cabin floor and were broken, leaving us in darkness, without anything to indicate the course. All hands were kept on watch; everybody was wet and miserable; the vessel's bow pitched into the seas frightfully, and there was two feet of water in the hold, which increased steadily in spite of two men working constantly at the pumps. The vessel was trimmed too much by the head, and I asked the captain about the stowage of the cargo. He said the forward part of the hold was full of soda-ash in casks, the midships contained the salt in bags, and the aguardiente and dry goods were in and around the cabin. A hasty survey through a bulkhead in the cabin showed the salt greatly diminished by the water in the vessel. It was being dissolved and pumped overboard; the after part of the vessel was being lightened, and the heavier cargo forward was pressing the bow under water. Still nothing could be done to alter the stowage in such a storm, and we watched, waited and hoped for morning and milder weather, in greater anxiety now that we knew the true condition of affairs below.

" It was a long and anxious night, but the sun came at last to dry our clothes and cheer us, the sea went down gradually, a fire was started in the galley, and coffee and hard-tack were served. The coffee had a foul odor and taste and no one could drink it. Gardner had watched its preparation and was sure that nothing but coffee, sugar and water had been put in the pot. The water was examined and found as filthy as sewage. It was in a cask that had held aguardiente, and had a putrid, sickening taste difficult to imagine. If the coffee was undrink-able, the water was more so, and there was no other beverage aboard but fiery Spanish rum. This was a great disappointment, because there is nothing so greatly relished by sailors as the early pot of coffee, and it was hard to do without it after the exposure and fatigue of the night. We were well water-soaked and not very thirsty, so concluded we could do without water until the short run of 175 miles was made to Key West.

"About three o'clock in the afternoon, the sea had become smooth enough to make it safe to take off the hatches, and most of the water in the hold had been pumped overboard; so I set the men to work under Sylvester's supervision, had the soda-ash stowed amidships and the remainder of the salt placed forward of it, thus lightening the bow of the vessel, bringing the stern down into the water, and fixing her in excellent trim for sailing. The bonnet was bent on the jib, the foresail hoisted, the reef shaken out of the mainsail, the gaff-topsail set, the deck cleared up generally, and we went bowling along right merrily and felt quite comfortable. The provisions were of the coarsest and meanest kind, and the only bread we had was the bag of hard-tack brought from the Nautilus, but we could endure privations for the glory of taking in a prize, and only longed for a good drink of water. There was,

'Water, water everywhere, and not a drop to drink,'

because the nauseous contents of the rum-cask we could not call water, much less drink it.

"The men were divided into watches which were set at 6 o'clock. I took the starboard watch from six till midnight; placed the rebel captain and Gardner, as lookouts forward, and let Sylvester and the port watch get some sleep. Sylvester took the helm and the port watch, with one of the sailors and the rebel mate on lookout, from midnight till six o'clock in the morning. The lazy Dago was permitted to sleep all night among his pots and pans in the little galley behind the foremast, but the trusted men slept upon the top of the cabin where they would be ready in an emergency. A pleasant breeze from the westward drove us on our course; the night passed uneventfully, and everybody felt rested and refreshed in the morning. Only our thirst began to be troublesome, and we were obliged to drink some of the filthy water to assuage it, for we could not bear the coffee. I had an opportunity to examine my orders and accompanying papers, which had been wet through in my coat pocket, and had remained there unopened till this time. The orders read as follows:

'U. S. Steamer Nautilus,
Off the Island of Cuba,
June 13th, 186-.

'Sir:

'Proceed with the Prize Schooner Fanchon under your charge to the port of Key West, and there deliver her, together with the accompanying papers (which are all that were found on board) and the persons retained as witnesses, to the Judge of the U. S. District Court or to the U. S. Prize Commissioners at that place, taking his or their receipt for the same. You will not deliver her, the papers, or the witnesses, to the order of any other person or parties unless directed to act otherwise by the Navy Department or Flag-Officer commanding the Squadron.

'The Fanchon was seized by this vessel, under my command, on the 13th day of June, 186-, off the Island of Cuba, for violating the rules governing the blockade at present instituted by the United States; and, of the circumstances attending the case, you are sufficiently aware, and will communicate them when required to do so by competent authority.

'On your arrival at Key West, and immediately after you have visited the Judge or Prize Commissioners, you will call upon the U. S. District Attorney thereat, show him these instructions, and give him any information concerning the seizure he may solicit. Then you will next report yourself in person to the Commanding Officer of the Navy Yard thereat, show him also these instructions, and ask his directions, when needed, as to the disposition of yourself and the rest constituting the prize crew. Finally, when duly notified by the Judge, Prize Commissioners, or District Attorney, that your services are no longer wanted by the Court, you will at once return to your vessel, taking with you the men under your command and the receipt above alluded to, unless otherwise ordered by superior authority.

'You will receive herewith a communication for the Secretary of the Navy, giving him a detailed account of the seizure. This you will mail immediately on your arrival at Key West.

'Your attention is called to the annexed 'Circular,' lately issued from the Navy Department, to which have been added, since it was issued, the words in the last paragraph, beginning with, 'together with a descriptive list,' etc.; which you will see is complied with, in every particular, before sailing with your prize.

'Very respectfully, your obedient servant,
Amasa Prescott,
Commander.
Commanding U. S. Steamer Nautilus.'

'To Ensign Harry Careswell,
U. S. Navy.'

"Statements of the men's accounts alluded to in the 'Circular,' the Fanchon's papers, a letter to the Secretary of the

Navy and another to Admiral Bailey, accompanied the orders. It was plainly my duty to get to Key West, but with only the sun and stars to steer by, the course could only be approximated. I had set my watch by the ship's chronometer before leaving the Nautilus, and, as it was getting towards eight o'clock, I prepared to take a time sight for longitude. What was my chagrin to find nothing but an old fashioned quadrant with no screw to fasten the index and vernier scale. I took several sets of sights, holding the index with my fingers, and worked them up carefully. The first series placed us in the longitude of the Azores; the second, in that of Texas. I tried several times and, in spite of the utmost care, could not get correct altitudes of the sun. It was just as difficult at meridian. The latitude from my observation was that of New York. Time sights at four o'clock were equally erroneous, and I gave up in disgust and threw the 'pig-yoke' into a bunk below.

"If there had been no sails, we could have made some out of clothing and bagging; if no rudder or spars, we could have fashioned rude ones from the topworks of the schooner; but without compass courses from which to work up the dead reckoning, without a good instrument to take altitudes and determine the latitude and longitude, scientific sailing was out of the question. I knew the swift currents of the Gulf would carry us to the eastward, and, with only the heavenly bodies to help us guess at a course, the chance of making a straight run for Key West was slight. I knew we could reach the line of keys, extending from Florida to the Tortugas, somewhere, and the schooner was kept due north all day and night, still not a sign of land.

"The bedding, clothing and arms were dried during the day; the revolvers and carbines were fired off, cleaned and reloaded; the hold was pumped dry, and some necessary repairs were made to the vessel's running rigging. The watches were kept in regular man-of-war fashion, during the second night and afterwards, and nothing broke the monotony of the summer sailing until six o'clock the second morning, when I was awakened by a cry of 'Sail ho!'

" 'Where away?' asked Sylvester.

" 'Four points on the port bow, sir!'

"I was up in a moment, and made out with a glass a small schooner standing to the southward. She was just the size, shape and general appearance of a blockade-runner, and I determined to overhaul her for two reasons: I wished to get some fresh water, and I hoped, if she was a dodger, to capture her and take in two prizes instead of one, though this was not in my orders.

"The Fanchon was brought to the wind and the sails trimmed on the port tack, which made her head nearly for the stranger. The latter kept on her course until she was only two miles distant, and we could see an unusual number of men upon her deck; then, when she had probably made out our few blue-jackets, the course was changed, her sails were trimmed on the starboard tack, and she began to run away from us. We tacked ship, crowded all sail in pursuit, and got the carbines up from below ready for a fight if necessary. The difficulties of navigating to Key West, the treachery of the prisoners, and the disloyalty of the Dago, were all forgotten for a time, and every effort was made, by trimming the sails and wetting them with buckets of salt-water, to get the greatest speed possible out of the Fanchon. She skimmed over the water and dashed into the moderate seas like a sportive sea-gull, and, for a time, it seemed she was gaining upon the chase, but, on board the stranger, the people were watchful of the sails and steering, and her admirable movements excited our approbation and envy.

"A stern chase is generally a long one, and it became evident towards noon, that the vessels were well matched and the result of the race would be doubtful. I thought I would try a ruse, so I had the Confederate flag hoisted to the main truck, where it could be plainly seen by those aboard the fleeing vessel. Though it was kept flying an hour, no notice was apparently taken of it. It was then hauled down and the stars and stripes run up in its place. This did not have the desired effect, but the flag was kept aloft till sunset.

"Slowly and surely the unsociable schooner drew away from us; she was five or six miles off at dark, when we gave up the chase and tacked ship to the northward. A whole day had been lost in a futile effort; we were now farther away from port than ever, and felt deeply chagrined at being beaten.

Even the rebel captain had taken much interest in the affair, perhaps, thinking a fight might give him a chance to snatch a weapon and win back his vessel. The night was clear and starry; the men slept about the deck comfortably notwithstanding the dampness, and the Fanchon made an excellent run which continued all the next day. We noticed before dark the next night that the water was changing color; the deep blue had become a yellowish-green, but no bottom was found by a cast of the lead at fifteen fathoms. The vessel was kept about northeast; the flying jib and gaff-topsail were taken in and furled, and everybody kept a sharp lookout for land. A light was seen at ten o'clock, and, at twelve, the white walls of a fortification, which I knew from its appearance must be Fort Jefferson, on the Dry Tortugas, were plainly in sight. It was dangerous to cruise in these unknown waters without compass and bearings, so I kept the vessel to the northward under easy sail till four o'clock, and then tacked and ran back, with the intention of calling at the settlement for water, a compass and sextant. No land was in sight at daylight, nor at noon, and, believing the current had swept us past the islands to the eastward, and the wind having changed, the course was made due east, and we went along lively. Several small, wooded, uninhabited keys were seen in the afternoon, none of which looked like the one we were in search of, but we approached the larger one in order to get some water, and, at five o'clock, ran ashore upon a snowy bank of coral sand.

"I had an anchor taken off immediately into deep water and tried to kedge the vessel off the bank, but could not, and the tide went down and left us fast. Fortunately the wind fell and the water became smooth, so that the vessel did not pound any. I sent the boat away to the keys for water, but she returned without any. This was a bitter disappointment to all. The men reported that the islands were mere piles of sand, covered by starving shrubs and mangrove trees, and containing central lagoons of salt water.

"The water in the casks had grown steadily worse by exposure to the sun, and the lapse of time. Eating salt provisions, washing in salt-water, breathing salt air, sprinkled by salt spray, blistered by the fierce heat of the sun, exposed to

the wind day and night, and depressed by anxiety and loss of
sleep, our thirst had become overpowering, and we had been
obliged to drink the filthy fluid. It had early caused nausea
and diarrhœa, and, to mitigate the evil, I had broached one
of the casks of aguardiente and mixed it sparingly with the
water. This compound was unsatisfactory, irritating and ag-
gravating. It quenched thirst for a time, only to increase it
tenfold later. It checked the diarrhœa, but burned our very
vitals. It gave a buoyancy and support to our flagging ener-
gies, but fevered our blood and scorched our brains. We were
conscious of our responsibilities, but moved, acted and thought
in a mild delirium. Things around us took fantastic shapes;
the islands seemed to rise and fall in the mist of evening;
the trees appeared like dark spectres, stretching out their arms
to seize us; the line leading away to the kedge anchor looked
like a monstrous sea-serpent, wriggling and writhing towards
us; the shallow waves became tongues of flame, chasing each
other restlessly onwards; the gentle ripples along the vessel's
side and under the stern sounded harsh and discordant; the
footfalls upon the deck smote the ears like the blows of a
sledge-hammer, and the fall of an oar made a sound like a
clap of thunder.

" Ever and anon a school of fish would rush into the shal-
lows around the vessel and spatter, clatter and beat the water,
until it shone like a shower of diamonds in a flash of sheet
lightning; a floundering turtle of gigantic size, would crawl,
flop and swim over the white sand, seeming like a nightmare,
until he worked into deeper water; a dark triangular fin
would cut the surface of the water like a razor, and a long,
slim, treacherous shark steal by without a sound, and make
us shudder at the thought that he might soon be tearing our
flesh down in a coral cave, surrounded by waving sponges.
The prisoners, fearful of our revolvers, and suffering and
sympathizing, made no more suspicious or seditious movements.

" The night was bright with stars that winked as if in
mockery of our misery, and it was only by a supreme effort
of the will that we could shake off the illusions of our over-
wrought and fevered senses and keep from going mad. Sick
in body and mind; far from human help; not knowing with

certainty which way to go; with only the heavenly bodies to
guide us, and our vessel hard and fast ashore, it was enough
to try strong souls and cause despair. I think some of us
prayed a little, but not aloud. Still hope did not forsake us,
and energy and courage kept us though that dreadful night.

"When the clouds seemed darkest, the silver lining shone;
the white sails of a vessel were seen in the distance, and the
rattle of her cable told us she had come to anchor. I sent
three men with a cask in the boat for fresh water, and they
returned before midnight with an ample supply of what seemed
to us the most delicious beverage in the world. The captain
and several men from the schooner, which was a turtler, came
on board soon after, and I made an arrangement with him to
lighten the Fanchon and help get her afloat, provided we
could not warp her off the next high tide. He informed me,
to my great surprise, that we were ninety miles east of Key
West. He said the currents along and between the Tortugas
and the different keys were rapid, and it required considerable
experience to estimate them. When we had stood to the
northward of Tortugas and then run back south to find the
islands, the strong easterly current had struck the vessel upon
the broadside, and swept her east almost as fast as she had
gone ahead. When I thought we were sailing south, we were
going southeast, and had been carried beyond Key West, probably in the early morning. This explained the mysterious
disappearance of the Tortugas from the face of the waters and
our non-success in reaching port.

"I shall always have respect for turtlers. If I had not
met this honest captain, I should probably have followed the
line of keys around the coast of Florida and perhaps lost the
vessel. I thanked him heartily for his information; gave him
a demijohn of the Cuban fire-water and some Havana cigars,
and he went aboard his own vessel.

"There was a high tide and spanking breeze early in the
morning, and, to our great joy, we succeeded in getting the
Fanchon afloat, and shaped our course for Key West. We
reached the light-house at dark and attempted to beat up the
channel according to the indications of a miserable chart,
feeling the water with the lead, but we nearly ran aground
several times, and at last considered it safer to anchor for the

night. In the morning the anchor was down, when we saw the Nautilus creep in past Fort Taylor and come to anchor. I knew you would give us up for lost and concluded to surprise you. You know the rest. Here I am, with tawny hands and a peeling nose, hungry as a wolf for all the good things of the wardroom mess."

Everybody agreed the experience was unique and perilous. Careswell had to repeat the story, with modifications, explanations and embellishments, to the people of Key West, and the ladies greeted him with their sweetest smiles and best cakes and wines. Madam Fontana called him a hero, and Laura looked upon him with admiration, but had little to say. They were in the garden one afternoon looking at a Victoria Regia, that Madam had nursed carefully into full bloom. It was growing in a tank of water; its large, lustrous green leaves floated around the snowy petals of this most magnificent flower in the world.

"How pure and sweet! How grandly beautiful it is!" ejaculated Careswell in his enthusiasm.

"Yes, Lieutenant," Madam said, "you can appreciate it and express sentiment over it, but most of the people about town think I was foolish to spend so much time and labor in bringing it to perfection. They say, 'it will last but a few days, then what is the gain?' My northern education has just destroyed my patience with some of these people. I long for the society of those who appreciate beautiful things, who like art, music and literature."

"I think I understand your feelings," said Careswell. "My mother was fond of flowers, and had a garden that attracted and deserved admiration. When I was a boy, I had to do a stint of weeding and digging every day before going to play. She considered flowers the glory of the earth, and always insisted upon their elevating and ennobling influence. Those who do not admire flowers have little taste for the refinements of life, and flowers may therefore be made touchstones for testing individuals."

"I love flowers," said Laura timidly.

"Yes, my dear, I know you do," said Madam, "you know there are exceptions to all rules. We are speaking of the masses. Mr. Bloss loves flowers, does he not, Lieutenant?"

"Certainly. He has the red rose you gave him, pressed in his diary."

Madam looked pleased at this evidence of remembrance, and said, " Why does he not come ashore oftener ?"

" I think he is not very well."

" Not well ? Then I must send him some guava jelly. It is delicious when one has not much appetite."

"Thank you. He will, no doubt, appreciate it."

" I wondered why he did not come to see my lily."

" Which one ?" said Careswell, looking at Laura.

"Oh, the Victoria, of course. Lilies do not last forever, and this one already begins to show signs of decay. Look at those little spots on this snowy leaf. See how rusty they are. In a short time this pretty white will be shrivelled brown, and I must remove the blossom to save the strength of the plant."

" Well, I shall tell Mr. Bloss to come immediately."

Clearly Madam was much interested in Mr. Bloss. It was not so certain that Bloss cared much for Madam. A day had been set for the ladies to visit the Nautilus, but she had gone to sea before the time. Careswell now appointed another day and then took leave. When he arrived on board, he learned that the ship was to sail at daylight for Charlotte Harbor, and he was therefore obliged to send his regrets and farewells ashore by letter.

CHAPTER XI.

THE Nautilus got underway at daybreak; steamed slowly up the coast, and, the next day, arrived and came to anchor in Charlotte Harbor upon the west coast of Florida.

A great number of islands of all shapes and sizes lie along this coast of Florida. The passages between these islands make an extensive network of inland waters, navigable by small craft, and, with the numerous broad, shallow rivers in the main land, furnish muddy homes for thousands of alligators, and gave, in war times, countless hiding places for blockade-runners. It was the boast of the men engaged in blockade-running from this region, that they could pole their vessels all the way inland around Florida until they reached the latitude of Nassau, when they could run across to British waters in one night.

The islands are composed of sand and the muck of vegetable decomposition; they are covered by stunted growths of mangrove, pine, cypress, palmetto and lime trees, and many of them contain pools of brackish water and swamps in the interior. The islands and coast are little above sea level, and the tide sweeps through all the passages and up all the rivers for many miles. Charlotte Harbor is land-locked by these islands. It is in reality a beautiful bay eight to ten miles wide and twenty-five miles long. Pease Creek enters its head, a narrow passage leads south and receives the great Caloosahatchie, and its principal outlet is towards the west. The rivers are broad, shallow, muddy and sluggish. Their bottoms are a slimy ooze, furnishing no support for the feet, and their banks are the homes of voracious alligators, so that fording was dangerous and alost impossible.

There were few inhabitants in this part of Florida during the war. An old Italian refugee, named Salvini, lived with his son and daughter upon Pine Island to the south, and a Mr. Bruno and wife had a small clearing upon the adjacent

10

main land. They claimed to be Union refugees and were
supplied by the naval vessels with regular rations. Being far
from Confederate recruiting officers, they were very friendly
and instructed the officers how to fish and hunt and were very
hospitable to visitors. They did considerable bartering with
the sailors, exchanging corn, sweet potatoes, melons, lemons,
limes and venison, for coffee, sugar, salt, flour, hard-bread,
clothing and tobacco. There were few people along the banks
of the Caloosahatchie. Fort Myers, the old defence against
the Indians, twenty-five miles up the river, with its stockade,
block-houses, barracks, officers' quarters and hospital, was deserted and in ruins. The large fish-curing house and wharf
near the mouth of the river, belonging to a Connecticut company, were in a fair state of preservation, though unprotected
by their owners; numberless coons were running boldly along
the river's banks, and flocks of curlew were piping shrilly about
the marshes.

There were a few families residing upon clearings away from
the banks, far up Pease creek, and a small guard of "Florida
Regulators," having two field-pieces, was camped behind a
rude earth-work upon the right bank at the junction of the
stream with the head waters of the bay.

Many wild cattle roamed over the meadows; red deer darted
about in the forests; coons rushed in packs from place to place;
sea turtles crawled up the sandy beaches to lay their eggs; land
turtle, called gophers, dragged slowly over the sandy soil from
hole to hole; black and green snakes wriggled in the tall
marsh-grass; alligators sunned upon the mud flats, or floated
with only their noses out of water; pelicans flew in long lines
across the bay to roost upon the mangroves; blue and black
herons flapped lazily from shallow to shallow, or stood in
silent astonishment at the appearance of man, and clouds of
pink and white curlew fed upon the marshes and, at night,
whitened the trees along the shores of the islands. There
were myriads of snipe, scarlet flamingoes, marsh-hens, quail,
plover, pigeons, ducks, blackbirds, shags, boobies, quacks,
gulls, owls, eagles and mocking birds. Muscles, quahaug and
oysters were plentiful on the island banks; tiger and shovel-
nosed sharks, porpoises, saw-fish, jew-fish, skate, sheeps-head,
cat-fish, toad-fish, sand-fish, red-fish, red grouper and mullet,

made the waters of the bay fairly alive with flashing fins and glittering scales.

Charlotte Harbor was a paradise for sportsmen, and the officers of the Nautilus had little to do, but watch the channels by night and fish and hunt by day. A single draught of the seine would feed the whole crew a day, and two hunters could shoot enough curlew in an evening to give all hands pot-pie for breakfast. There was only one dangerous animal in this Eden—it was the mosquito. Tropical heat develops the harmless hundred-legs of the North into the venomous centipede. The moist, warm climate of Florida changes the mosquito into a demon of persecution. It augments his size, elongates and sharpens his instrument of torture, increases the virulence of his venom, and elevates his musical hum to clarion tones. It was necessary to close up the bunks with nettings and to seek for each intruder with a club. The wardroom after dark sounded as if it contained a liliputian brass-band; the lamps were clogged with victims; the deck was so thronged that the insects struck against the face like rain drops, and the sand beaches were covered by clouds of voracious blood-suckers. Before measures had been taken for protection, the suffering from mosquitoes, when there was little wind, was almost unendurable. Officers and men climbed about in the boats, tops and cross-trees, vainly seeking escape and needed sleep. Some men were nearly smothered beneath head wrappings and improvised tents; others dressed in complete suits of oil-clothes or rubber, and a few covered their faces and hands with petroleum and shrouded themselves in tobacco smoke. The loss of sleep made the men unfit for duty; discipline was relaxed, and the daily drills were for a time suspended.

The Nautilus had been ordered to the Florida coast to relieve temporarily the sloop-of-war R——, which sailed for home the next day after her arrival. The rebels at Tampa Bay had been sending expeditions to Pease creek and Charlotte Harbor to forage and to capture refugees and man-of-war's-men. They had already caught several refugees from the main land and shot them as deserters. They were guarding the creek, protecting blockade-runners while discharging and loading cargoes, and accompanying them in force until they were well started upon their voyages. It was supposed that there were many boats and some vessels far up the creek ; that there were dépôts of cotton and stores in houses back in the woods; and that an old Indian fort at the forks of the creek was held by a small force, in frequent communication with the fortified works at the head of the bay.

It was resolved to strike a blow at the Florida Regulators, who were not regularly enlisted men, and, therefore, did not expect quarter nor give any. They were mostly cattle-drivers, who knew every foot of the country, and were supplied with fleet horses. It would have been madness to have followed them into the forests and attacked them where they chose to make a stand. It was necessary to go up the river in boats in order to clean it out, and the service was particularly dangerous, because the bush-whackers could shield themselves by bushes and trees and have the sailors, crowded in a small space, at a disadvantage.

It was reported by a refugee, who came down to the ship in a dug-out, about a week after the arrival of the Nautilus, that a sloop up the creek was nearly loaded with cotton and getting ready to sail for Nassau. One of the cutters was manned, armed and equipped, and sent in charge of Master Sanborn to reconnoitre and blockade the mouth of the creek. The next afternoon, the boat returned with two men wounded, which caused considerable excitement aboard the Nautilus, as this was her first real war casualty.

Mr. Sanborn reported that he had reached the head of the bay after dark and laid at anchor in the mouth of the creek all night without seeing or hearing anything of the enemy. Just before daybreak he landed upon the point of what he supposed was an island near the right bank of the river to make coffee and dry the clothes of the men, wet by a light shower. He posted four men on picket across the point, two hundred yards inland, and left two in charge of the boat, while the remainder proceeded to make a fire and cook breakfast. Nothing happened till ten o'clock to disturb the comfort of the bivouac, and Sanborn was congratulating himself that he had found a secure hiding-place for his boat during the day, when the coxswain of the boat, who had strolled out near the picket line, called to him that one of the pickets wanted to see him.

He went out immediately, after ordering the men to take their rifles and gather near a clump of bushes. The land beyond the pickets was covered by tufts of grass and small bushes, and beyond these, there was a meadow of tall grass. The picket reported that he had seen cattle moving about in the latter, and that they were approaching the camp. Sanborn used his marine glasses and caught occasional glimpses of dark forms which he decided were horses. He reasoned quickly that, if these were horses, their riders were with them, and, as there was not a stump nor tree upon the point for shelter, it would be better to embark and get out of range as soon as possible. He moved the pickets within fifty yards of the boat; ordered them to fire upon the first appearance of an enemy, and set the coxswain to getting everything into the boat as soon as possible. This was soon accomplished; the pickets were called in, and sturdy arms soon sent the boat over the water, just as twenty men, each one leading his horse, came obliquely over the sand hill and discharged a volley of rifle balls and buckshot after her. Their weapons were poor and their aims hasty, but two of the sailors received slight wounds, one in the shoulder and the other in the groin. Four men were kept at the oars and the remainder of the crew fired their Sharp's rifles and soon drove the enemy from the hill, killing one horse and wounding two of the riders, one mortally. There was nothing to be gained by remaining in the region during the day, and Sanborn had returned aboard for the sake of the wounded. The affair showed lack of discretion in Sanborn, in landing and building a fire that would by its smoke betray his position, but no one doubted his courage, and he was complimented upon his management in bringing his men away without serious loss.

Everybody was full of revengeful feelings and wanted to have a chance at these Florida Regulators, as was abundantly proved when Lieutenant-commander Felton had the officer-of-the-deck pass the word forward by the boatswain's mate: "All who wish to volunteer for an expedition lay aft to the mainmast!" The whole crew, boys and men, cooks, stewards and petty officers, came in a hurrying crowd, each anxious to be first accepted. A careful selection of tried and experienced men was made for two boats; the first and second cutters were provisioned and armed; Ensign Careswell and Midshipman Edgewood were ordered to take command, and instructions were given them to lie in the channels and capture any boats or vessels that might appear. Mr. Weston, a refugee from the region, was taken as a pilot, the boats cleared away with three cheers from the ship, spread their sails and at dark were far up the bay.

Careswell stationed Edgewood's boat in a channel behind the islands to the south, and anchored his own in the entrance of the creek. The camp-fire of the rebel guard upon the right bank was seen with men moving about it, but nothing happened to disturb the serenity of the night, except the occasional jumping of a fish out of water and the splashing of alligators along the muddy shores. Before daylight the boats were pulled to a small, wooded island, drawn well into the weeds, and covered with branches of trees, while the crews made a camp back among the mangroves, and a lookout was sent into the top of a tall pine. Loud sounds were not permitted and the day passed uneventfully. The boats were anchored out at night as before, and the next day was spent in the snug retreat upon the island. The third evening, Careswell, Edgewood and Weston discussed the situation, and concluded, as the sloop had not appeared, they would go up river and find her. The oars and rowlocks were wound with strips of canvas to muffle their sounds; the arms were carefully examined, and, at eight o'clock, a long course was pulled down the bay and around to the right shore below the guard at Fort Winder, in order that they might ascend the stream in the shadow of the bank.

Cautiously and quietly the boats crept along, the oars not making much more noise than the ripples, and the dark shadows of the bank and trees enveloping them in obscurity. They passed the fort at the mouth of the river so near that the voices of the men around the camp-fire were heard, and went onwards hour after hour, struggling against a strong current, and, with rifles in hand, scrutinizing anxiously every stump, bush and prominent tree along the bank. A dozen times were rifles cocked and revolvers grasped to fire at some compact bush or decaying stump, that, in the general apprehension of danger, took the rough semblance of a man. An image passed, all felt relieved and half ashamed of their fears, but the next suspicious object excited them again.   It was a new experience for all aboard the boats.   They were men who had been bred to arms and were ready to face any danger, yet, they shrank from this exposure in open boats to a fire from a concealed foe. The uncertainty of where and when they might be attacked; the ignorance of the country and the forces along the river; the silence maintained aboard, and the deep darkness along the shore, all added to the general uneasiness.

Careswell's boat led the advance, and, in the struggle with the current, the other boat dropped far behind.   Suddenly, in turning a bend in the river about ten miles from its mouth, a fire was seen upon Hickory Bluff, on the right bank, and men were moving around it.   The boat was stopped and Careswell and the pilot held a consultation.   It was decided to wait awhile for the other boat before proceeding.   After a delay of half an hour, the boat not appearing, they pulled cautiously along to reconnoitre and soon discovered a sloop anchored in the stream about a hundred yards from the bank.   The people ashore were evidently having a jollification.   They were eating, drinking, dancing, laughing and singing. and their movements could be plainly seen by all aboard the cutter.   Weston said it was customary for friends and a guard to accompany a vessel down to this place, and have a good time with the crew just before sailing.   He thought there were not many aboard the sloop, and that the officers and men were in the crowd around the camp-fire.

Careswell resolved to take the sloop without waiting for Edgewood.   Four men were kept at the oars and ordered to remain in the boat with the pilot; the rest were detailed by Careswell to follow him aboard the vessel with rifles in hand. The boat was run along the outer side of the sloop, thus making her a bulwark for protection from a fire from shore, and Careswell, with revolver in hand, sprang upon the deck of the vessel followed by the men.   Not a man was on deck.   Careswell rushed to the cabin gangway, pushed back the slide, opened the doors and shouted, "Come up out of there!"   A negro rushed up, ran his woolly head against the cold muzzle of Careswell's revolver, dropped on his knees upon the stairs and cried in piteous tones: "Mercy! Massa! Mercy! Lord 'a

mercy! Don't shoot, Oh, Massa Linkum, don't shoot! Massa
Linkum, don't shoot a poo' nigger!"

"Tell me the truth then and I will spare you," said Careswell sternly.

"Yes, massa! Oh don't shoot, massa! I'll tell de whole
truf."

"Is there anybody else aboard this vessel?"

"No, Massa."

"Where is the crew?"

"On shore, Massa, sayin' Good-bye to de women folks."

"How many men are there?"

"There's Captain Money, and Massa Brown, and Massa—"

"Never mind their names. How many are there?"

"Five, Massa."

"Who else is on shore?"

"De women folks, Massa."

"Who else?"

"Some ob de regerlaters."

"How many men altogether?"

"Dunno, Massa, spects 'bout fourteen."

"Have they guns?"

"Yes, Massa."

"What is the name of this vessel?"

"De Record, Massa."

"What have you aboard?"

"Eight and a half bales ob cotton and some pertaters,
Massa."

"Have you any guns?"

"Yes, Massa, seberal rifles an' shot guns."

"Where are they?"

"In the cabin, Massa."

"Very well, get into that boat and keep quiet and you shall
not be hurt."

The poor darkey was ash color; he trembled for some time
violently, and watched everybody anxiously.

Careswell took the helm; ordered two men to slip the rope
cable and hoist the jib, and the remainder to lie down upon
the deck. The rattle of the hanks, as the jib ran up the stay,
made a noise that was heard ashore, and then only the rebels
discovered that something was wrong aboard the sloop. Sev-

eral yelled, "Here you nigger! what you doin' thar?" No answer was returned, but the jib was hoisted and drawn over to windward, there being a light breeze off shore. The keel of the vessel just scraped the muddy bottom; she payed off very slowly, and, for a few anxious moments, it was a question whether she could be floated off. The mainsail was quickly hoisted; a few puffs of stronger air came opportunely and turned the sloop faster; she swung off into deeper water, and began to move towards the middle of the stream. In the mean time, the crew upon the bank had rushed into a small boat and started to paddle out to the sloop, but when they saw the heavy mainsail hoisted so quickly, they knew the negro was not alone in running away with the sloop, and went ashore again. Then the whole party opened fire with rifles and shot-guns upon the receding vessel, and the bullets and buckshot sang through the air and whistled across the sloop's deck, cutting the rigging and wounding several men. Coxswain Wilcox was shot in the neck; seaman Smith got a bullet through his hand, and Careswell received a slight flesh wound in his side. The men were now ordered out of the cutter and she was towed astern. Then Careswell shouted, "Now, my lads, give it to them! Load and fire as fast as possible, and aim low!" The flash of ten rifles answered him, and, still holding the tiller, he emptied his Colt's revolver upon the enemy. The shore fire ceased immediately; the camp-fire was deserted, and the rebels rushed to the cover of the trees. A few more volleys were fired from the sloop, then the command was given to cease firing, as she had struck the strong current in the middle of the river and was fast getting out of range.

The Record went rapidly down river; the wounds were dressed, and a sharp lookout was kept for the missing boat. Fort Winder was passed safely before daylight, a good run was made down the bay, and the sloop was brought to anchor near the Nautilus late in the afternoon. Nothing had been seen of Edgewood's boat. Her disappearance was incomprehensible.

Careswell and his men were congratulated heartily upon the success of the expedition; the two wounded seamen were placed in snowy cots down in the sick-bay and tenderly cared for by Dr. Willett and his assistants: the arms were cleaned, and the cutter was prepared for an immediate return to the head of the bay in search of the missing boat. Every one felt anxious for her safety, as the country was aroused by the capture of the sloop, and it was feared, not knowing this, Edgewood might go on up river in search of the first cutter and meet with disaster. Careswell said nothing about his slight wound, and insisted upon his right to go in charge of the boat, though the captain was inclined to send Mr. Bloss. A call was made for volunteers. Every one of the previous crew, except the wounded men, came aft and was accepted, and the vacancies were filled by selecting two men from the dozens who offered their services. The boat got away at four bells, and reached the head of the bay about nine o'clock. The right shore was searched to Fort Winder, then the boat was pulled across to the left bank of the creek, where there was a wharf, and there the missing cutter lay, with the whole crew sound asleep. It did not take long to awaken them and to hear their explanation. They had pulled against the current half the night, but not seeing anything of the other boat, concluded it had been passed in the darkness or had been captured, as they heard the firing far up the river, and had returned to the wharf on the safer side, where they had kept guard all day, until overcome by fatigue, even the man left on watch had succumbed to the drowsy god.

Edgewood and his men were much chagrined, when they learned that the sloop had been cut out and taken down to the ship, and they were eager to proceed up the river and wipe out their failure of the previous night. Careswell and Weston thought the capture of the sloop and her sailing down the bay would lead the people along the creek to think the object of the expedition had been accomplished, and they would be off their guard, so that a further exploration might be made without much risk. It was decided to go up the river; the muffling of the oars was repaired, and the boats advanced cautiously along the left bank until near morning; then Weston conducted them to an island, where they were pulled up and completely covered by branches of trees, and a camp was formed among the mangroves. A fire was started immediately in a dense thicket, which prevented its light being seen from

the shore, and thus early, because the men were suffering for
hot coffee, and it was necessary to have the fire out and the
rising smoke dissipated before the dawn, otherwise it would
attract attention to the hiding place. Pickets were posted
after breakfast, and the day was spent in rest and sleep. The
camp was broken up and the boats were manned at dark, and
the ascent of the river was continued slowly and cautiously.
When they came to a branch, one boat would remain at its
mouth, and the other go up to its landings and destroy with
axes, sink or take in tow all the boats which could be found.
This was done upon both sides of the stream by the boats'
crews in alternation, until they approached Fort Morgan, the
remains of an old Indian fort, situated upon a point of land
in the fork formed by the two largest branches which united
to make the creek. This was considered the head of navigation for blockade-runners, though they could be poled up the
branches and half over the peninsula of Florida if necessary.
Here they were loaded with cotton, hauled in from the country
upon a fairly good road. A guard of regulators occupied the
log houses of the old military post. The point was firm,
arable land, considerably elevated above the level of the creek,
and, therefore, could be easily defended from an attack by
boats. It was easily reached from all parts of the adjacent
country by boats and teams, and a force of bush-whackers
could be assembled there at short notice. Weston thought it
probable there might be several vessels by the bank and twenty
or thirty men guarding them. The boats were run in to a
fallen tree and the plan of attack was determined.

It was very dark along the river. The stars were veiled
by clouds. The gentle night breeze hardly stirred the mossy
boughs of the cypress and pine or the broad leaves of the palmetto. Not a sound was heard save the crackling of leaves
and sticks beneath the feet of stealthy animals, and the occasional grunts and splashes of alligators. The officers and men
examined their revolvers and rifles, girded their sword-belts
tighter, and piled their overcoats beneath the seats. The two
bow oarsmen in each boat crouched down with their rifles
ready; the officers and coxswains grasped their revolvers, and
Careswell gave the order, "Give way!" The boats moved
along, Careswell upon the right, and Edgewood upon the left

bank of the river. Careswell ran his boat up the right branch
two hundred yards and landed his men quietly, leaving three
to guard the boat; Edgewood proceeded up the left branch
the same distance, landed, and left three men with his boat.
Unfortunately one of the men let his oar fall upon the gun-
wale, which made a noise that was heard across the point.
Then both landing parties, led by their officers, ran in single
file towards each other, leaving a man behind every ten paces
as a picket, until the officers met and exchanged the countersign, "Lincoln." Then the pickets faced the log huts and
advanced upon them, gradually closing the line as they
marched, and the fort was captured. Not a man was seen,
not a gun was fired. The camp-fire was a bed of live coals;
the rude beds upon the floors of the cabins were warm from
their recent occupants; men's and women's clothing was scattered all about; provisions, camp utensils and ammunition,
even, were abandoned; all indicated the recent and hasty flight
of the garrison. There was not a bale of cotton nor a vessel
at the landing. The disappointment and chagrin at this fruit-
less and bloodless victory were universal. The clumsy lubber,
who had dropped the oar, had awakened the rebels, and they
had had time to get out of the trap set for them before the
picket line had been completed. They were far up the road,
and pursuit of them would have been useless and dangerous.
Tigers fight best in their own jungles.

A council was now held with Edgewood and Weston, and
the latter made a singular proposal. He said, "Lieutenant, I
have a sister living up the road about a mile whom I am very
anxious to see. I have heard but little from her since the war
commenced. She is loyal to the United States, and can give
us information of everything in this section. If you will let
me have two men, I will go and see her and return within an
hour. I know all the cowpaths, and think there will be little
danger in the attempt. If we are discovered, we can hold a
whole company back with these excellent arms. These fellows
around here are not soldiers; though they are good shots at a
deer, they are afraid as death of the crack of a Yankee gun."

Careswell and Edgewood were much astonished at this
proposition. They could not question Weston's loyalty, because he had run away from this country and had served the

naval forces well. He was known as a refugee by his former neighbors, and his life would last only while they were hunting a rope, should he be captured by them. He knew the danger he would incur, yet, love for his sister and a desire to serve his country prompted him to run the risk. Careswell was anxious to learn if there were any more vessels up the river, and his sympathies were aroused for Weston, but he was cautious and suspicious, and hesitated to give his consent to so desperate an undertaking. He did not like to order two men upon a perilous mission that was not strictly a part of their duty. While he was considering the conflicting impulses of his mind, Carey, the coxswain of his boat, touched his cap and said, "I will go with him, sir." Then several other men offered their services and the case was decided. Carey and Ferguson were ordered to accompany Weston, and to obey all reasonable and proper orders from him. Careswell was still uneasy, and took Carey aside and said to him, "Keep a sharp lookout upon the way you go, so as to be able to find your way back alone. Keep your eyes upon Weston's actions, and, if you see any treachery in his conduct, shoot him immediately; then return here as quickly as you can. We will wait for you." The countersign "Lincoln" was given, the men passed through the pickets and were out of sight in a moment.

It was a dreary watch that night, forty miles from the ship and far into the enemy's country, and Careswell made the rounds from boat to boat along the picket line several times, anxious and impatient at the slow passage of time. Once there came from inland the deep baying of hounds, and the melancholy sound served to make the night more dismal and the picket-guard more alert.

"What is the time?" asked Edgewood of Careswell.

"One o'clock, and they have been gone an hour."

"Halt! Who comes there?" called a picket sharply.

The officers drew their revolvers, and the sharp click of cocking rifles was heard along the line.

"A friend!" was the answer.

"Advance, friend, and give the countersign!"

"Lincoln!" Weston and his escort passed into the camp and were greeted heartily.

"Lieutenant, we must get out of here as soon as possible,"

said Weston. "There is hard riding up the road. A messenger has gone to Tampa Bay where there is a company of cavalry. The whole country will be alive by daylight, and we may have trouble getting out of the river. I will tell you more aboard the boat"

The stores and ammunition were seized; the fort was left as it had been found; the pickets were marched to the boats; the men embarked and bent to their oars, and they were soon going down river at a lively rate.

Careswell and Weston conversed in low tones for some time. Weston said there were no blockade-runners in the creek and very few boats of any kind above Fort Morgan. The dozen regulators, who had been in the fort, had retreated to a house three miles back from the landing. The whole country had been excited by the capture of the sloop in home waters, and sixty regulators, comprising all the active men about, had been notified to meet at Jackson's plantation, at 7 A.M. that very day to organize and settle upon some plan for more effectually guarding the river. The meeting would be a failure, because most of the boats had been destroyed or removed, the muddy branches were full of alligators and could not be crossed without them, and it would take many days to ride around their head waters. Jackson's plantation was two miles below the fort and a mile and a half back from the river. It was a place of storage for all the supplies brought into that part of the country by the blockade-runners. It was the headquarters of the regulators, and a rendezvous for all the rough riders of the region. There, deeds of valor were related and acts of treason hatched and nourished. Its destruction was justifiable as an act of war, and it would be a fitting climax to the expedition.

Careswell resolved to make the attempt, and was encouraged by the ready assent of Edgewood and Weston. The seven captured boats, which had been fastened to a tree upon the bank, were towed down to the entrance of a little inlet that led to Jackson's landing, passed without examination in going up the stream, and anchored some distance off shore. The two cutters entered the inlet and their crews were landed quietly. A large boat that lay high up the bank was stove with axes. Five men were left in charge of coxswain Ferguson to guard

the cutters and protect the retreat, "Nautilus" was given as
the countersign, and seventeen men took up the line of march
along a miserable road, sometimes in water a foot deep, leading through tall pine trees back to the clearing. Careswell
and Weston led the advance, the men followed in single file,
keeping a sharp lookout to the right and left, and Edgewood
brought up the rear. Just before reaching the opening, the
men were halted and the plan of attack was explained. Weston and six men were detailed to surround the clearing and
let no person escape; Edgewood and four men were ordered
to search the outbuildings, ascertain their contents, and capture any person found; and Careswell and four men were to
enter the mansion, seize the occupants and then join Edgewood.
The force marched on again, and as it approached the clearing,
three bloodhounds burst down the road and were beaten back
by the sailors' cutlasses. The clearing, perhaps a hundred
yards square, was reached and quickly surrounded by the
pickets; the remainder of the force ran to the buildings in the
centre. Edgewood entered the smoke-house and kitchen
without opposition, took three men prisoners who were sleeping in a corner, noted the quantity of provisions, salt, matches
and dry goods stored within, and then withdrew his men to the
front of the house. Careswell ordered two men to enter the
mansion by the back, and he with two men went in at the
front door. The doors were fastened and it was necessary to
force them open. A heavy piece of timber was used as a bat-
tering-ram; the front door flew inwards, and Careswell and
his men rushed immediately into the dwelling with revolvers
in hand, and saw by the light of a bull's eye lantern, carried
by one of the sailors, two men sitting up in bed. They
reached under their pillows for their revolvers, but the stern
command of Careswell to get out of bed at the peril of their
lives, and the persuasion of three revolvers pointed at them,
induced them to surrender. They arose, dressed, and were
placed with the other prisoners under guard of two men upon
the edge of the clearing towards the boats.

There were no other persons at the plantation; the prisoners
were of the opinion a few more men would be there during
the day, but it was not deemed advisable to wait for them. A
few revolvers and guns were taken from the buildings; two

horses, discovered under a shed, were turned loose; some
women's clothing was placed in trunks and left in the road,
and Careswell ordered the three buildings to be given to the
flames. Edgewood set fire to the two log outbuildings, and
Careswell and his men ignited the more pretentious, match-
boarded dwelling. The men gathered kindlings and a quantity of tallow in one corner and set fire to the pile, while
Careswell, impatient at the delay, lit the cotton curtains and
straw of the bed with a candle, and the smoke and flames soon
drove the legal incendiaries out into the night. The pine
structures and their contents burned furiously; the flames
curled, leaped, crackled and shot upwards a hundred feet in
the still air; the light illuminated the whole clearing like the
sun, and danced upon the sun-browned faces, the blue uniforms and the polished arms with a weird glamour, while the
men stood silent and awe-struck at the magnificent spectacle.
The pickets were called in and the men were formed in the
road in double file with the prisoners and Weston ahead, still
no order was given to march—every face was turned towards
the burning buildings. The log houses were pictured in
flames; the frame of the dwelling was nearly denuded of its
covering, and still spread its fiery network of beams across the
dark background of pines. Suddenly a column of flame shot
upwards; a loud explosion smote upon the senses; the burning timbers flew high in the air and to the remotest parts of
the clearing, and not even the foundations of the house
remained. All was level with the ground. Careswell looked
at the prisoners for an explanation. They said a magazine of
powder beneath the floor of the house had exploded.

The order was given to march; the boats were reached
without accident, and the party embarked immediately. The
streaks of dawn were creeping up the eastern sky. Fort
Winder was still below, and it was advisable to get out of the
river as soon as possible. The captured boats were taken in
tow; the men bent to their oars; the boats fairly flew down
the current, and before daylight were past the fort and far out
in the bay. The guard had left the fort—at least there were
no signs of life about it—and had probably gone to swell the
martial array at the ruins of Jackson's plantation. Then the
sails were set, vigilance was relaxed, a cold breakfast was

eaten, the breaker was tapped and a tot of whiskey served to every man, not forgetting the prisoners, and, with story and song, the day was spent in sailing down the bay, so that it was dark when the boats drew near the Nautilus.

The nine boats approaching the ship made a formidable appearance.

"Boats ahoy!" came the sharp hail of Mr. Felton.

"Aye, aye, sir!" answered Careswell, the usual reply of a wardroom officer to indicate his rank, when he is the senior aboard a boat.

"Keep off or I will fire into you!"

"Aye, aye, sir!" was the reply.

Careswell and his comrades were astonished. What did this rough greeting mean? The oars backed water and the boats were stopped.

"What boats are those?" Felton asked.

"Two naval cutters and seven river boats," Careswell answered.

"How many men are there aboard?"

"Twenty-eight, sir; twenty-three belonging to the Nautilus and five prisoners of the United States."

"Very well, sir; you can come alongside in the cutter, and leave the other boats in charge of Mr. Edgewood."

"Aye, aye, sir!"

The first cutter was pulled to the starboard gangway, and Careswell climbed up the ladder and stepped gaily down upon deck. He touched his cap to Mr. Felton and said, "I report myself aboard, sir." He noticed that Felton had his sword on, all the men were at quarters, and the guns were run out and depressed.

"You will report to the captain, sir," said Felton severely.

"Aye, aye, sir!" Careswell walked aft where Captain Prescott stood, saluted him and said, "I report myself and crews returned, sir!"

The captain returned the salute and answered sternly, "Consider yourself under arrest, sir! Go to your room!"

Poor Careswell was struck dumb by this extraordinary reception, and looked for comfort at some of the officers stationed near, but all maintained a cold demeanor, and he went down to his room with an aching heart. He could not understand the matter at all, and the more he thought over it, the more he was puzzled. He heard the battery secured, the men dismissed from general quarters and the boats hoisted up, but the wardroom officers did not come below, and, weary and wretched, he fell into a feverish sleep. How long he had slept, he did not know, when a knock at his door awakened him. "Who is there?" he called.

"It is I, the doctor," was the reply. "Open the door, I want to see you."

Careswell leaned out of his bunk and turned back the bolt. Dr. Willett came in, shook hands and said, "My dear fellow, I am glad to see you back safe. You have given us quite a scare. Here is something you must take right away. It's a dose of quinine and whiskey. You can't knock around in these Florida rivers without an antidote to their malaria. Drink it down, and then I'll open this bottle of sherry. You poor lad, you are feverish now." The doctor passed his hand softly over Careswell's forehead and then felt his pulse. Tears came into Careswell's eyes, and a choking sensation in the throat nearly prevented his swallowing the potion. The doctor was busy drawing the cork from the sherry bottle. He poured out half a tumblerful of the wine and handed it to Careswell, saying, "There! that's the stuff for you; that will take the bitter taste out of your mouth; now you will feel better, and wake up all right in the morning."

"Thank you, Doctor. How are the wounded getting along?"

"Very well. I was obliged to amputate Smith's hand."

"Were you? Poor fellow! I'm so sorry for him. Will he get well?"

"Yes, but we will be obliged to send him North."

"Is Wilcox hurt much?"

"No, only a flesh wound, but it is in a bad place and very painful. He will come out all right."

"That's a comfort. I've a little scratch myself for you to patch up to-morrow."

"You? Where?"

"Here in my side, only through the skin. I got several bullet-holes in my coat."

"And you went back with that hole in you? You careless

fellow! If that ball had gone half an inch deeper, it would have killed you."

"'A miss is as good as a mile,' Doctor. I tipped the ball out with my knife-blade and kept a little oakum over the place."

"Why didn't you tell me of this before?"

"I forgot all about it in my anxiety to get Edgewood out of his danger."

"Well, you're a trump."

"You say I have given you a scare. What do you mean?"

"Why, we thought you and your boats had been captured, and the flotilla you brought down to-night was full of rebels coming to take the ship. We watched for you all yesterday and last night and to-day gave you up for lost. We saw the boats coming down the bay before dark, but they were too far off to make out who was aboard of them, and we went to quarters at dark. The ship was bristling with arms when you arrived, and, if you had been rebels, you would have got 'Hail Columbia.'"

"Didn't you hear my men singing 'Landlord fill the flowing bowl,' etc., just as they have so many times aboard the Nautilus?"

"Yes, but we considered that a ruse of the enemy to throw us off our guard."

"Pshaw! You must have been scared to so lose your judgment. It would have taken more than a million rebels to have made my men sing when prisoners. Am I under arrest for scaring you?"

"No, not exactly; but for disobeying orders."

"How did the captain know I had disobeyed orders?"

"He knew you must have done so, because you were gone so long and brought down so many boats. You mustn't mind being under arrest; it will not last long. The whole ship's company knows the history of your expedition now from your comrades, and it is too much credit to the Nautilus for the captain to ignore it and punish the commander. He can't ignore it; it must be reported, and Admiral Bailey will not permit you to be punished for your brave conduct."

"I would like to know what the Navy is going to do, if its officers are not to be governed by circumstances and to act in

emergencies.   There was an excellent opportunity to clear out
the river, as the result proved.   I should like to see any one
daring enough to attempt it to-morrow.   The whole country
is in arms, and a hundred cavalry from Tampa Bay are now
patrolling the banks of the river.   This conservatism and
servility to tradition are the curse of the service.   If an officer is only to follow the letter of the law, and not its spirit;
if he is only to do what he is ordered to do, like a machine;
farewell all ambition, all hope of glory !"

"Yes, there is too much old fogyism.   The powers will
blame you for assuming responsibility in one instance, and
reprimand you for not assuming it in another.   There is too
much red-tape; too much jealousy of the high prerogatives
of rank."

Just then a form in night-shirt appeared at the door.   It
was the paymaster.

"I came in to give you a good shake, Careswell," whis-
pered he.   "I heard you talking and I couldn't sleep till I
saw you and told you how unjustly I think the captain has
used you.   Edgewood and Weston have told us all about the
expedition, and you deserve praise instead of blame.   The
officers all think so too, except Ashton, who seems to have a
special spite against you.   I judge it is jealousy on his part.
The captain took Weston below and had a long confabulation,
and I think he is sorry for his hasty action."

"All right, Pay., I've done my duty, let the consequences
be what they may."

"Pay., we mustn't keep Careswell awake any longer; he is
weak and wounded, and needs rest and sleep, or he will be
on the sick-list.   We can talk matters over to-morrow."

"Wounded?   You don't say so !"

"Yes, but only slightly."

"I am sorry to hear it, and I'll not disturb him a minute
longer."

Good nights were said and the gentlemen retired.

Careswell went to sleep immediately and, by the doctor's
orders, was left undisturbed till ten o'clock the next morning.
He turned out feeling a little stiff and stupid, but pretty well
considering what he had passed through, and was greeted
warmly by most of his brother officers.   After he had eaten

breakfast, his colored boy told him the captain had sent down word that he wanted to see him as soon as he was about. Careswell went into the cabin and Captain Prescott shook his hand heartily and said, "Mr. Careswell, I relieve you from arrest. I was hasty last night and am sorry for it. Take a seat. Steward, open a bottle of sherry."

Careswell said coldly, "I think you were hasty, but I forgive you."

The gentlemen sat down at the table, sipped the excellent wine, and had a long talk about the expedition. The captain's manner was so frank and friendly that Careswell soon forgot his resentment, and, when he arose to go on deck, he thought his commander one of the best of men. It was decided that a boat should be stationed in the channel behind the island, south of Pease creek, to intercept any inward bound vessel, and that Careswell should, in a few days, take the Record to Key West with dispatches for Admiral Bailey.

The following day a sail was discovered outside and the armed launch was sent in pursuit. She had a long chase but finally caught the craft off the southern end of Uzeppa Key. She was a boat the size of a ship's cutter; the cargo consisted of one barrel of turpentine; the crew of two men, and the destination was Nassau. She was probably the smallest blockade-runner of the war.

The U. S. supply steamer Union arrived in the afternoon, and two boats were sent out for the usual supply of fresh beef, potatoes, canned goods, wine, ice, and the mail. The day of her arrival was always a red letter day for blockaders. The good things she brought were doled out sparingly and made to last until she came again; the newspapers were read and re-read by officers and men until they were worn out, and letters were perused over and over and parts of general interest made common property. The supply steamer was the link that connected the isolated and weather-beaten sailors with the dear ones at home, and when she was delayed beyond her regular time, complaints along the coast were loud and bitter.

Occasionally a vessel on her way to some up coast station, or a cruiser with a roving commission, would stop off the coast and signal for a boat, or come into the harbor and drop anchor for a day or two, sometimes bringing a little later news and the gossip of the fleet, but besides these angel-like visits, there was little to interrupt the daily routine of a station. An occasional chase, an expedition to the mainland, the appearance of some hungry refugee from the interior, and fishing and hunting, lessened the monotony at times, but the interest and excitement passed quickly and the old machine-like life was continued. The large amount of leisure permitted much reading and writing, and the officers were busy when off duty in keeping diaries, getting up letters for home, studying science and languages, and devouring every novel aboard. Even the men forward developed quite a taste for literature, and were well supplied with books by their sympathizing superiors.

The boats came back from the Union at dark, the stores were taken aboard, the large mail-bag was carried down into the wardroom and emptied upon the table, and the paymaster and his clerk proceeded to distribute the mail. First came a small bag for the captain, which was immediately sent into the cabin. Then the newspapers and letters were gone over carefully. Those for the men forward were put in one pile; those for the steerage officers in another, and those for the wardroom officers were delivered immediately. The paymaster's clerk took the sailors' mail to the officer-of-the-deck, who sent for the master-at-arms, the chief-of-police of the berth-deck, who distributed it below. A steerage officer was generally waiting in the country, and to him was given the precious package for his shipmates.

When sailors get letters at long intervals, they do not tear them open roughly and read them hastily. That is too summary treatment for such precious missives. They slip away quietly to their state-rooms, or, if they have none, get in some out of the way place where they may remain undisturbed, and read them slowly, carefully, thoughtfully, having each sentence and phrase 'like sweetness long drawn out.' After the letters are read, the newspapers are gone through hastily, and, perhaps, an hour after the mail has been given out, if no bad news has been received, all the officers assemble in their quarters, and the men gather in little knots, and all talk of home and what has happened during the last month.

CHAPTER XII.

THE wardroom officers gathered below after the mail had been disposed of and discussed the war news and indulged in jokes and general hilarity. The U. S. army had been successful in several important battles; the *cordon militair* had been drawn closer around the rebellious states; the blockade had become more effective; a number of new vessels had been put in commission; the Vanderbilt had gone after the Alabama; many valuable prizes had been taken by the navy; promotions were becoming frequent, and there were rumors that the Nautilus would soon go home. This was enough to make everybody rejoice, and the sailors on the spar and berth decks and the gentlemen in the two steerages and the wardroom were having a jolly time.

The paymaster had received a bunch of ripe bananas from Miss Garver; Mr. Bloss, a basket of fine oranges from Madam Fontana, and Careswell, a large, rich fruit-cake from home. These were placed upon the table, a gallon of iced claret punch was made, and the captain and the gentlemen of the two steerages were invited into the wardroom. The good things disappeared rapidly and were praised extravagantly. It was hard to determine which was appreciated most: the luscious fruit of the South, the familiar cake from home, or the delicious ice-cold punch. All were the greatest luxuries to the weather-beaten blockaders, who exchanged scraps of news, cracked jokes, told stories and sang songs till nearly midnight. The captain withdrew early; the wardroom officers contributed their share to the sport with easy dignity, and the steerage gentlemen just let themselves loose for a good time. Mr. Bloss was in his element. He had a joke, a gibe, a piece of poetry or a story every few minutes.

Careswell had received twenty letters; sixteen of these had accumulated at Havana and been forwarded to the fleet, two had come directly from the North, and two were from Key West. He had long grieved over the apparent neglect of his

Northern friends, but now he rejoiced in the knowledge that they had written to him regularly, and the Post Office officials were responsible for the non-delivery. This miscarriage of letters was very common on the blockade, and men sometimes were months without any news from home. When letters did finally arrive, they occasionally contained news that near and dear relatives had died months before. One expects such things on a foreign station, but the blockaders could hardly realize at first, being on their own coast, that they were as much removed from loved ones, as if the broad ocean rolled between. Lawson had, also, received a large mail, and Bloss said to him, "Lawson, I am glad to see industry has its reward."

"What do you mean?" asked the chief-engineer.

"Why, that your indefatigable letter writing has brought fruit in return."

"I don't write any more than the rest of you."

"You don't? There's not an hour in the day that you don't jot down an item for your inamorata." The wardroom officers smiled and Lawson looked confused.

"Well, that's the way to write," said he; "put down all your ideas just when they come into your mind. I could not sit down and write a letter all at once that would be readable."

Lawson kept a sheet of foolscap fastened to his desk and filled one daily. He would come in from the engine-room and make a note, lay down his cigar, come below and make another, and even leave the mess-table to crystallize a thought upon the paper. His letters were copious and ponderous. What he found to write so much about was a marvel, and he was frequently quizzed by his brother officers upon his idiosyncrasy.

"It's a mistake to say too much in a letter," said Bloss. "One should give a bold outline of the situation, and not fill in details. Leave something to the imagination. Girls don't write much. Careswell's letters are all thin. I'll bet they contain a heap of sweet things." This caused a laugh. Bloss continued, "Do you remember what Byron says of a woman's letter, Careswell?"

"No. What does he say?"

" He wrote,

> " ' I love the mystery of a female missal,
> Which like a creed ne'er says all it intends,
> But full of cunning like Ulysses' whistle,
> When he allured pure Dolon : you had better,
> Take care what you reply to such a letter.' "

" Well! take care what you reply to Madam then, for I saw her handwriting on one of your letters," said Careswell.

Every one laughed and Bloss replied lightly,

> " ' I'll write her a sonnet,
> Upon a new bonnet ;
> I'll let free my muse,
> And speak of her shoes ;
> I'll enclose a caress,
> For her beautiful dress.' "

" That puts me in mind of an excursion through an orange grove with a party of ladies," said Ashton. " I was sauntering along with one of the young ladies somewhat behind the rest, and we came under a fine tree loaded with fragrant blossoms. I plucked a sprig and handed it to the lady. She took it, placed it over her forehead and said, ' How do you think I would look under a wreath of them ?' ' Lovely, of course,' said I. ' I suppose I shall never wear them,' she said sadly. I did not continue the subject. I thought it was getting a little too confidential."

" Your conceit matched her sentiment," said Mr. Felton. " Some men think the ladies are all in love with them. Women are not such fools. They are like quail, shy and easily frightened. They wait until a man shows some interest in them before they are attracted. Then they make up their minds in regard to a fellow, and repel or accept his attentions according to circumstances."

" It is certain that quite a number of our army and navy men are finding their affinities down South," said the doctor. " I know several very improper alliances already. Some finely educated officers of excellent family have married Southern women whom they will be ashamed to take home with them. I have no doubt some of the gentlemen have broken their vows to Northern sweethearts."

"They might have broken them if they had stayed at home," said Bloss. "Holmes says,

'Ah! that's the way delusion comes, a glass of old Madeira,
A pair of visual diaphragms revolved by Jane or Sarah,
And down go vows and promises without the slightest question,
If eating words won't compromise the organs of digestion.'"

"Forever harping upon love and marriage and woman! I do wish you'd find something else to talk about," said Paymaster Horton impatiently.

"What shall we talk about? We are deprived of the charming society of ladies and must have some recompense," said Sanborn.

"Better talk of the Sphinx, the Exodus from Egypt, and the Holy Sepulchre," said Ashton sneeringly, hinting at the paymaster's love for ancient history and the Bible.

"I have a story," said Careswell.

"Let us have it then," said several.

"An Irish sailor fell off of the mizzen topgallant yard; he plunged down a little way and struck a stay which turned him over, then he caught upon some of the running rigging which helped to break his fall, and when he reached the quarter-deck, he came down rather forcibly bolt upright upon his feet before the captain, who was walking up and down.

"The captain started back in alarm and shouted, 'Where did you come from, sir?'

"The Irishman, stunned and dazed, saluted his commander and replied, 'From the north of Ireland, sir.'"

When the laughter had subsided, Bloss said that reminded him of one.

"Mr. Bloss! Mr. Bloss!" called out the middies. Bloss began:

"I had a maiden aunt, who went from Portland to Boston in a small schooner. The wind was dead ahead going up Massachusetts Bay, and the vessel beat in during the entire night. The violence of the wind and sea, the noise upon deck tacking ship, and the strangeness of her surroundings, made the old lady so anxious that she could not sleep. She had a great story of the dangerous journey to tell her friends after she arrived home. She said, 'A sailor's life is a terrible one, and I do not want any of my kin to go to sea. Every little while, during that awful night, the poor sailors were called to turn the vessel around, but there were two who must have been worked nearly to death, poor fellows, they were named ' Ready About,' and ' Hard A. Lee.' "

Shouts of laughter greeted this good yarn, and everybody drank to the health of Bloss' aunt. Then Bloss repeated,

" ' My aunt! my poor deluded aunt!
Her hair is almost gray;
Why will she train that winter curl
In such a spring-like way?
How can she lay her glasses down,
And say she reads as well,
When, through a double convex lens,
She just makes out to spell?' "

The mirth over this appropriate quotation subsided, and then Captain Prescott said,

"Commodore Pearson was on his way to China in one of our frigates and stopped in at Cape Town for supplies. The English admiral requested him to take the mail to China and he consented. The mail-bags were delivered and the messenger requested Pearson to sign a receipt for them. "Take your receipt back,' said the commodore, ' and tell your admiral that flag which floats over us is sufficient guaranty that his mail will be safely delivered.' The admiral apologized immediately, and laid the blame upon the messenger."

The officers applauded by clapping hands, and the captain soon after retired to his cabin.

Sanborn then related the following:

"A square-rigged brig was running with all sail set and the wind and sea on her quarter. You know these vessels are exceedingly difficult to steer before the wind, because the few fore and aft sails draw little and cannot counteract the yawing caused by the square sails upon the mainmast. The man at the wheel had worked so hard to keep the vessel on her compass course, that he had discarded all his clothes except his shirt and pants, and stood bareheaded and barefooted, rolling the wheel to the right and left rapidly and laboriously, as a puff of wind came or a sea struck the brig under the counter and pitched her round.

"'The captain came up in his nightshirt and took a look at the compass just as the vessel had been knocked off her course three points. He looked into the binnacle sharply, noted the deviation from the course, and yelled at the helmsman, 'Why don't you keep her on her course, you lubber?' The helmsman, worn out and dripping with sweat, responded, 'How can I keep her on her course, when every few minutes she turns around and looks me in the face?'"

This yarn was appreciated and heartily applauded. Then Mr. Felton described a total eclipse of the sun, which he had witnessed when he was cruising in the Caribbean sea.

"I was coming home from a four years' cruise in the China seas, and the ship touched at Rio de Janeiro for fresh provisions and water. After a few days' delay, we put to sea, crept away to the northward in sight of the beautiful coast, passed to the eastward of Trinidad, and entered the blue Caribbean between Antigua and Montserrat, two of the loveliest isles of the Caribees.

"It was one of those clear, balmy days that make the latitude of the southeast trade winds so delightful. The softly-shaded, feathery clouds were piled drift upon drift in endless banks of silvery gray; the sun shone brightly down upon the deep blue of the island sea, and the stately ship moved quietly along, rolling slightly to starboard and port, as if making courtesies to the summer billows. A flying-fish would occasionally slip from a wave crest, dart sportively along the rippling surface of the waters and bury himself when weary in his ocean home. The sea gulls floated lazily around in circles and parabolas, now near, now far away, and the chirping Mother Carey's chickens flitted in the wake of the vessel, catching the food that the lolling boys of the ship always saved from their allowance to feed to them.

"About ten o'clock in the morning, a lurid red glamour of light and shade fell upon the waters; the clouds and sky became of a deep dark purple color, and, looking upwards to the source of all light and heat and life, we noticed for the first time a dark body partly covering the face of the sun. Little by little it crept onwards until the bright orb became a dull leaden ball, surrounded by a broad halo, or corona, of silver and gold, with fiery radiating needles and rose-pink flames, shading into outer circles of gray and terminating in blackness. A dark shadow swept across the ship and sea so rapidly, as to make us feel we were moving sideways at terrific speed. We were in the hundred and fifty mile wide path of the moon's shadow. The stars came out suddenly and twinkled with their old midnight glimmer; the birds ceased their chirping; the gulls settled upon the waves with folded wings, and something awful seemed impending.

"The sailors, impressed by feelings of awe and reverence for unseen power, stood motionless in groups about the deck, with their livid white faces and anxious eyes turned heavenward. The clanking of the engine, and the dull thud of the screw blades seemed frightful sounds to the painfully acute ears, and the plash of the waves, as they broke against the wooden walls of the ship, had a mournful sound. It was a solemn moment, and everyone felt his insignificance in the presence of this phenomenon of nature.

"Then the leaden moon moved across the face of old Sol; lay in his crescent arms awhile, both bodies showing a most exquisite play of colors, and was finally pushed off by fiery darts into invisibility, while the stars faded quickly away, and the glorious sunlight chased the melancholy shadows from the tropic sea. A weight seemed lifted from our throbbing hearts; speech returned in subdued tones which seemed harsh in contrast with the previous stillness; the chickens began to flit and chirp astern, and the bewildered gulls commenced another day of ceaseless soaring.

"I had watched through childhood and youth, with bits of smoked glass, upon cloudy and disappointing days, for partial eclipses of the sun. There, in the Caribbean sea, I was gratified by the sight of a total eclipse—a great movement of nature —observed under circumstances which greatly increased its magnificence and grandeur."

The gentlemen were greatly pleased at this recital and clapped their hands and stamped noisily. After some conversation, the doctor was called upon for a story and related the following:

"A poor Irishman, who lived on an estate some distance from Dublin, was taken sick in the night and the village doctor was called. He found the patient suffering from crapulent colic, the effect of an overindulgence at supper, told him he must take an emetic, administered it with his own hands and returned home.

"Patrick vomited freely, became very weak and fearful, and had his friends send to Dublin for the city doctor.

"The latter came, examined the patient, looked grave, shook his head, wrote a prescription, and was about to depart, when Patrick called him. 'Doctor dear,' said he, 'do you think I'll get well?'

'I hope so, Patrick,' was the reply.

'Doctor, what is that ye's a givin' me?'

'It is an emetic.'

'Och! Doctor dear; it's no use to be a givin' me that; the other doctor gave me one and it wouldn't stay on my stomach at all, at all!'"

When the laughter and fun over this story had quieted, everybody looked at the paymaster and he told his story.

"I made a cruise in the Practice Ship with a hundred or more middies once, and a livelier set of mischief-makers I never saw. We were serving grog one day. You know how it is done. A rope was led across the port side from the mainmast to the rail about three feet above the deck; the tub of spirits and pile of little tin cups were placed just aft of it; Mr. Buttons, my clerk, stood by them and Jack-o'-the-Dust gave each man his tot, as he came under the rope and went around the mainmast forward. Mr. Buttons took a pint pot full of whiskey out of the tub for his own use, before he began serving, and set it under a gun-carriage to his left hand. There was always a crowd of middies on the port side, watching the grog drinking, and they gathered close about Buttons and between him and the gun on this occasion apparently much interested.

"Several of the men had been detected in doubling, that is, coming under the rope and getting an extra tot on several former occasions, and Buttons watched his list and the faces sharply to catch the rascals.

"When he had served all hands, he and Jack lowered the tub down through the hatchway into the store-room, put on the padlock and returned to the deck. He stooped down, reached under the gun, seized his dipper and went below. The middies had all disappeared, and I saw them down in the steerage below the berth-deck passing something around and keeping very quiet.

"Pretty soon Buttons came from his quarters forward, looking as dark as a creole, and began to question everybody about deck in regard to who had been in proximity to the gun. No one knew anything. There had been a number of midshipmen about, but no one could say who they were. Finally Buttons let out the secret of his wrath. He had found after he arrived at his mess-room that his dipper contained good ship's water. Some one had smuggled the dipper below, emptied out its precious contents and filled it with water.

"The store-room could not be opened again; there was no help for it, and Buttons and his messmates had to do without their whiskey that day. No one except myself ever knew who were the guilty parties, and I never told anybody."

"Three cheers for the paymaster!" cried an excited middy. All enjoyed the tale exceedingly.

"Now, who do you suppose took Buttons' whiskey?" asked the paymaster, turning to the midshipmen.

"The engineers, of course," answered one.

"The ship's cat," said another.

"Some powder-monkey," said a third.

"The poor middies always have to bear the blame of every mishap in the ship," said a fourth.

The engineers were silent. Indignation prevented utterance. The majority of the gentlemen present affirmed the ship's cat was the guilty party.

Mr. Lawson was called upon for a yarn and responded readily.

"Two boats were racing on the Mississippi river; one of them exploded her boilers and threw passengers, pilot-house, hurricane deck and timbers high up in the air. The pilot went up some distance and, during his fall downward into the water, met the clerk going up. 'It's no use to try to find safety in that direction,' he shouted, 'there's too much unclaimed machinery and too many lumber-yards flying around up there!'"

This raised a laugh, but all complained the story was too short.

"Well, I'll tell you a true one," said the chief.

"We had a new clerk in the steerage last voyage who was exceedingly gullible. We were pumping out the bilge one day and the measured sounds of the pump attracted his attention.

"'What makes that noise?' he asked of a third-assistant.

"'That's the donkey.'

"'The donkey! Have you a donkey down there?'

"'Yes, of course. Don't you hear him stamping?'

"'Ye—s; but what do you keep him down there for?'

"'To drink up the bilge-water.'

"'You do? What do you feed him on?'

"'Oh, the cook gives him the potato peelings and other waste.'

"'I'd like to see him.'

"'Well, you may sometime.'

"The verdant one looked thoughtful, and asked several engineers if there was a real donkey down below. They were all in the secret and swore it was true.

"We crossed the equator a few days later, and the sailors celebrated the event by bringing Neptune over the bow, shaving the uninitiated with a piece of iron barrel-hoop, and marching about the ship. They had in the parade an elephant, a donkey and several monkeys made for the occasion. Men were covered by tarpaulins, rigged out with leather, rope yarns and swabs, and the two men who personated the donkey had belaying-pins in their hands, which they struck upon the deck as they went along to imitate the tramp of the jack. The curious cortege, led by a band of music, marched all round the ship, and in the darkness made a deceptive appearance and a great deal of fun.

"The unsophisticated clerk was very curious; he examined the animals closely, and took hold of the donkey's swab tail, but he received such a kick from the hinder belaying-pins, that his investigations suddenly came to an end. The next day I took him down into the fire-room and showed him the donkey-engine used for pumping the ship."

While everyone was laughing and quizzing the chief about his made-up yarn, the bell upon the forecastle and the one by the binnacle began to strike rapidly—ding—ding—ding, and a shout rang through the ship, "Fire in the fore-hold!" The gentlemen turned pale, sprang from their seats, ran to their rooms, grasped their side-arms and rushed to their several stations. The sailors poured up the hatchways, joined the watch on deck, and all hastened to their duties. The captain and executive were already upon the bridge, the latter giving orders in quick, firm tones. Each officer and squad of men had a division of labor to perform. Hose were led out, pumps manned, and streams of water sent forward; the magazine was flooded; (?) the boats were lowered and manned; provisions and water were hoisted out and lowered into them, and nautical instruments, log-books, charts and flags passed down by hand; the smoke and flames drove the men aft; (?) it was found impossible to save the ship; (?) the officers and men were ordered to the boats; the executive took charge of the first cutter; the captain stood in the gangway a moment, took a last look at the vessel, raised his cap, descended into his gig, and asked the executive, "Are all embarked, sir?"

"Aye, aye, sir!" was the reply.

Then he gave the order, "Shove off!" This was repeated by the officer in charge of each boat; the oars fell, and strong strokes sent the boats twenty fathoms from the ship, when an order was given to stop rowing. The stars were shining brightly; there was not a breath of wind, and the Nautilus lay motionless and deserted upon the water.

The whole time consumed, from the moment the bells had rung out their terrible alarm, until the boats had reached a safe distance from the vessel, was only eight minutes.

The Nautilus was not on fire; the men had only made believe flood the magazine; no smoke and flames had been seen; it was not impossible to save the ship; but it was several minutes before the men found out that the alarm of fire had been made simply to test their efficiency in the "Fire Drill." The captain thought it would be a good opportunity, as most of the officers were awake and dressed, and he had ordered the deck-officer to sound the alarm. The boats returned to the ship before eight bells (midnight), and were unloaded and hoisted up; the decks were cleared up, and all except the mid-watch turned in.

12

CHAPTER XIII.

THE pretty, little sloop-yacht Rosalie, carrying a 12-pounder howitzer and a crew of twelve men, had been sent to Charlotte Harbor to act as a tender to the vessel upon the station. She was commanded by Acting Master Coffer, a thorough Massachusetts sailor from " behint Nantucket pint," and was stationed by Captain Prescott inside of Punta Rassa, in the estuary made by the Caloosahatchie River. The Rosalie had not been long upon the station before she gave a good account of herself. The rebels far up the river put thirty regulators below the deck of a small schooner, called the Georgie, dropped her down to Fort Myers, and anchored near the shore. The Rosalie frequently ran up to the fort and stayed a day or two in order to get early news of any blockade-runner loading up river from the refugee families which had been transferred from the harbor to the barracks, and the rebels thought they might get an opportunity to board the little craft and capture her. They had not long to wait. The Rosalie was seen coming up the river one afternoon, but she anchored at dark half a mile below the fort without having discovered the Georgie. The rebels got underway about ten o'clock, sailed close along the right bank of the river until just above the Rosalie, and then steered directly for her. The wind was light and the current strong, and, unfortunately for the well-planned attack, the Georgie was swept below the other vessel almost as soon as she came out from the shadows of the trees. At the same time she was discovered by the Rosalie; a rattle was sprung; all hands were on deck in a moment, and the volley of the attacking party was answered by the sharp music of several revolvers and rifles. The Georgie was a long musket-shot away before her men could reload, and their second discharge went wild. Coffer answered it with a shower of canister from his howitzer, which hurt several rebels, drove most of them below, and scared the captain so badly that he ran the schooner ashore. Another quart of canister flew around the schooner, and the captain and his men took to the woods and scattered. Coffer dropped his vessel down abreast of the schooner, shelled the bank awhile, then sent in a boat and brought the prize out to anchor.

The next day he returned to the mouth of the river; the following day, sailed his two vessels up to the harbor and came on board the Nautilus to report, looking as proud as the captain of a sixty-four gun frigate. He was congratulated by the wardroom mess over a bottle of sherry, dined by Captain Prescott, and, after two wounded men had been transferred to the Nautilus, he took the Rosalie back to her station in the afternoon.

Coffer's exploit was the talk of the ship for several days. It was the first time he had been under fire, and, although he was a volunteer officer, a so-called mustang, he had acted with the coolness, energy and circumspection of a regular. Such conduct was expected of a regularly educated naval officer, but some surprise was expressed that a man who had been all his life in the merchant marine should be able in a trying emergency to handle his vessel and crew so skilfully.

All along the blockaded coast from Norfolk to the Rio Grande, the volunteer officers were distinguishing themselves by their efficiency and courage, in blockading, cutting out vessels, and actual fighting upon sea and land, and the feelings of superiority, contempt and hauteur with which the regulars at first regarded them, soon gave place to respect and admiration. After the first year of the war, the volunteer and regular naval officers were a band of brothers, vying with each other in honorable ways, as to who could serve the country best.

Coffer had a good time upon his independent station and everybody envied him. In the day-time, his men raked oysters, dug quahaugs, fished with lines, drew the seine, and shot curlew upon the marsh behind the Connecticut fish-house, which Coffer, in memory of a famous Boston hotel, had named in large black letters across the front, "Parker House." Some days he would run up the Caloosahatchie and search its branches for a blockade-runner, and others, put to sea in chase of a passing sail.

The west coast of Florida was a fine place for sportsmen; the rivers, inlets and smooth waters of the Gulf made a safe and pleasant cruising ground; the islands and coast furnished firewood, camping places and some supplies; the heat was tempered by delicious breezes; the storms were mostly of rain and rarely violent; the mail came so seldom that everybody was isolated from the cares and troubles of the world, and man was left face to face with nature and the mosquitoes.

"By my tarry top-lights and top-gallant eyebrows!" said old Harrington, the senior quartermaster, one night on watch, "I never saw such blood-thirsty villains as these mosquitoes. There's no getting away from them. If a fellow was up to his neck in salt water, they'd cover his head like the front of a bee-hive and dive for the bottom of his trousers. The men below sleep half the time and fight mosquitoes the other half, and look as if they were just getting over small-pox."

"You don't think this is a happy life then?" asked Careswell, who had the deck.

"Not much, sir! There's no such thing as happiness on a ship. It is simple endurance of misery."

"You seem to like misery pretty well, old fellow, since you have come back to it every time you've been paid off."

"I had to come back. An old barnacle like me can't get anything to do ashore. About all an old sailor could do on land would be to work along the docks, and to get in coal for gentlemen. There are too many longshore-men now, and the niggers do all the rest of the work. We are going to free the niggers to make the white men slaves. That's my opinion. If I was only twenty years younger, I'd live, I would."

"Well, you live now. How would you live?"

"I'd make a long cruise to China, save my pay, come home and buy a farm. Then I would get some snug, clipper-built, little woman to be Mrs. Harrington, and settle down to raising potatoes and pigs."

"You would give up salt water?"

"Not exactly; I should have a water front to my place, where I could keep a sail-boat, do some fishing, and see the big ships going to sea."

"You'd get mighty homesick with no smell of tar and bilge water, and wish yourself aboard every vessel that passed."

"No I wouldn't, sir, begging your pardon."

"I think you would. Every sailor longs for a farm, and plans what he will do when the cruise is over. It seems as if the deprivation of some emanations from the land makes him eager to possess some, and, if long continued, brings on scurvy. I have seen a sailor after a long voyage rush on shore, drop on his knees, smell the fresh soil eagerly, fill his hands and mouth with it, and even swallow some. When a sailor gets ashore with a pocket full of hard-earned dollars, he forgets all about the country life he has longed for when on the ocean, gets into bad company, spends his money recklessly, soon finds himself hard up, and is obliged to ship again."

"Some sailors do that, but there are others who look after their kin, help educate a sister, set a brother up in business, support a widowed mother, or give the old man a lift."

"They are mighty few, Harrington," said Henderson, the captain of the afterguard, touching his cap to Careswell. "The Lieutenant is right. Everybody in this world is made for something, and we are made for the sea. When we get ashore we are like fish out of water, with bleared eyes, livid gills and rough scales. We can't breathe freely in the dirty roads and narrow streets. There's no use kicking against nature. It's our part to take the ships around the world, and it's the part of other men to plow, sow, reap and look after cattle. I am satisfied where I'm put. I'd rather weigh anchor, than pry out a stump; tar down a stay, than hoe a row of corn; and reef topsails in a gale of sweet wind, than feed the pigs and be poisoned by their stink."

"Oh, go away, young man! wait till you've been to sea as long as I have; then you may talk," replied Harrington.

"That reminds me of an old doctor, who was a poor logician and very proud of his diploma," said Careswell. "Occasionally some sharp fellow would corner him in argument, then he would close the conversation by saying, 'It is very plain to me you have not had a regular medical education.' How long have you been to sea, Henderson?"

"Going on nineteen years, sir; twelve years in Her Majesty's Navy and seven years in ours."

"Ours? You claim the United States as your home then?"

"Yes, sir; I have taken the oath and I mean to stand by it."

"You are a Scotchman, I believe?"

"Yes, sir; I am a native of Glasgow."

"Why did you change your country?"

"Well, the truth is, Lieutenant, I was tired of a country where the poor are trodden under foot, and of a service in which the sailors are treated like dogs."

"It looks very much as if we were going to have war with Great Britain. Which side would you fight with in such an event?"

"Which side, sir,? Why, on the side of the United States, of course. I don't owe the English navy anything. They fed us poorly, watered our grog, and flogged us for the slightest offences. They never tried the cat on me but once, the scoundrels! I did not deserve it, and I deserted a few days afterwards."

"We have many British sailors in our navy. Do you think they all feel as you do?"

"Yes, sir; to a man. I have talked with many of them, and I know it. Treat them like human beings; give them good grub and plenty of grog, and they will fight as long as the ship will hold together."

"Eight-bells, sir!" said the quartermaster, touching his cap.

"Very well, make it so. Tell the boatswain's mate to call the watch, and you wake up Mr. Bloss," said Careswell.

The after bell was struck, the bell on the forecastle answered, the lookouts called their stations, "Starboard cathead," "Port gangway," etc., the boatswain's mate's whistle sounded in the hatchway, and his voice was heard calling, "All the starboard watch!" Then the men came on deck grumbling and cursing; the port watch went quickly below; Mr. Bloss relieved Careswell, who turned in, and all became quiet except the steady tramp of the men on duty.

The next day Careswell was relieved from watch and was busy putting provisions, water, instruments, baggage and crew aboard the prize sloop Record, and getting her ready for sea. He started early the next morning for Key West, with orders to turn the vessel and cargo over to the Prize Court and to return to the ship by the first conveyance. He had a bundle of dispatches for Admiral Bailey, including his own report of the expedition up Pease Creek, Coffer's report of the fight and capture upon the Caloosahatchie, and a general report from Captain Prescott. The run to Key West was made in thirty-six hours, the sloop delivered to the prize commissioners, the evidence given to the district attorney, and the dispatches handed to the admiral. The sailors were sent aboard the Tahoma, and Careswell took up his quarters at the Russell House, which was anything but comfortable.

Madam Fontana and Laura were very glad to see him, and had numerous questions to ask about the coast, the service, the danger, Mr. Bloss and the Nautilus. Careswell visited the ladies and went to ride with them frequently; dined aboard the different naval vessels in port and with the officers of the garrison; supped with Captain Temple and the admiral; smoked, played cards and read the papers at the Naval Club, and managed to fill up the time so well that he was almost sorry when the Union came along after three weeks to take him back to the Nautilus. He visited the admiral to say good-bye, received a bundle of dispatches for Captain Prescott, and was given a fine double-barreled shotgun, captured on the Record, as a memento of the fight up the creek.

"Tell the gentlemen up the coast, if they want promotion, they must fight for it; there's a document for you in the captain's package," said the kind old admiral with twinkling eyes and a significant smile at Captain Temple.

Careswell bade adieu, went aboard the Union, and arrived on board his own ship without mishap. The mail was delivered, and soon after he was summoned to the cabin.

"I have the honor to present to you your promotion to the grade of Master, with my hearty approval and congratulations," said Captain Prescott, handing Careswell an open envelope containing a folded document and shaking his hand cordially.

"Thank you, sir!" he answered joyfully.

"I want you to dine with me to-day, sir, and tell me the news and all about Key West."

"I shall be most happy, sir; but I would like to go and read this now."

"Very well; two o'clock, remember!"

Careswell retired, opened the envelope in his room and read:

"U. S. Flag Ship Dale,
"Key West, September 12th, 186-.
"Sir:
"In consequence of the special recommendation of your commanding officer, Captain Prescott, you are hereby promoted to be a Master in the Navy of the United States; subject, however, to the approval of the Secretary of the Navy.

"Respectfully,
"Theodorus Bailey,
"Rear Admiral.
"Commanding E. G. B Squadron.
"Master Harry Careswell, U. S. N.
"U. S. S. Nautilus."

Naval officers serve their country from patriotism and a sense of duty, but they look for reward in promotion. It is the incentive to study, to drill, to battle with the elements and to face the cannon's roar. It adds insignia to the uniform, importance to one's position, and more money to the pay. It is the goal of honorable ambition, and the sheet of parchment that conveys the official news is a precious document to the owner. If there is anything dearer than a love letter, it is a commission of higher rank to an officer.

Careswell read his commission over and over again, now stopping to note the words carefully, now looking at the page with satisfaction and delight. He had his reward for faithful service; the news was too good to keep; he sought his brother officers, and showed them the document. He was, of course, congratulated, and it was impressed upon him immediately, that, according to an old naval custom, he must "wet his commission." So he ordered out some sherry and submitted gracefully to the toasts of his shipmates, wishing him " health, long life and frequent promotion."

Considerable change had occurred in and about Charlotte Harbor during Careswell's brief absence. Many families of refugees, men, women and children, had come down from the main land and squatted upon the islands. They claimed to be loyal to the United States, and affirmed they had always been loyal, but had been obliged to remain at home on account of the difficulty of getting transportation and the vigilant watch kept over them by the rebel forces. They had finally escaped in dug-outs and upon rafts, and had poled and paddled from island to island, until they had been seen from the ship and rescued. They took the oath of allegiance to the United States, and were, thereafter, supplied with regular ship's rations. They cleared some of the fertile spots upon the islands; planted sweet potatoes, beans and melons; built huts with poles, grass and palmetto leaves; bartered fish and game with the sailors for tobacco, and settled down into the indolent life of the Southern cracker. They cooked the tops of young palmetto trees, caught gophers and fish, shot curlew, drew their rations, and lived better than they ever had before. Their clothing was ragged and variegated. As piece after piece disappeared before the thorns of the thickets and the tooth of time, they were supplied with the cast-off garments of the sailors, which were worn indifferently by both sexes and all ages. The effect of this mingling of Florida styles and naval fashions was exceedingly grotesque.

These people were thin, yellow and tough; of a low order of intellect; unable to read or write; ignorant of the world and its inhabitants; licentious, indolent, selfish and filthy. They represented the lowest order of crackers. They had no conception of the nature of an oath or of fealty to the Government. They were starving upon the main land; they heard the naval vessels would feed even the slaves, and, therefore, made their way as rapidly as possible to the source of such extraordinary and munificent bounty.

The settlements were not intended to be permanent; they depended upon the blockading vessels for support and protection, and, without them, the choice would have been starvation or emigration.

Uzeppa Key (Lacosta Island) lies just south of the principal entrance (Boca Grande) to Charlotte Harbor. It is legendary among the natives of Florida, that it was formerly a rendezvous and hiding-place for pirates of the West Indies. The largest squatter camp was located upon its inner shore; a small one was upon a little island near Punta Rassa; another was at Fort Myers; a few huts were scattered at other convenient points, and Salvini remained monarch of his own little realm.

A Captain Crine had been in command of a company of volunteers during the Seminole war and knew every foot of the west coast country. He had lived at Tampa Bay with his family before the war, and had entered the United States service early as a pilot. He knew all the crackers by name and reputation, and his services were valuable in regulating them and settling their differences. He was looked upon by them, as chief of the nomads, and they were ready to do his slightest bidding. The refugees were numerous at every blockading station and at Key West, and had become a great burden upon the resources of the squadron. It was resolved to organize the able-bodied men into a company; uniform, equip and drill them, and make them useful upon the rivers of the peninsula in enticing rebels to desert and in catching wild cattle. They were sent to Key West, the old men and boys were left to care for the families, and Captain Crine was selected for the command. He had a difficult task, but after some weeks the force was considered able to take care of a post, and was sent to Fort Myers.

There were several families already at the fort; some others were permitted to remove there from Charlotte Harbor, and these, with the garrison, made the most important settlement on the coast south of Tampa.

The block-houses in the angles of the stockaded fort were occupied by squads of men; the river bank was patrolled, and the Rosalie was brought up and anchored off the fort to cover it with her single gun. Captain Crine took up his quarters in the old hospital and maintained martial law. Nothing occurred to disturb the serenity of the garrison; few deserters came in; no cattle were found near, and the whole region seemed abandoned by the Confederates. This inaction did not suit a man of such ardent and energetic character as Captain Crine, and he made raids far away from the fort in search of cattle and rebels. Some cattle were shot and several men captured, but he met with no resistance. The news of his doings finally reached Tallahassee, and a company of mounted infantry was gathered in the interior and sent down the Caloosahatchie to check his operations and drive him from the fort. The refugee soldiers knew the fate that awaited them if they should be beaten, as some of their neighbors had been captured awhile before upon Pease Creek and shot. It was supposed they would fight, not only for themselves, but for their families.

The rebels made an unexpected night attack, captured some

of the block-houses, tore down a part of the stockade, drove
the soldiers into the buildings along the river, and endeavored
to fire them.   Captain Crine rushed here and there, urged the
men to resistance, stormed at their cowardice, cursed the women
and children who were clinging to the men, and exposed himself recklessly to the fire of the enemy.   A boat was sent to
the Rosalie with an order to fire over the houses ; a shower of
canister rattled through the woods ; the refugees took courage
and began a brisk fire of-musketry, and the rebels were finally
forced to retire, having lost several men and horses.   A few
refugees were killed and wounded and one man was missing.
This was a man who had spied all along the coast, gathered
up all the information he could, and deserted to the enemy.

After this example of rebel courage and refugee cowardice,
Captain Crine, who, upon the same ground, had helped to
whip the Seminoles years before, did not take much interest
in raiding, but kept his men within the stockade and repaired
the breaches.   The post had been garrisoned by the enthusiastic and brave captain for a specific purpose, and his great
expectations had not been realized.   He informed the admiral
of the attack and narrow escape, and of the unreliability of
his raw recruits, and advised the abandonment of the fort.

A few weeks afterwards the place was evacuated ; the soldiers
were distributed to the different stations and permitted to re-
lapse into cracker barbarism ; the Rosalie returned to her station at the mouth of the river, and no further attempt was
made to establish an army of occupation.

"Shiver my timbers, if I see any sense in painting the
Nautilus lead color?" growled old Brenneman one night by
the mainmast to Mr. Bloss who was on watch.

" Paint the ship lead color?   Who ever mentioned such an
idea?" asked Bloss.

" The executive told me to-day the order came up by the
last mail."

" Well, well ! the ways of the Department are past finding
out.   Here we are fitted up to imitate an Englishman at short
notice, and now they want to paint us like the bummers
that lie against the mud-banks of the Mississippi.   The next
thing will be to paint vessels that sail among verdant islands,
green ; those that skirt rocky coasts, brown, and the open sea

cruisers, dark blue. We shall have a picturesque fleet, and care must be exercised in selecting their crews to have their complexions agreeing. You can then sing,

> " I once sailed in an old lime-juicer,
>   Now I belong to a dark blue cruiser;
>   I receive good grub and excellent grog,
>   And I'm a merry old sea-dog."

"Ha! ha! ha! but you *are* a poet, Lieutenant. Do you think we shall stay here much longer, sir?"

"I think not. They have built many new ships at the North; Richmond is pretty well scared; the war must soon be over, and we need repairs greatly."

"If we stay here much longer, we will ground on the beef bones, sir. When the cook brought the men's beef in the skid to the mainmast to-day at seven-bells, to be inspected by the deck-officer, he said it was the last chunk of the old Texas bull. Mr. Sanborn tasted it and said it came from Portland. What did he mean by that, sir?"

"Why, did you never hear about the old horse, Brenne?"

"No, sir; what about him?"

"Why this, a sailor asked his junk of beef,

> " ' Old horse, old horse, how came you here?'

"The beef answered,

> " ' From Saco Head to Portland Pier,
>   I've carted stone this many a year,
>   Till killed by sorrow and sore abuse,
>   They've salted me down for sailor's use.' "

"Ha! ha! that's good! I've eaten a great deal of salt-horse in my time, but I never thought it was real horse meat," said Brenneman.

"Neither is it, but horse meat ought to be good."

"I suppose it is as good as the alligator steaks you had in camp last week, sir."

"Yes, and the porpoise cutlets we tried off Hatteras."

Mr. Bloss walked away aft, took a look all round the ship,

and noticed the lookout on the midshipman's deck leaning across the spanker boom fast asleep.

Did he report him, have him court-martialed and put on bread and water, or order him triced up in the rigging? Not at all; he picked up the end of a rope and laid it across his legs vigorously, so that the youngster danced a hornpipe.

"Sleep on watch, will you, you vagabond?" said Bloss. "Take advantage of my back being turned and neglect your duty? Lay across that boom in this heavy dew and dream of home, and let the rebels come up astern and blow the ship out of water?"

"Couldn't sleep below, sir, on account of mosquitoes."

"You couldn't, hey? Well, you'll get your death of cold and give the doctor a job. You'll be sent to Davy Jones' locker the first thing you know. You lazy, good-for-nothing lubber! Get up on the boom now and straddle it, and stay there till eight-bells! Do you hear?"

"Aye, aye, sir!"

"Keep a sharp lookout then!"

"Aye, aye, sir!"

Mr. Bloss walked the quarter-deck for half an hour, thinking of the difference between moral suasion and the persuasion of a rope's-end, and between colored and white slaves, occasionally humming an air from *Faust* or *Il Trovatore*.

"Poor fellows," thought he, "they *do* have a hard time of it. When they were freezing up North, we had a red-hot shot to toast our shins by in the wardroom. When they were sweltering on the berth deck north of Cuba, or nearly roasting at the furnaces in a temperature of 134° F., we were fanning ourselves under the windsails and sipping iced claret and sherry. Now they are pestered and deprived of sleep by the mosquitoes, while we get in behind our nets and slumber peacefully."

He stopped by the after howitzer and said, "Dyer, come down out of that and come here!"

"Aye, aye, sir!" said the youngster, hastening down.

"Are you sorry you slept on watch?"

"Yes, sir."

"Will you promise never to do it again?"

"I'll try, sir."

"Very well.   Go and call the ship's cook and the stewards, it's nearly four-bells."

"Aye, aye, sir!"

"Four-bells, sir," said the quartermaster.

"Make it so.   Pierce, tell the boatswain's mate to get out the buckets, brooms and holystones, and wash down the decks and scrub the paint."

"Aye, aye, sir!"

Mr. Bloss took off his shoes and stockings, turned up his pants, and pattered around the deck looking after the work. The firemen hoisted up and dumped the ashes overboard; the gunner's mate cleaned the guns; the boys scoured the brasswork, and the watch dashed water, sprinkled sand, dragged the holystones back and forth, and scrubbed the decks and bulwarks till they were as clean as a dresser in a Pennsylvania farm-house. About six-bells work was temporarily suspended, the men got some coffee, and Mr. Bloss had a cupful with some hard-tack brought to him by his colored wardroom boy; then the cleaning up was finished; the ropes were hauled taut and coiled down; the boatswain went out ahead of the ship in one of the cutters and whistled and made signals with a flag to one of his mates, who squared the yards; the hammocks were piped up and stowed in the netting; the watch below was piped to breakfast; the executive came on deck and relieved Bloss to make his toilet, and the booby, that roosted nightly on the starboard foretopsail yard-arm, flew away to get his breakfast. When the colors were hoisted at eight-bells, there was not a cleaner or trimmer ship than the Nautilus in the United States Navy.

And this beautiful vessel was to be painted lead color. That fact made all the officers groan. She was painted, nevertheless, the next week, and her inhabitants could not recognize their home afterwards, so great was the change in her appearance.

CHAPTER XIV.

THERE was considerable growling amongst the wardroom officers at the caterer, who had served ever since leaving Philadelphia, because of his heavy assessments. The paymaster had that honorable and lucrative office, and had charged each member of the mess fifty-five dollars a month for grub and wines. He said the wine bill was heavier than the food bill, because so many officers and other visitors had been entertained from the very start. This was true; there was no redress for the entertainers except to growl, and growl somebody did at every meal. A sailor who cannot growl has something serious the matter with him.

The doctor started the talk one day at dinner by saying, "The paymaster calls himself a Christian and charges the mess for pickles."

"Well, pickles cost, and I don't know anyone who eats more of them than you do," was the paymaster's reply.

"You promised to keep run of the wines ordered, and to credit those who did not drink and charge those who did," said Lawson.

"I have been trying to do that, but haven't found anyone yet who belongs to the credit side."

"We're a band of brothers," observed Bloss.

"Seriously, Pay., you do give us too many beans," said Careswell. "Now, for my part, I can stand them often, but when we get them twenty-one times a week, it's a little monotonous."

"You ought not to complain, Careswell; you know you were brought up on them. Beans and codfish are the usual aliment of New Englanders," answered the paymaster.

"Well, give us some codfish occasionally for a change; I've not seen a Cape Cod turkey for a year."

"No, but you've had lots of Florida chickens."

"Chickens? Not one."

"Yes, sir; Florida chickens are gophers *alias* terrapin."

"They are the first four-legged chickens I ever saw."

"You know that large one the captain had running around the deck?"

"Yes."

"I harnessed him to a camp-stool and he drew it all about. He raised himself with George Washington, who weighs a hundred pounds, standing upon his shell, and moved ahead a little. If an elephant had proportionate strength, he could haul a meeting-house. One of the boys, I guess it was George, painted C. S. on his shell in lead color. He said it was for Confederate States. The captain was wrathy when he saw the decoration."

"It will not hurt him for soup," said Bloss.

"What time does the evening train pass?" asked Ashton.

"About sunset," answered Bloss.

"What is the evening train?" inquired the paymaster.

"The pelicans that cross the harbor to roost in the trees on Mangrove Island," said Bloss. "They fly in a straight line near together, and go so regularly that we call them the evening express train."

"Oh, yes, I have seen them."

"When in camp the other day, I shot one through the bill with my revolver at a hundred yards distance," said Careswell. "He was on the river, and just swam round and round in a circle until I went out in the boat and caught him. We kept him in camp some hours and then he flew away. The hole will not prevent his catching fish."

"Which side did the bullet enter?" asked the doctor.

"The right side."

"Which way did he turn?"

"To the left."

"That's correct; the concussion caused agitation and a current in the horizontal semicircular canal of the internal ear; disturbed the equilibrium and sense of space, and induced the peculiar gyrations."

"All right, Doctor," said Bloss. "The hypothenuse of the diatom came in collision with the diæresis of the ventriculum, and caused a parallax of the proboscis."

Everybody laughed heartily, and Ashton said, "It's my opinion, he swam around to the left to get away from the injury that he felt from the right, and I think he was right in going to the left."

This unexpected play from so stern a man as Ashton evoked applause.

"Why don't you give us a pelican stew, Pay.?" asked Bloss.

"Are they good to eat?"

"Certainly; they are excellent, only a little fishy."

"Don't do it, Pay.," said Careswell; "he's joking. Pelican stew! If you feed this crowd on such stuff, you'll be impeached. They are worse than crow."

"Have you tried them?" asked Bloss.

"Yes; we cooked one in camp, when fresh grub was scarce. He did not need seasoning."

"How about alligator steak?"

"Oh, it is delicious and smoky, especially if old. Young ones ought to be tolerable."

"What a blessing it is to have canned things. I think the blueberry pies our steward makes are delicious."

"So say we all of us," said Lawson.

"There are too many necks in the canned chicken," said Careswell.

"Yes," replied Bloss, "it is often neck or nothing."

"Joshua, give Mr. Bloss a glass of my sherry, he has been to a necropsy," said the doctor.

"All right, Doctor; here's your health, and I hope you'll not have any on us fellows," said Bloss.

"Your health, Bloss," said the doctor, emptying his glass.

"What do you think of Quaker color for a fighting man-of-war, Mr. Felton?" asked Ashton.

"I don't like it. It's a notion put into the Secretary's head by some of the Mississippi captains. I don't like Quaker colors or Quaker principles. Quakers are a set of religious fanatics, who stick to their colors, but would not fight for the flag."

"No, but they are doing as much good at home as they could in the service. They are taking care of the sick in the hospitals, and contributing largely to the support of the Sanitary Commission. If they are not in arms, they are giving aid and comfort to those who are."

"That's a fact," observed Careswell; "I saw many Quaker ladies visiting the Cherry St. and Catherine St. hospitals, in Philadelphia, and carrying in baskets filled with dainties for the poor wounded fellows."

"Well, I suppose they are useful there," said Felton, "but I am opposed to so much sectarianism in religion. Why can't all the people belong to the Episcopal church? It is the old historic church purified, and its service is beautiful and satisfying."

"Just because that church requires decided convictions of sin and a belief in fixed formulas," remarked the paymaster.

"That's all right. It is better to have formulas fixed by the Apostles, than to let sinners fix them to suit themselves, and then get ministers with elastic consciences to rehearse for them. I believe in one church."

"So we all do, except Lawson, and he's going to perdition anyhow," said Bloss.

"Come, let's go and smoke," said the doctor; "I don't eat dinner because I want it, but in order to have a smoke afterwards." The gentlemen pushed back their camp-stools and chairs and went up on deck.

"Did you hear about the captain's fishing, Lawson?" asked Careswell.

"No; was he fishing?"

"Yes, over the stern, and he had a bite that nearly pulled him overboard."

"Did he? What was it?"

"A Jew-fish. He got him aboard with the help of a harpoon and a boat-hook. Guess what he weighed."

"Fifty pounds."

"No, sir! He weighed exactly two hundred and thirty-one pounds."

"The dickens! What did he do with him?"

"Threw him overboard. Jew-fish are coarse and not good eating."

"Is that a fish story?"

"No, the absolute truth, isn't it, Pay.?"

"Yes."

"Lawson, how did you catch that lovely sheepshead to-day?" asked the paymaster.

"I pitched him a piece of pork on a hook, just off the point of Uzeppa Key, and he took it like a gourmand."

"Did you fish from the shore?"

"Yes; I just walked along and threw the line out as far as possible."

"Is that all you caught?"

"Yes, but I had lots of bites from mosquitoes and sand-fleas."

"He will make a delicious breakfast for the whole mess."

"Yes, and I won't charge you for him. Did you ever see fish so plenty as they are in this harbor? It is alive with them, and, when porpoises, sharks and dog-fish come swimming in, they rush in such shoals as to make the water fairly boil. I never thought I should like fish so well. I prefer the mullet to all others, they are so delicate and juicy. They can be fried in their own fat, but a little pork improves the flavor."

"Yes; they are to my taste better than trout or salmon, and a single cast of the seine is sufficient to load the boat half full of them. The men enjoy them very much; all the messes have commuted some of their rations this month. Salvini says they used to ship large quantities of them to Havana before the war, and the principal business done at the fish-house on the Caloosahatchie was in salting and packing them in barrels for the New York and West India trade."

"That pig Salvini gave us jumped through a gun-port to-day and swam a mile before he was caught," said the doctor.

"Did he cut his throat?" asked Bloss.

"No; I don't believe they hurt themselves swimming. It's all moonshine. This pig swam almost as fast as the boat went, and hadn't a scratch."

"He evidently don't like man-of-war life."

"No; swill is scarce and there's no dirt aboard."

"You always see everything, Doctor. I wish I had nothing to do but loaf about decks as you do."

"Loafing is sorry work, Bloss. I'd rather be a watch-officer than a surgeon, as far as work is concerned."

"Well, I'll trade professions with you."

"Salvini has taken quite a fancy to Careswell because he talked French with him," said the doctor. "The old man has not heard the familiar tongue since he came away from Corsica, twenty-eight years ago."

"He wants me to buy a schooner," said Careswell, "and come down here after the war and carry fish to Havana. He says he and his son will help, and I can clear two or three thousand dollars a year. What a prospect for a naval officer!"

"And what about the daughter?" asked Bloss.

"The lovely creature was not mentioned."

"He expects you will marry Marie."

"Of course, he does," said the doctor, "and there's your fate and fortune all mapped out for you."

"Yes, but I don't fancy the life nor the alliance.

> " ' Better twenty years of Europe,
>   Than a cycle of Cathay.' "

"Ah! Careswell, you know the girl is lovely," said Bloss, "and rather more intelligent than the average Floridian, yet, you turn up your aristocratic nose at such prospects.

> " ' A simple maiden in her flower
>   Is worth a hundred coats of arms.' "

"The offer is open to any of you who can navigate," replied Careswell.

"Your heart is not your own," said the doctor; "it's my opinion you are engaged to that Philadelphia girl or else dead in love with Laura."

"Oh, it is Laura, of course," said Bloss.

"Well, have it your own way," said Careswell coolly, knocking the ashes off of his cigar. "It's my opinion from sundry *billets doux* that I have seen come and go, not to mention the basket of oranges, that madam has struck you in a vital part."

"That's in his stomach," said the paymaster; which allusion to Bloss' corpulence and love of good living caused shouts of laughter.

That night everyone in the wardroom had turned in except the Paymaster and Careswell, who were writing letters upon the table and conversing in low tones about their friends in the North. It had been very sultry during the evening, and the black clouds of one of those sudden squalls so common in the latitude began to pile up in the west and blot out the stars. The blackness soon spread across the heavens; the wind rushed over the waters in violent gusts that made the ship's rigging vibrate in mournful tones; the lightning flashed in broad sheets behind the clouds and darted from cloud to cloud and earthward in fiery lines, and a few large rain-drops pattered upon the deck—the advance guard of the torrent to follow.

Suddenly a vivid flash of light filled the ship, a smell of ozone was in the air, a terrific crash smote the ear, and the two gentlemen, stunned and terrified, rushed upon deck, followed by the awakened sleepers. The bells rang the fire-alarm, and all the officers and men were soon at their posts prepared to fight the flames. An examination showed that the lightning had shivered the foretopgallant mast into splinters, run down the foremast, and scattered upon the chain cables upon deck and in the boxes below, but had not started any fire. Just behind the boxes was the magazine, containing several tons of powder and loaded shell.

The escape from instant destruction was miraculous, and there were many pale faces and trembling voices both forward and aft, as the men were piped below.

The first death in the ship occurred the next day. A poor, decrepit negro, named Jacob, who had come down to the station in search of food and freedom, succumbed to debility, occasioned by many exposures and an untreated ague. The carpenter made him a neat pine coffin, and he was taken ashore and buried on the sandy point, where Mr. Sanborn read the Episcopal burial service and the boat's crew acted as chief mourners.

He had not been long on board and was not much missed, but the event caused a general sadness that lasted several days. Death on board a ship is like death in a little village, where neighbors are knit together by the strongest ties of interest and brotherhood, and departure leaves a void which is painfully apparent.

The U. S. S. James Battles was signaled outside the next morning, and quite a communication was held with her by means of the signal flags and book. She was bound up the coast and soon disappeared.

In the afternoon the Tahoma and the Honduras came in from Key West and borrowed Mr. Crine, as pilot for an expedition against the rebels at Tampa Bay.

They sailed the next morning, and cheers were given aboard the Nautilus and returned by them as they passed out to sea.

The next week the U. S. schooner Sea Bird, Capt. Clark, dropped anchor for a day, and brought the news that the expedition to Tampa had captured a steamer loaded with cotton, burned a steamer and a sloop, and whipped the rebels badly, with a loss of seven men, ten being killed on the other side—a small loss, considering the danger of cutting out vessels protected by shore batteries.

Everybody aboard the Nautilus envied the men who had taken part in the fight. They lamented their inactivity and "inglorious ease" upon a dull blockading station, and would have preferred a fight with all its attendant risks to life to the humdrum of the daily routine.

"'I thought to stand where banners waved,'" said Careswell one day at the dinner-table, "and I find nothing but the wash-clothes drying in the rigging. I think I'll apply for an ironclad."

"Well, you're a queer one, anyway!" said Bloss. "Here we live on the fat of the land with home trimmings; get our regular mail and sleep; drill a little; shoot, fish, swim and boat to our heart's content; have little to do but fan ourselves and smoke good cigars, and you are not satisfied. You wish to be on the go. You want excitement, and danger, and bullet-holes in your bread-basket. Byron says,

"'The path of glory leads but to the grave.'

Why can't you be content and settle down to steady habits?"

"I don't know, old man. 'What's bred in the bone —'"

"What are you gentlemen doing with Brenneman's coon on deck in the night watches?" asked Mr. Felton.

"Letting him tear our trousers to keep us awake, sir," answered Bloss.

"Does he bite?"

"Well, I should say he did.   Zip is not vicious, but he is the most persistent little rascal you ever saw.   He will jump at you and chew your shoestrings and clothes every time you poke a foot at him.   If it were not for him, I don't know how we could keep awake these warm nights."

"He ought to be promoted to midshipman then, as the chief service of a middy on watch is to keep the deck-officer awake."

"They had a lively time in the starboard steerage to-day," said Careswell.   "The gentlemen put Zip and one of the captain's roosters in there and laid wagers as to which would whip.   It was a good fight, but Zip chewed his opponent's head off in about fifteen minutes.   They are a queer lot in there and indulge in much chaff.

"'I'll bet a broadside of grog on Zip,' said Cozzens.

"'Whiskey is dead,' answered Hanson.

"'The mourners are sincere,' observed Edgewood.

"'I must tell Jane about this,' said Webster.

"'Who's Jane?' I asked.

"'Oh, she's my Dulce, my Future.   Jane and I are engaged.'

"'No fellow has a right to be engaged till he can raise a moustache,' said White.

"'May you never know the sorrow of an unthrifty whisker,' answered Webster sadly.

"'White has been eating peanuts to make his voice short,' observed Cozzens.

"'Go in Zip!' yelled his backers.

"'Give it to him Shanghai!' cried the opponents.

"'Who wouldn't be a soldier laddie?' asked Gardner.

"'I wouldn't,' answered Cozzens.

"'Why not, my salt-water sonny?'

"'Don't like the pay and prospects.'

"'Pay is good and promotion rapid.'

"'Yes, thirteen dollars and found.   Found with your head off in the morning.'

"'Oh, go away; that's too sanguinary.'

"'Why didn't you invite the captain in?' I asked.

"'Oh, he'd take too much interest in the affair.'

"'This being captain, sitting alone in regal state and having

nobody but the servants to talk with, is not much comfort.   I
have no doubt he would enjoy the sport,' said I.

"'Perhaps.   Don't you tell him, Mr. Careswell.'

"'Of course not,' I answered."

"What did they do with the rooster?" asked Felton.

"Pushed him out the dead-light.   They said the captain
might see him floating away and think he had been drowned,
but probably would never miss him."

"How did they get him?"

"Bought him from the captain's steward for a dollar.
Don't you tell the captain, Mr. Felton."

"Not I; I've been in the steerage myself, but I must keep
an eye on that steward."

"Short, spirited drills are to be encouraged," says the *Naval
Manual*, but the executive generally forgot the advice and
made them long and exhausting.   The principal drill of a
man-of-war, and the one in which everybody took the most
interest, was General Quarters.   This included many of the
other exercises, and the men had been brought to a rare degree
of perfection in performing their duties.   The captain loved
surprises and did not always inform Mr. Felton what he
wished to do.   Everybody except the watch on deck was fast
asleep one night, when at midnight the drum and fife called
to quarters.   The officers sprang into their clothes, thinking
an enemy was at hand, grasped their side-arms and buckled
their belts, as they hastened to their stations, where the men
were already gathering.   The ship's company went through
the following drill: the battery was cast loose; the guns were
loaded and fired rapidly; the pivot guns were pivoted to starboard and port; disabled guns were removed and replaced by
others; wounded men were taken to the cockpit on stretchers;
fires were extinguished; boarders were repelled, and boarders
rushed over the rail with pistols, cutlasses and pikes; the
sharpshooters and marines kept up a rattling fire; spars were
fished; shot-holes were plugged; the pumps were manned;
the cable was slipped; sails were loosed, trimmed and furled;
tacking and wearing ship were accomplished; a train was laid
to blow up the magazine, and the ship was abandoned in the
boats.

The whole drill occupied an hour and a half, and the exercise of firing seventeen shell to a gun was performed in fifteen minutes. The night was cool and pleasant; every one entered into the spirit of the occasion and did his best work, and the officers were highly pleased with the result. If there had been an enemy about, he would have fared badly.

"Up all bags!" shouted the boatswain's mate one forenoon, and the spar deck was soon covered with men, each one having his long, black, numbered bag with him. The master-at-arms was ordered to search each bag for a pair of shoes that had been stolen from one of the cooks.

A sailor's bag is his dressing-case, tool-chest, bureau and trunk all together. He keeps in it everything that belongs to him except his bedding, which is slung up in his hammock at night, and lashed up and stowed in the netting during the day.

The master-at-arms made every man empty his bag and exhibit his shoes. The missing ones were found at last in the possession of a man named Pennock, who boasted of having been many years in one of the merchant ships of the famous Black Ball line, running between New York and Liverpool. He was a lazy, sulky fellow, who had made considerable trouble already in the ship, and had been several times in double-irons, on bread and water, for various offences.

He was brought to the mainmast by the master-at-arms, and Mr. Felton asked for an explanation. He said the shoes belonged to him, and he had received them from the paymaster the previous month. The paymaster examined the books and reported that he had not delivered them. The man affirmed the truth of his statement with several oaths and much loud talk. Mr. Felton ordered him to be quiet, and the master-at-arms took hold of his arm, when he sprang at him and knocked him down. Several men were called, who assisted the master-at-arms to put him in irons and take him below to the brig. Some days afterwards, five of the wardroom officers were ordered by the captain on a court-martial for his trial. The specifications were, theft, insubordination, and mutinous conduct towards his superior officers. The court was held in the wardroom during the forenoon; the evidence for and against the prisoner was presented and considered carefully; a verdict of guilty was rendered, and a sentence to one month's confinement in double-irons, in the brig, upon bread and water, and loss of pay for the time, was pronounced. The prisoner said nothing, but scowled his hatred; he was conducted below, and a marine was posted before the grating of the brig to keep watch over him, and see that the sentence was properly executed. When he was released at the expiration of a month, he was delicate and white, and was ever afterwards a respectful, obedient and efficient seaman.

An unstimulating beverage and vegetable diet, taken with manacled hands in the narrow confines of the brig, have a wonderful influence upon hot blood and a rebellious spirit, and are a much more humane and effective punishment, than tricing up in the rigging or the application of a cat-o'-nine-tails.

Minor offences in the navy were punished by setting the culprit to walking the deck with a handspike or a heavy shot, sending him up aloft, putting him astride a boom or yard, giving him extra duty, or reducing his rating and pay. Serious offences were atoned by confinement in the brig, single or double-irons, and restricted diet. Very grave offences brought imprisonment in a penitentiary, or death by shooting or hanging at the yard-arm. It speaks well for the *esprit de corps* of the United States Navy, that grave offences were almost unknown in it, during the entire period of the war of the rebellion.

All over the sandy islands of the west coast of Florida the gophers were numerous, and had as many holes to run into as the blockade-runners. The most successful way to secure them was, not to seek them through the weeds and underbrush, but to hunt their holes and close them up. When a certain area had its holes blocked, a drive was organized and the clumsy walkers were taken before their own doors. The officers and men were always eager for a gopher hunt and often secured forty or fifty in an afternoon. Terrapin stew is the delight of the gourmand at the North and is certainly a most delicious food anywhere.

CHAPTER XV.

Rumor had reached the Nautilus by several visiting men-of-war that she was soon to be relieved. Blockade-running upon the station had ceased; the regulators along the river banks had withdrawn inland; the sports of the region had become tiresome; the gophers were fewer; the curlew and snipe were wilder; the deer had been frightened away by target firing with heavy guns; the alligators had learned to drop their noses beneath the water whenever they heard the rhythm of oars, and everybody was weary of watching when there was nobody to watch, and desirous of leaving the peaceful scenes for more active service. It was just when everyone was so tired of the monotony that he would have engaged in the most desperate undertaking for a change, and when the long separation from loved ones had begun to make the heart ache with ceaseless longings, that the whole ship's company was excited by the appearance of a bark in the offing. She came boldly into the harbor with all of her sails spread and shining in the sunlight, flying her signal number, the long pennant, and the starry flag, and dropped anchor a few cable's lengths from the Nautilus.

It was the U. S. S. R——, carrying eight long 32-pounders, two 24-pounder howitzers, and a 30-pounder Parrott. Her captain came on board and was received at the gangway by Capt. Prescott, Mr. Felton and the officer-of-the-deck, and conducted to the cabin, where there was a long conversation over a bottle of sherry and sundry dispatches from the admiral. The good news soon spread through the ship that the vessel had come to relieve the Nautilus, which was ordered to Key West and was there to prepare to go North. Its effect upon everybody, from the captain to the smallest powder-monkey in the ship, was remarkable. It seemed as if all hands had just been let out of a minstrel show. There was lively movement, animated conversation, much joking and general hilarity. Every one felt a kindlier interest in his shipmates, and all rejoiced at the prospect of speedy departure. In the evening the sailors danced, sang and played instrumental music till ten o'clock, and the officers cracked several bottles of wine with their visitors and smoked and talked till midnight.

The next day the Nautilus was prepared for sea, and, the following day when the tide served, she steamed gaily out of the harbor with her flags flying, receiving and giving cheer after cheer till she was beyond hearing distance. The run to Key West was made without notable incident, and, the next afternoon, she came to anchor under the guns of Fort Taylor. Captain Prescott made his official visit to the admiral and returned with a confirmation of the report that the Nautilus was ordered home. Active preparation of the vessel for the voyage was made; the bunkers were filled with coal; the water casks were emptied and filled; the stores were replenished, and some of the officers and men were allowed a run on shore every afternoon and evening.

The officers were received by their army and civilian friends with the greatest cordiality, and it seemed almost like getting home again to meet old acquaintances with whom so many pleasant hours had been whiled away.

Key West had received a large accession of citizens during the period the Nautilus had been up the coast, and business was flourishing and social life very gay.

The officers of the Nautilus had wished for some time to make a worthy acknowledgment of the kind attentions they had received on shore, and, after much discussion, it was decided to give a party on board of the ship. Captain Prescott gave his permission cheerfully; Mr. Felton promised to do all in his power, and a committee on refreshments was given carte blanche to provide the good things. The steerage officers submitted the names of the friends they desired to invite; the wardroom officers revised and approved a list, and the paymaster wrote the invitations and sent them ashore. The event was fixed for Thursday evening, and the announcement made a great sensation in society circles on the Key.

Preparations were commenced the next morning, and the whole crew was employed in beautifying the ship. The paint was scrubbed clean and touched up here and there; the brasswork was scoured bright; the guns and arms received a careful overhauling; the decks were holystoned clean and white; the awnings were spread over the quarter-deck; the running gear was coiled and flaked in fancy figures; the dishes were arranged with care; the silver plate was given an extra burnish; the rooms were all put in good order; colored and battle lanterns were hung all about the rails and rigging; signals and the flags of all nations were draped about the gangways and steps, and large flags separated the quarter-deck from the forward part of the ship. A place between two guns was then set apart for the musicians; the starboard steerage was arranged for the gentlemen's dressing-room; the captain gave up his cabin for the ladies; the wardroom was devoted to the refreshments; the boats were cushioned and carpeted to bring off the people from shore, and all hands were dressed in full uniform.

The guests from the ships and the shore began to arrive at 7 o'clock, and the quarter-deck was soon covered with a merry party of ladies and gentlemen. There was great curiosity to see all parts of the ship, and groups of visitors were conducted around by the officers, who answered all the questions, entered into elaborate descriptions, and displayed their familiarity with naval technology.

A lady said the figure-head was so named because it was placed ahead, and the cutwater was not sharp enough to cut anything. Another knew there was a cat-o'-nine-tails for whipping sailors, and asked, if the catheads upon the forecastle belonged to cats that had nine tails. Some could not see the sense of calling the forward deck the forecastle, as there was no castle there, and observed if it had been made level, the pivot gun could have been moved around easier. Others thought the brig was a chicken-coop, and were much surprised to learn that it was a prison; the apothecary's room was too small, and the sick-bay did not resemble a bay at all; it was too bad to make the sailors hang up under the deck to the iron hooks; the magazine was too far away from the guns, making too hard work for the poor, little powder-monkeys; the galley was the biggest stove they had ever seen, and the kettles were large enough for a sugar-house; the engine was awfully complicated, and the fire-room was a dreadful place to work in; the guns were much better than those on the fort, but they

must split the ears when fired; the state-rooms were very cosy,
and the officers must be dreadful flirts, if the pictures upon
the walls were all sweethearts; the cabin was too pretty for
anything, and even women might go to sea in such elegant
apartments.

Such innocent observations were heard upon every side, and
the old salts, who were standing around with their caps in
their hands, smiled secretly and shifted their quids in silent
derision. It was as amusing to listen to the chatter of the
land-lubbers, as it was interesting to them to learn the object
and use of everything that attracted their attention.

"Why do you call that semi-circular thing up there the
top?" asked Mrs. Dr. Edwards.

"It is near the top of the mast," replied Mr. Bloss.

"But the top of the mast is away up there."

"No, that is called the truck."

"Does anybody ever go up there?"

"Certainly; the pole must be painted, and sometimes the
halyards must be rove. The ship's boys often climb up and
hang their caps over it for fun and to see who can do it the
quickest."

"Is it possible! It looks very dangerous."

"Do you keep all the powder and shell in the great magazine?" asked Mrs. Fortescue of Lieut. Ashton.

"No; there is a smaller magazine under the wardroom for
these howitzers," was the reply.

"Isn't it dangerous to have powder so near the stove?"

"No; the fires are all put out before the magazine is opened.
The men in the magazine wear canvas slippers without nails,
and have no metal about their persons, not even a button."

"Do you officers have any stoves in the winter?"

"No; they are not allowed."

"How do you keep warm when you are in a cold climate?"

"We heat a solid shot in the furnaces and keep it in a tub of
sand. It throws out heat for a long time and warms the
rooms well enough."

"That's a queer way. Suppose the ship should get on fire,
with all this powder aboard, what would you do?"

"Put the fire out."

"Suppose you couldn't?"

"We would flood the magazine with water. There are stop-cocks outside to turn water into them."

"Wouldn't it be dangerous, with so many loaded shell?"

"Yes, rather; but the fire would probably drive us into the boats before it had reached the magazine."

"Do your men cook nice things?" inquired Miss Peterson of the paymaster.

"Of course. Do you think we live on salt-horse and hard-tack?"

"No; but you have so many to cook for and so little room, I thought you couldn't have pies and cakes and such things."

"Well, we do; we have lots of them. I am caterer, and I would be keel-hauled, if the stewards did not supply our aristocratic crowd with regular desserts."

"Keel-hauled? What is that?"

"Dragged along under the ship's bottom—a nautical way of drowning a man for punishment."

"How terrible!"

"Pay. has charge of the tea-kettle halyards," observed Sanborn, laughing.

"Oh, belay your jaw-tackle," answered the paymaster.

"How do you load one of these guns, Mr. Careswell?" asked Madam Fontana.

> "Two midshipmen and a master's mate,
> Two round shot and a stand of grape;
> Ram home the charge,"

was the reply.

"A pretty heavy charge that, Careswell," observed Col. Gordon. "I would rather stand before the gun, than behind it, in such a case."

"Oh, pshaw! That is only some of the Lieutenant's nonsense; he likes to tease me," said Madam.

"Do you ever allow shore people to see you drill?" asked Mrs. Loudon of Captain Prescott.

"Not often; they would be in the way," was the reply.

"Oh, I should so like to see the sailors work the guns."

"Would you? Well, wait awhile," said the captain significantly.

The men composing the band had taken their places between the guns and now commenced to play a quadrille, and

the gentlemen and ladies formed sets and danced for some
time.   Then two of the sailors danced a hornpipe in the gangway, and, afterwards, several of the men danced singly a great
variety of peculiar steps, which excited the admiration and
applause of the visitors.   Then there were more dances by the
guests and officers, interspersed with instrumental solos and
nautical songs by the sailors, followed by a march around the
deck, pensive watching of the waves through the gun-ports,
enthusiastic study of the constellations through the spy-
glasses, and romantic tête-à-têtes, sitting upon the gun-car-
riages.

The discipline of the ship was still maintained; men were
on watch as usual; lookouts and marines were stationed; Mr.
Sanborn was in charge of the deck, and the bells were struck
regularly.   This continuance of order enhanced the interest of
the shore people, and they were much pleased to see hammocks piped down, and the men take their snugly-lashed rolls
of bedding from the netting and march below.

Supper was announced at 10 o'clock, and the wardroom
and cabin were filled with guests and their attendants.   The
paymaster took charge of the table and the stewards and
waiters distributed the bountiful repast.   The handsome
dresses of the ladies, the plain suits of the civilians, and the
showy, gold-ornamented uniforms of the army and navy officers, formed striking contrasts in colors, which were heightened
and beautified by the green, blue and red signal lanterns that
illuminated the scene.   'It is little that makes the glad laugh,'
and witty speeches, happy repartees, and short stories, caused
merry laughter, that awoke the solemn echoes of the broadsides and went rippling from gun to gun to the forward part
of the ship.

The band upon deck played appropriate selections from its
naval repertoire; several of the ladies sang solos and duets to
guitar accompaniments, and some of the gentlemen repeated
humorous, sentimental and declamatory pieces of poetry.

The event of the evening was the singing of " *Ave Maria* "
by Miss Laura.   Madam Fontana had been talking to her
earnestly and, assisted by Careswell, had gained her consent to
favor the company.   She took up the guitar and swept her
fingers rapidly over the strings.   Her expression had been one

of timid reserve, but now it became sad, her eyes seemed to look far away, her head was thrown slightly back, her lips parted, and the full rich tones of her voice filled the listeners with such emotion, that they could hear nothing but their own heart throbs and the delicious harmony.

When the last sweet tone had ended and the tinkle of the guitar was stilled, a storm of applause arose that filled the ship, the captain said it was the finest song he had ever heard, and everybody crowded around and offered thanks and praises. Laura was urged to sing something else, but her feelings were too profoundly stirred, her mind was too full of busy thought. She yielded to the clamor, however, and played an exquisite fantasie upon the guitar which was heartily applauded, and then busied herself looking over an album of photographs, seeking to withdraw from the conspicuous position in which her musical talent had placed her.

Toasts were drunk in sherry and champagne, pretty compliments were passed between the guests and their hosts, the captain and lieutenant-commander excused themselves and went upon deck, and the ladies began to think it was time to depart, when suddenly the sharp whistle of the fife and the rattle of the drum shocked the night air and spread consternation below.

"It is a call to General Quarters," said the paymaster; "you had better all go up and see the manœuvers."

The visitors were escorted upon deck; the officers of the ship seized their arms and hastened to their posts; the men rushed to their stations; the battery was cast loose, and the motions of loading and firing, transporting guns, boarding and repelling boarders, putting out fire and handling the sails, were performed with precision and rapidity, while the guests looked on with astonishment and pleasure, receiving explanations from the naval officers belonging to the other vessels. Then rockets were sent up; different colored Coston signals were burned, in communicating with the other ships, which answered in the same way, and, lastly, while the ladies were intently watching the fire-works and the whole harbor was illuminated, one of the quarter-deck howitzers was discharged. It was so unexpected and so near, that the ladies shrank into a compact crowd and uttered cries of alarm, and then asked

their attendants if the magazine had exploded or what was
the matter. They soon saw and learned the cause of their
fright, and feeling ashamed of their timidity, laughed hysterically and chatted with more volubility than ever. The battery was secured; the music sounded the Retreat; the officers
clustered around; the captain asked Mrs. Loudon with a sly
smile how she liked the drill, and the visitors were profuse in
their thanks to him for the fine exhibition that he had afforded
them. Then the boats were called away; good nights were
said, and the precious freight was taken ashore safely just as
eight-bells, midnight, struck. Never had a naval vessel given
so generous a party. Never had the people of Key West enjoyed themselves so much.

CHAPTER XVI.

THE next few days the officers remained aboard ship getting her ready for sea, and receiving flowers, fruit, notes and farewell visits from their many friends. Then a day or two was devoted to leave-taking ashore, and one evening the captain announced that the Nautilus would sail for New York the next day.

In the morning some discharged men were received as passengers, the boats were hoisted up, numerous signals were made with the vessels of the squadron, the anchor was weighed and catted, and the good ship turned her bow seaward.

As she steamed slowly out of the harbor, the flag of Fort Taylor was dipped, the crews upon the men-of-war cheered, and a crowd of people along the shore waved handkerchiefs, hats and umbrellas. The happy men of the Nautilus responded to these tokens of regard by lusty cheers and swinging their caps, and a group of officers upon the midshipman's deck shook their handkerchiefs and watched their friends with glasses.

As soon as the Nautilus was fairly at sea, the sails were set and the fires banked, the screw was hoisted up, a lookout was sent up into the fore-topmast cross-trees, and everything was made snug.

Three strange looking objects were seen ahead during the afternoon, which upon close acquaintance proved to be waterspouts. Their summits were enveloped in storm clouds, their bases in cones of foam, and the great columns of water turned and twisted and swayed about like monstrous pythons in agony. They approached the ship for awhile, and a gun was cast loose and loaded with solid shot to fire at them should they come too near, but the precaution was needless, as the cyclones soon lost their force, the upper parts of the waterspouts were drawn up into the clouds, and the lower cones settled down to the sea level in great masses of foam.

The Nautilus was homeward bound, and the knowledge sent a thrill of gladness through the crew, which far surpassed

that occasioned by a double allowance of grog or the capture
of a valuable prize.

> " Home, whispered in some foreign scene,
> Sweetly it falls upon the ear;
> Like fairy visions that have been,
> Or mournful music floating near."

As a general thing Jack Tar does not care much where he
is, provided he has plenty of money and a free run ashore,
though he has a preference for a seaport in his own country.
Many of the sailors of the Nautilus were different, however,
from the usual type. They had homes by the rivers, around
the great lakes, and in the smaller places upon the coast, and
had left them to fight for the preservation of the Union. Now
they were going home, intending to resume the occupations
from which they had been driven by necessity and patriotism,
and their hopes and anticipations made them active in their
duties and merry in their pastimes. Every evening there was
music and dancing; the officers sat about the deck listening
and looking on, and all planned what they would do when the
ship went out of commission.

The Nautilus was kept under sail when the wind was favorable, and under steam when unfavorable, and, aided by the
current of the Gulf Stream, made north latitude rapidly.
There was little to break the monotony of the homeward passage, and it seemed interminably long to everybody. Occasionally some merchant vessel would be overhauled and
boarded, only to find that she belonged to a neutral power or
the United States, and a cruiser or blockader would chase
and challenge the Nautilus to give an account of herself,
then bring aboard a bag of letters for home and wish her
" *bon voyage.*"

The Sunday inspection was rigid, that a good appearance
might be presented in port, but the long service and the sea
air had made the uniforms look seedy and taken the shine
off of the buttons and gold lace of the officer's coats. It
was apparent to even a casual observer that all were veterans.
At 9 A.M., the ship was as clean as a new pin, and word was
passed, " All hands to muster! " The officers formed a line
on the starboard side of the quarter-deck, the marines on the

port, and the sailors gathered in the port waist. The executive read some of the *Articles of War*, and the paymaster, selections from the *Episcopal Prayer Book*. The paymaster's clerk then called the roll, and each sailor passed around the mainmast to the starboard side and forward, under the critical eyes of the captain and executive. The marines and officers answered to their names and were inspected and all were dismissed. The captain and executive then examined the ship from stem to stern, alow and aloft.

Sunday in the service is an off day after inspection ; there is little ship's work done, and the sailors get up their bags, overhaul and repair clothes, read, write, and spin yarns all day. The officers read, write, talk, smoke and get extra sleep. This is the manner of observing the fourth commandment in the U. S. Navy.

A New York pilot-boat was spoken Monday morning; a pilot with a pocket full of newspapers was taken aboard, and the course was shaped for Sandy Hook. During the night, the Highland Lights were made and passed, and the Nautilus came to anchor before daylight off Staten Island Quarantine Station.

When the morning dawned, all eyes and hearts were gladdened by the rugged hills, the rich green verdure and foliage, and the lovely forts and villas of the Narrows. A brief visit was made by the officers of the port; the anchor was weighed ; the ship's signal number was hoisted; the vessel proceeded slowly up the magnificent harbor, and came to anchor off the Brooklyn Navy Yard.

How indescribable the feelings of a wanderer upon his arrival in his native land ! How the hearts of these heroes of the war swelled with emotion and pride, when they thought of the perils they had passed and of the glory of their common country. No one can have a proper conception of what love of country is, and how much he has of it, until he has been abroad awhile.

The Nautilus was home again, and all was excitement and anxiety to get the ship's mail, and to learn the latest news of the war, though some had been gained from the pilot and his papers. Everybody was desirous of stepping upon a shore not pressed by traitor's feet, and of getting into the well filled stores, where money would bring its worth of honest merchandise, but there were certain formalities to be observed before the prisoners of the sea could be liberated.

The gig was called away, Captain Prescott made his official visit to Admiral Paulding, and kindly brought the mail back with him. Then there was a call to quarters; the broadside guns were cast loose, and the customary admiral's salute of thirteen guns was fired. The discharged men were then transferred to the receiving-ship North Carolina; the sails were loosed, dried, unbent and stowed away below; the gangways shipped; the booms swung out; the boats put overboard; the awnings spread; the windsails hoisted in the hatchways; the yards squared, and all the ropes hauled taut. These duties kept every one busy all day, and the tired crew was glad to turn in early without giving the usual musical entertainment.

The next few days there was free communication with the shore; leave parties scattered about the two cities, gazed with delight upon the splendors of the great metropolis, and tasted once more the pleasures of nineteenth century civilization. Orders came the second week to put the Nautilus out of commission preparatory to docking her; to transfer the crew to the North Carolina, and for the officers to await orders at the yard.

All hands were called to muster and the captain made a speech:

"MEN OF THE NAUTILUS.—It is with feelings of sadness that I announce to you the time has come for separation. The Nautilus goes out of commission to-day. I thank you for your observance of the regulations of the ship, and for your efficiency and courage in times of danger. You have the proud consciousness of having served your country in her need, and she will reward you for your patriotism. I shall always be glad to hear of your welfare. And to you, my officers, I owe much. You have ably performed the duties required of you, and have been industrious, zealous and brave throughout the cruise. Such conduct will bring its reward in consciousness of rectitude and in deserved promotion. The naval examining board is in session. I shall ever be ready to advance your interests, and trust that the ties of affection that bind us may never be loosened. Farewell!"

"Three cheers for Captain Prescott!" shouted Mr. Felton, jumping upon a gun-carriage. The loud hurrahs burst from more than a hundred lusty throats and swept across the river.

"Three cheers for the Nautilus!" he cried, and they were given with a will.

"Pipe down!" he said to the boatswain. The shrill whistles sounded and the men retired. At meridian, the flag and pennant were hauled down—the official life of the Nautilus was ended.

The ship was hauled alongside the dock and delivered to the ship-keepers; the stores were formally turned over to the yard officials; the men were sent to the receiving-ship, and the officers took carriages and went to their hotels. A week or two later, some of the officers found the Nautilus a dismantled, disordered hulk. The hatches were off and the hull was empty; the anchors and guns were on the dock; the yards and topmasts were down, and the rigging was lying about in snarls. The ship was nearly ready to go into the dry-dock. The officers were given a month's leave and then ordered to different ships. Careswell was promoted to lieutenant, made another cruise, and captured several valuable prizes. The war went on furiously and every man was needed upon the blockade, and he was not one to neglect his duty or to remain inactive, but in the lonely watches of the night his thoughts often turned to the little island in the gulf and he longed for peace.

FINIS.